What Makes You Tick

(Ed Case: Book 10)

John Morritt

Copyright © 2024 John Morritt

All Rights reserved.

ISBN: 9798326692474

DEDICATION

This book, and all future books, are dedicated to my father, David William Morritt, who I have to thank for my starting my writing career after a gin-fuelled bet in 2010. Sadly my father passed away in 2019 after losing his fight against cancer. I lost not only a father but a best friend. Rest in peace Dad.

OTHER TITLES BY JOHN MORRITT

Black Cockles (Ed Case: Book 1)

Nine Lives (Ed Case: Book 2)

Vengeance

Inglorious (Ed Case: Book 3)

Full Circle

The Last Hit

Nobody's Heroes (Ed Case: Book 4)

Nobody's Heroes Part II: Retribution (Ed Case: Book 5)

Last Man Alive (Ed Case: Book 6)

Relentless (Ed Case: Book 7)

The Box (Ed Case: Book 8)

Inside Outside (Ed Case: Book 9)

www.johnmorritt.com

ACKNOWLEDGMENTS

As always I would like to say thanks to all the people that read and buy my books, and to those that give me support and the inspiration to continue writing. I would like to thank Tracey O'Connor for her help with the editing process, critical review and input into making this book so much better. Thanks to all the individuals I have met in my life that I steal a little part of, and pen into the characters in my work. Thanks also to all my friends and family for being supportive and patient when I am absorbed in my work and for the honest feedback. Special thanks to photographer Josh Redd for making his photographic work available on Unsplash free of charge, which I used to create the cover for this book.

.

CHAPTER ONE

Padstow present day

Death; Mick Woods prayed for a swift death. He was sure that death would be the outcome of his ordeal, despite not having been subjected to any physical violence; not yet at least. Why else would he be pinned to the floor, spread-eagle and naked as the day he was born, in his own living room?

The nylon cable ties that bit into his wrists and ankles were coated in a sheen of blood where he'd futilely tried to break the bonds that secured him to the concrete floor with masonry nails. His mouth was bone dry as were his sore and cracked lips from the makeshift gag made from one of his own socks that had been roughly rammed into his mouth. He desperately needed to urinate, but that was the least of his problems; he was about to lose his life, why should he concern himself with losing his dignity?

Mick could hear his tormentor in the kitchen, whistling a tune he knew but in his heightened state of panic couldn't recall. Perhaps it was a song by Queen? "I want to break free" came to him in a moment of clarity. He heard the kettle boil and then the sounds of his tormentor making a cup of tea or coffee. A few minutes later the man entered the living room and made himself comfortable on the sofa.

'How are you feeling, Mick?' the man asked.

Mick turned his head and stared at the man who'd asked the question. Despite the gag that stretched his lips and cheeks, his eyes portrayed fear and hate in equal measures.

'Oh, I'm sorry, Mick. How rude of me. Perhaps I should

remove the gag so we can have a sensible conversation. I'm warning you though, if you scream or shout, I'll kick you so hard between the legs that the next time you need to scratch your balls, you'll have to loosen your tie. Do I make myself clear?'

Mick nodded his head, happy to comply, if only so he could swallow and lick his parched lips. His captor took a sip of his coffee and placed it on the nest of tables beside the sofa he was sat on. He leaned forward and with his gloved hand removed the sock from Mick's mouth. Mick pulled in a deep breath and spent a few seconds trying to generate saliva to moisten his mouth and lips before finally speaking.

'Who are you and what do you want?' he asked. His voice sounded alien, as if it belonged to a stranger.

The man who'd retaken his seat nodded and smiled back at Mick. His mouth and eyes were all that Mick could see. The black ski mask that the man wore made his teeth seem unnaturally white. He couldn't make out the colour of his piercing eyes due to the poor lighting in the room. Perhaps they were grey, Mick thought.

'Both good questions. One is largely unimportant and that's what my name is. To make things cordial you can call me John. To answer your second question, I want to know what makes you tick. What makes a man like you who he is, or perhaps more relevant would be, what he's become? Call it research,' John replied.

His eyes bored into Mick's as he tapped a finger on his chin.

John crossed his legs and picked up his coffee and took a sip.

'I don't understand why people who drink instant coffee buy cheap, supermarket own-branded, when other brands are much nicer. Oh well it's wet and warm,' John said and shrugged his shoulders.

'You said research. What do you mean? What research involves nailing a man to the floor?' Mick asked. Questions would stall for time, he thought, as he strained at his bonds to no avail.

'Trying to escape will do you no good. I've tested this method of restraint at home and it'll take a much stronger man than you to break free. Just concentrate on answering my questions for now.'

John leaned forward then poured the almost full cup of coffee over Mick's abdomen. The liquid scalded on contact and burnt its way down to his genitalia. Mick hissed in pain and stifled a scream, uttering a noise that resembled a deep growl, remembering the threat John had given him about shouting or screaming. He clenched his fists and gritted his teeth, and waited for the liquid to cool and the pain to abate before speaking.

'What the fuck was that for?' Mick asked. His eyes were screwed tightly shut still trying to cut out the pain.

'Being punished and not knowing what you're being punished for. Not a nice thing to experience is it? What a pity you never thought about that before and maybe you wouldn't be where you are now.'

'You're fucking mad,' Mick replied.

John stared back at Mick, seeming to be deep in thought, trying to decide if he was indeed mad or not.

'Isn't everyone a little mad? Everyone has a madness within them, but for most people it's repressed, only coming alive in dreams, and for others it manifests itself in other ways. I don't understand racism, hating someone for their skin colour. I don't understand bullies and paedophiles, but I'm not sure that makes them mad or not. To some it might seem like madness to others perfectly normal. I guess it's all down to morality and how limited your imagination is. I'll let you think about that while I go make myself another coffee.'

As soon as John left the room, Mick once again began to pull at his restraints. There was no slack; his arms and legs were pinned down securely and the only result of continued struggling was to cause the bleeding to restart. His wrists and ankles were on fire and blisters were beginning to form on his abdomen and penis from the hot coffee. Hopelessness began to creep up on him with every futile tug of his bonds.

John returned, once more whistling the same tune. Mick let out an involuntary whimper. A single tear escaped when he screwed his eyes shut. They sprang open when John kicked him in the ribs with some force. Even before the audible snap, Mick knew from the excruciating pain a rib had been broken.

'I've just remembered where we were going with this conversation. I was saying to you, how it's confusing to be unfairly punished and not knowing what you're being punished for. Wouldn't you agree, Mick?'

'Yes,' he eventually managed to reply. He was close to tears, knowing what he'd experienced at the hands of this madman so far was likely to be just the tip of the iceberg.

'You're married aren't you, Mick?'

'Separated,' Mick managed to say. Every breath hurt like hell from his broken rib.

'Ah yes, I forgot. How long were you married?'

'About ten years,' Mick replied, wondering where this line of questioning was going.

'Why did you separate?' John asked, his voice becoming intense as he leaned forward and scrutinised Mick like an apex predator would look at its prey before striking.

'We grew apart. She became sullen, wouldn't do jobs around the house or did them badly and withdrew and would hardly speak to me or make love to me,' Mick replied.

John wasn't slow to pick up on the bitterness in his voice.

'Is that so?' John asked and leaned further forward. 'It'd be a very bad idea to lie to me Mick.'

'It's the truth; I swear it's the truth.'

John pulled a masonry nail from his pocket and picked up the hammer he'd used to secure Mick to the floor. He placed the tip of the nail gently on Mick's kneecap and hefted the hammer in his other hand.

'I heard differently. Your wife stated that you abused her both physically and mentally. If a job wasn't done or done to your satisfaction you beat her and sometimes you raped her if you wanted sex or perhaps just wanted to degrade her further. You were the one who became moody and withdrawn and used your wife as a channel for your aggression and inadequacies. Isn't that more the truth? Think hard about your answer, Mick,' John warned and applied a little pressure to the nail.

Mick nodded and sniffed back a tear. 'Y…y…yes,' he managed to stammer.

'Now we're getting somewhere. Why, Mick? Why did you beat your wife?' John pressed, leaning further forward, now just inches from Mick's face, staring intently, the nail and hammer forgotten for now.

'I…I…I did it because I loved her….'

John was unable to hide his surprise and laughed but there was no humour in his laughter. It chilled Mick.

'You beat her, raped her and humiliated her because you loved her? What kind of sick, twisted logic is that?'

Mick stared back; tears now flowed freely down his cheeks. He sniffed again before replying.

'Gillian was popular. She had lots of friends and I was scared I would lose her. I treated her badly and threatened her so she'd be too scared to leave me. I loved her. I never wanted to hurt her but things… things got out of control…'

'Out of control? I guess that's one way of describing it. Did you know you were out of control? Did you care? Did you do anything to stop this cycle of violence? Did you?' John pressed.

'Y…yes, I knew… but… but by that time it was too late. By then it was the only way I could keep her. I fucking knew, OK? But I couldn't stop.' Mick said between sobs.

'Couldn't stop or didn't want to stop?'

'I…I…couldn't. If I stopped she would've left me.'

'And why would that be a bad thing?'

'I loved her, she was mine. If she left she would've found someone else.'

'She was yours? She was your wife not a possession.'

'I know…I know…'

'Did you enjoy beating her?'

'No, not at first, but… but it became the norm and yes, I enjoyed it and hated myself for it. I'm sorry, really I am.'

Mick sniffed and began to cry.

'You really are a pathetic excuse of a human being, but I guess you already know that. Thank you for your time and your honesty. I think I know what makes you tick. Goodbye Mick.'

John had heard enough. He gave Mick a look of contempt and swung the hammer down with as much force as he could into Mick's face. His lips were pulverised as were most of his teeth. Mick was unable to scream as splinters of teeth were choking him. He managed to turn his head and spit pieces out before John crammed the gag back into his mouth, careful not to catch his fingers on the jagged remains of Mick's teeth. Mick's muffled scream was short-lived as he thankfully passed out.

That's when the real torture began. The hammer smashed down onto Mick's lifeless body.

CHAPTER TWO

Crete

The cool breeze was taking the heat out of the midday sun as Ed and Angel sat gazing out from their elevated view point over the crystal clear, blue water of Mediterranean Sea and the bay of Elounda below. It'd been a long hot walk from the town, but once the path began to ascend the air began to cool and they were treated to a gentle breeze.

It was their first holiday together as a couple, in a relationship that had been ongoing for a little over a year. Angel's job as an MI5 agent often took her away for long periods where she faced untold dangers as she and the rest of the team sought out members of the Illuminati to thwart their quest to set up a new world order. Ed had always assumed the illuminati were a thing of fiction but now knew better. He despised the group that had set about destroying his life and would've achieved it, if it wasn't for Angel and Team Nemesis and their boss Jack Griggs. All that seemed a lifetime ago. Ed's past was complicated and littered with personal disasters and worse, and was, for the most part, something he did his best to try and forget. He just took every day as it came and lived it to the fullest.

He and Angel had an easy going relationship. Angel was a highly trained and highly skilled soldier and a lethal killing machine. When she was at work she came across as cold, heartless and ruthless, as her job and training expected of her. Ed knew her better and under the surface she was a kind and caring person. Ed, despite not being a soldier, had experiences that few civilians would ever encounter. Like Angel, Ed had killed men with his bare hands, and more recently, thanks to his experiences with Team Nemesis, with all manner of handguns. Also, like Angel, underneath the surface he had a warm and generous nature. They made a perfect team and Ed was once again happy with life. Everyone needed an Angel in their life.

He put an arm around Angel's shoulders and gave her a brief hug and kissed her tenderly on the cheek.

'What was that for?' she asked.

'Do I need a reason to kiss my beautiful girlfriend?'

'You're going soft. You need another mission with Team Nemesis to toughen you up,' she replied and nudged him playfully with her shoulder.

'I seem to recall it was only a couple of months ago that I spent a week in prison to help out your boss, Jack Griggs, and MI5. That was a week to remember. I slept with one eye open and my arse cheeks tightly clenched.'

'I was so worried for you. I know you're capable of looking after yourself and are good at adapting to different environments but even so. It was the longest week of my life.'

'I think it was a lot longer for me. Prison was about the most hostile environment I've been in. Anyway enough talk of prison and the director general of MI5. We're on holiday, no talk of missions or anything else work related. Let's just soak up these beautiful views and enjoy the time together.'

'OK, agreed. It's been a great week. I wasn't sure about doing a road trip around the island. I was thinking of just lazing around the pool all day, drinking cold beers or wine, or being on a beach working on my tan.'

'Well we're staying in Elounda for a few days so you can do just that and you finally get to meet your hero, John Stone.'

'He's not my hero. All I said was that in the army he was something of a legend as he was one of the best snipers they ever had. He shot a man...'

'Yeah I know. Through the heart from over a mile. So you keep telling me and he told me that too. You'll get to meet him later so you can get his autograph, take a few selfies together and make all your old army buddies jealous. Maybe he'll give you a signed photo of himself. Maybe if you're really lucky he'll even give you a kiss if you ask him nicely.'

'Ed Case, as much as I might miss you, if you don't shut up talking about John Stone, you'll be going over the edge of that cliff in a minute.'

'OK, OK, so you won't want the gift that I bought for you?' Ed replied and grinned.

'You bought me a gift?'

'Sure, I've just been waiting for the right moment to give it to you. Before I get pushed off the cliff would seem like as good a time as any, else it'd be a waste of money.'

Ed rummaged around inside the small backpack he kept water and other essentials in. He pulled out, and handed Angel a small, velvet box and smiled.

Angel opened it and stared at the gold ring inset with diamonds and other gems, which Ed assumed were rubies, sapphires and emeralds.

'How did you know I liked this… and when did you buy it?' Angel asked as she slipped the ring on her ring finger. It was a little too big but fitted nicely on her middle finger. She held her hand up to admire it.

'I saw you looking at it in that jewellery factory we visited and could tell you really liked it, as you went back and looked at it a second time. When we were having dinner later on, I said I needed to go to the bathroom as I'd got a bad stomach. I went out the back of the restaurant and ran like a man possessed to the factory, which wasn't that far away and bought it. I guessed the size, but we can resize it when we get back to the UK, if you want to wear it on another finger. I've never seen you wear jewellery apart from earrings very occasionally. If you don't like it or want it we can change it on the way back to the airport next week.'

'It's perfect and I love it and you. I still think you're going soft,' she replied and kissed him passionately.

'From zero to hero just like that. Wonder if I'll ever make it to legend status like my mate John?' Ed replied when they pulled apart.

Angel shook her head, stood and pulled Ed to his feet.

'And you can just as quickly go from hero back to zero,' Angel said with a smile. 'Come on, let's go so we can have a drink by the pool before we go and meet Frank and John.'

Ed didn't need to be told twice when it came to a cold beer.

It was strange to see Angel nervous. Usually it was Ed who was nervous before an event. However, with Ed it was always before a confrontation, which he'd seen his fair share of over the years. Angel was a trained soldier, a perfectly honed killing machine who he'd seen in action many times. She'd shot men, slit their throats and killed in unarmed combat. She was always cool under pressure and unfazed by anything. This evening, however, she was a bag of nerves and just because she was meeting John Stone. Nervous was a rare emotion for Angel and seeing her like this was rather amusing, when all she was doing was meeting one of his mates. Ed told her so and risked a slap as he laughed at her discomfort.

'I'm not nervous, I'm excited,' Angel replied tetchily.

'You're forgetting that I've seen you both excited and nervous or apprehensive if that's a better description. When you're excited you smile and fidget a lot. When you're nervous you don't smile and you sit perfectly still; and if you grip that glass any harder, you'll shatter it and we'll need a trip to the hospital to get your fingers sewn back on and then you won't get to see your hero,' Ed replied and gave her leg a squeeze. The muscle was as tense as her face looked.

Angel frowned and then gave Ed a warm smile, seeming to relax a little.

'You're right and I know it's stupid but he's a legend in the army. Guys who joined long after John left still talk about him. So yeah it's a big deal getting to meet him.'

'A legend like me, you mean? That guy in Emmanuelle's said I was a legend.'

'As I said at the time, I think you misheard him. He actually called you a bell-end. You don't become a legend by giving Keith Fulton a slap.'

'I'll have you know, I've played my part in taking down a number of notorious mafia types, it's not just about giving Keith a good going over,' Ed replied feinting hurt feelings. He didn't care if he was a legend or a bell-end in Angel's eyes. They were together and he'd not been this happy in a very long time.

'OK, I admit, you're something of a legend,' Angel said begrudgingly.

'Good, now drink up or we'll be late. It's a twenty minute walk back into town and we don't want to keep that other bell-end waiting, do we?'

Angel punched him on the arm and called him an arsehole, before kissing him on the cheek. Ed put his arm around her and pulled her tightly to him as they set off on their evening out.

It was a pleasant stroll into the town. They walked hand in hand from their hotel to Frank and Emily's restaurant, which was easy to find being on the main road right opposite the quaint harbour, filled with fishing boats, speed boats and even a couple of larger pleasure boats.

Ed and Angel stood outside appraising Frank and Emily's business. It was called "Luca's" after the previous owner who'd sold up to spend his long overdue retirement on mainland Greece to be nearer his family. Ed recalled Frank telling him that they'd decided to keep the original name as it was a renowned and popular bistro with lots of returning clients, both locals and tourists alike, and also had great reviews on the internet for both food and its relaxed easy-going ambiance. They even retained the two staff Luca had employed so they could learn how to cook Greek food and provide the same standard of food as it was before they took the business over. It was a ploy that worked well and the business was thriving. Neither he nor Emily needed the money thanks to Frank's inglorious past as an enforcer for an infamous gangster and a notorious string of hits on security vans which netted him a share of twenty million pounds. It'd cost him a twenty year stretch in prison, but he'd got his money…eventually. Ed wondered how he'd coped. He spent a week in prison to help out Jack Griggs and had hated every second. How Frank coped with twenty years was beyond his comprehension. He'd ask him later; he was curious.

Ed gave Angel's hand a tug and they made their way across the road to Luca's. Frank, Emily and John were sitting at a table towards the rear. Frank was easy to spot from his size. Frank was six feet tall, but weighed around fifteen stone; all of it muscle. His huge shaved head sat atop of a thick neck. He looked like rugby prop forward. John, like Ed, was unremarkable, average height and build, but Ed had to admit, handsome. Emily was diminutive next to Frank and twenty years his junior. They'd met when Frank was released from prison and he walked into the Three Tuns pub in

Southwark, London for a pint and found out her mother, Maggie, had died and Emily was now the landlady. Despite the age gap they hit it off and were now married.

John noticed them and obviously said something to Frank who got up to greet them.

Ed shook his hand and Frank enveloped him in a hug, which threatened to break his ribs.

'Great to see you, Ed. So glad you came to see us,' Frank said before turning his attention to Angel.

Frank took her hand and shook it, albeit a lot more gently than he had Ed's and then kissed Angel on both cheeks.

'I can tell from Ed's description of you, you must be Frank. Nice to meet you,' Angel replied.

'I actually said you were a fat, old bastard with a big, bald head,'

'Still as charming as ever,' Frank replied and smiled broadly.

'If I changed you'd be disappointed,' Ed replied.

'That's true. Come on, I'll introduce you to John and Emily, Angel,' Frank said.

They walked to where John and Emily were standing, waiting to meet Ed and to be introduced properly to Angel.

When John shook her hand, Angel smiled back and grinned broadly. Ed had never seen her lost for words.

'Nice to meet you, Angel,' he said and kissed her on the cheek.

'You've just made her dream come true,' Ed said to John who gave Ed a look that suggested he didn't know what he was on about.

'John, you're Angel's hero. In the army you're something of a legend apparently, due to your marksmanship and skills as a sniper.'

'Really?' John replied, seemingly shocked by this revelation. 'I was a pretty bad solider in all other respects.'

Emily interrupted, as John seemed a little embarrassed as did Angel, who shot Ed one of her looks.

'Rather than spending time looking at the menu, I've pre-ordered. You didn't say that either of you had any dietary issues or things you don't like when I asked Frank to ask you, so hopefully the food will be to your taste.'

'We eat just about anything. Thanks Emily,' Angel replied.

'We were in Corfu a little while ago on business and got a reminder of how good Greek food is. While we were there we got talking and Angel said she'd love to meet you all, so here we are,' Ed informed his friends. He bit his tongue and didn't add, especially her hero, John.

'I won't ask as I'm sure it's classified,' John said.

Ed shrugged and looked at Angel, but when Angel didn't embellish John with any details, he assumed it was classified.

'Why did you leave the army, John? You were the best sniper the army had and I would've thought you had a long career in front of you. I've always been curious about that,' Angel asked.

'I joined the army because it was what I needed in my life back when I was a teenager. I'd spent years in and out of institutions and foster homes. I didn't fit in and needed discipline to keep me on the straight and narrow; a common reason for many new recruits. I didn't have a happy childhood and was a little wayward. The army was my new home and it felt right. It turned out that firing a gun seemed to be something I was naturally good at, although I only found out after a few times on the range when I was getting better marks than my peers and some of the instructors. So, a sniper I became.

I was enjoying army life for the most part and then one day in the Balkans my company was tasked with clearing a village of Serbian separatists who we were told were hiding out there. I was some distance from the village tasked with taking out any hidden snipers they'd got in the area and to take out any rebels that made a run for it. Anyway, the area was cleared and I was called back in and saw that the entire village had been rounded up. The interpreter was asking questions and my captain suspected they were lying and shot one of the villagers. He ordered the rest of the company to slaughter the villagers; every man, woman and child. They froze; torn between murdering the villagers and disobeying a direct order. The captain began shooting randomly, screaming for the company to shoot. Some of my company followed the order, but fortunately just a few. I shot my captain in the head from some distance away to save the villagers.

While I was making my way back to the company I bumped into a couple of kids. One was a young teenager and the other his even younger sister. They were petrified and I reassured them both that all would be OK and I wouldn't let them come to any harm. I directed them away from the rest of my company who were looking for the gunman that had shot the captain. At the time nobody knew it was me. I think later I was a suspect, but because of what Arnott had done, nobody asked; you know how it is in the army. Anyway, I joined in the search and steered them away from the direction the kids went.

Captain Arnott was buried with full military honours. I put in a request to leave the army and it was given with no questions asked. As you can imagine, I'd lost all respect for authority. I'm sure I was a suspect in Arnott's murder, but because of the scandal it would've caused, nothing was said, and the records show that Arnott was killed in action by a rogue sniper. If I was tried for murder, Arnott would have been posthumously dragged through the mud along with the army and his wealthy, well-connected family so all that was buried. As far as everyone was concerned, Captain Arnott was killed in action, end of story.'

It was the first time John had told anyone this in a very long time, but he seemed unmoved by getting it off his chest.

'That's a good reason to leave. I think anyone would've done the same in your position. If I saw a member of my team slaughter innocent people, I wouldn't hesitate to kill them,' Angel said.

'I'll be sure to warn the others next time I see them,' Ed said to Angel.

'You shot one of your own, but for the right reason and you helped a couple of kids. That makes you one of the good guys in my book,' Emily said.

'I rue the day I saved the kid and her older brother,' John paused for dramatic effect, and left everyone wondering. 'The girl's name was Kristina Kovac,' he eventually replied and gave a wry smile.

'No fucking way!' Ed said completely shocked by this revelation.

'I didn't recognise her but she recognised me when we met years later. I'm not sure if that was the reason she plotted my death or if that was a coincidence. Small world isn't it? She got her comeuppance, eventually. You did London a favour killing that nasty bitch, Ed. You should've been awarded the freedom of the city for that,' John said, his hatred of the woman undisguised.

'I know all about your antics with Kovac and Miles. Ed told me. He also told me about how you took her out and about you helping Ed with taking down Greenfield. What I don't know is how you all met,' Angel asked.

The three men looked at each other wondering who was going to start the tale.

'I reckon Ed should start,' Frank suggested.

'Kovac was after me for taking down her business in Aldbury House, as you know, and she sent a hit team to my home where Bob and I saw them off. We decided to go to London and find her. Pandora's boyfriend gave me a list of places we'd be likely to find her, and we went to check out this Italian restaurant in the East End,' Ed started and then looked to John and Frank.

'I'd just bought this place and John came in one night and again the next day, and we struck up a friendship; you know how it is fellow expats from the smoke? That evening I got a call from a friend telling me that my oldest friend had been murdered by Kovac. John overheard me and asked how I knew her. We talked and he told me how she tricked him and left him for dead on the bank of the Thames and we decided to go to London to kill her.

By a very strange coincidence we went to the same restaurant in London that Ed and Bob were checking out. John asked Ed what he was doing and Ed in his usual fashion got defensive and squared up to John. I came along and Ed turned his attention to me and chinned me. Hardest punch I've ever been on the receiving end of. He packs quite a punch for a little guy. Anyway, Bob came along, who I remembered from twenty odd years previous and calmed it down and we formed an uneasy alliance to take out Kovac and Miles, who was one of yours as I'm sure you know. By the end we all had a lot of mutual respect and became good friends and here we all are. I suggest we lay the past to rest, forget about it and enjoy the here and now and look forward to the future. Yamas,' Frank said and raised his glass.

CHAPTER THREE

Padstow Cornwall

Phil Reynolds was a contented man. His fiancée, Emma James, had moved in with him a couple of weeks ago and they were starting their new life together. The next step would be marriage, but that hadn't really been discussed at length. Both were happy with the current situation with each of them enjoying life as a proper couple. It was just like being married without the paperwork and expense of a wedding. They had an easy going relationship and they knew that one day they'd be married. Until recently Phil had been in a rented flat in one of the newer developments in the Padstow area, which was costing him a considerable chunk of his policeman's salary, even for a detective inspector, due to the popularity of the quaint harbour town with second home owners and tourists alike. Emma had been living with her good friend, Chris Stevens, in her spare bedroom over her shop also in the town, in a prime position overlooking the picturesque harbour. She wasn't paying a fixed rent, but helped out in the shop and made jewellery and also gave Chris a percentage of any of her paintings that were sold, which were becoming increasingly popular as her reputation gathered momentum. It was working out well for both of them, but it was time to move on, especially as Chris' fiancé, Lionel, had moved in; both women needed their personal space. Phil's mother had died, and being an only child, Phil had inherited her cottage on the edge of the old town, in addition to a nice cash injection into his bank account, which would pay for redecorating and refurnishing the cottage to bring in into the twenty-first century and more in tune with their more modern tastes.

The cottage itself was detached with a nice size garden both back and front. The garden was well maintained as that was his mother's pride and joy almost up to the day she died of a heart attack. In the garden there was a summer house, which Emma would use as her studio, as the two bedroom cottage had no room inside for a studio as they wanted to keep the spare room as a guest room.

Today was Phil's day off and he was stripping wallpaper in the spare room, while Emma was painting the newly papered main bedroom. Phil joked that as Emma was the painter it was only right that she should paint the bedroom as she was more skilled with a brush. Emma gave Phil a sarcastic laugh, but was more than happy to paint as she hated stripping walls and didn't have a clue how to hang wallpaper, not even lining paper which had no patterns to match up and which Phil seemed to have a natural flair for.

Today, despite being his day off, they'd got up early to work on the house. Emma entered the room with a cup of tea and a bacon sandwich as they'd skipped breakfast. Phil smiled as Emma put the cup and plate onto a chest of drawers pushed into a corner of the room.

'I could get used to this,' Phil said and kissed Emma on the forehead and gave her a hug.

'Don't,' she replied. 'I'm only doing this as you've got to keep your strength up. I want this bedroom finished the day after tomorrow so we can start on the stairs, hall and landing.'

'And there was me thinking you wanted me strong for another reason,' Phil replied and winked.

'There's that too,' Emma replied and looked up at Phil and gave him an alluring smile.

Phil bent forward and kissed her. His hands travelled slowly down her back to caress her buttocks. Alas, Phil's hands never made it that far as his mobile phone rang. He muttered an expletive, pulled it from his pocket and stared at the caller display; it was work. He swore under his breath and hoped it was nothing serious; he really wanted to get this room finished today or at least stripped.

'Hi Evelyn,' he said knowing Evelyn Hardy was the duty sergeant today.

'Hello, sir. Sorry to bother you on your day off but there's been a murder and the Super wants you to run it. The DCI is away on a course as you know, and that makes you the most senior man,'

'OK Evelyn, give me the details of where,' he said and grabbed an old piece of wallpaper from the floor and the pencil from behind his ear and began scribbling.

Phil ended the call and apologised to Emma. She and Phil had been an item long enough to know that this was the way things were sometimes and as disappointing as it was, she could live with it.

The Camel Trail was used by walkers, cyclists and horse riders, but today access had been granted to the emergency services and was guarded by a uniformed officer whose job it was to disappoint tourists by informing them the trail was closed today. Another officer was stationed at the other end tasked with the same. Phil passed a few disgruntled tourists, joggers, dog walkers and cyclists heading back to Padstow, having been turned back by the officer stationed on the perimeter of the crime scene.

Phil pulled up behind a squad car and made his way to the police crime scene tape. The uniformed constable recognised Phil and wished him a good morning as Phil ducked underneath the tape cordoning off the crime scene and made his way towards the forensic team in their white suits, and waited. It was a short wait before Mark Wilton, the chief forensic pathologist approached him.

'Hi Phil,' he said cheerily to his old friend. 'I see you got the short straw as the DCI is on his training course.'

'Hi Mark. Yeah and I can't say I'm too pleased as it was my day off and I was in the middle of stripping the walls. I was hoping to get both bedrooms complete before going to work in a couple of days; guess that's never going to happen. What have we got?'

'I hope you've not had a big breakfast as it's quite gruesome. Anyway, you'll see for yourself soon enough. We have a male in his mid to late thirties. He was killed elsewhere and then taken to the A39 and thrown over the wall where he rolled down and came to a stop just before the path. The forensic team found nothing along the trail and the broken bushes and position of the body are all consistent with being thrown from the bridge. The forensic team are making their way back up to the road to see if they can find any evidence,' Wilton replied.

'Great. I'll see what the traffic cameras have picked up. You said he was mid to late thirties so I assume there was no ID on him?' Phil asked.

'No. He'd absolutely nothing on him at all, and by that I mean absolutely nothing; we found him as naked as the day he was born, which also suggests being killed elsewhere and dumped.'

'Great! Why do I always get these cases? I guess we'll waste dozens of man hours contacting dentists to find his dental records, assuming he's got a dentist. Plenty of people don't these days; too bloody expensive.'

'Well actually, Phil, I've got some bad news for you, I don't think you need to trouble any dentists. You see our man was tortured, quite extensively, and there isn't a great deal left of his teeth. I think you best take a look, but prepare yourself. You know me, I'm not in the least bit squeamish; you can't afford to be in my job. However, this one made even my stomach lurch.'

Phil was filled with dread. If Wilton, who cut people open, weighed and dissected internal organs, struggled to keep the contents of his stomach down, he was in trouble. He remembered as a uniformed constable seeing a decapitated body as the result of a gruesome road traffic accident and had thrown up. He'd seen many more experienced officers do the same over the years. He steeled himself for the worst.

Wilton stopped and looked down gravely. Phil stepped up beside him.

'Jesus fucking Christ,' he said softly and instinctively turned his head away and took several deep breaths to compose himself.

'I warned you, it wasn't a pretty sight.'

Still looking away from the corpse, Phil asked, 'What was the cause of death?'

'That's a very good question. I won't know until I've completed an autopsy, but if pushed, I'd say that most likely he was asphyxiated. His teeth were smashed, with what I suspect was a claw hammer. You can see the corner of the mouth was torn away on the left hand side of his mouth. I'd guess that the hammer was smashed down with some force, shattering the teeth, and when the hammer was pulled out it ripped the side of the mouth and lip away. Then the gag was reinserted so it's quite likely, he may have choked on his own teeth.'

Phil nodded. 'Good god! What else is a likely cause of death?'

'Well it's difficult to say at this point. The red marks on his chest, stomach and genitals are scalds from hot liquid of some description. A number of his ribs are broken so he may have a punctured lung. Those other marks along his legs and arms are impact marks, which I assume are from the same hammer that shattered his teeth. Judging by the bruising and swelling, I'd say the person who inflicted these wounds broke just about every bone in his body. We can't rule out shock being the cause of death or loss of blood through internal bleeding. If I had to guess right now, I'd say he choked on his teeth and everything else was inflicted after death.

'What kind of sick bastard would do that and why?' Phil asked rhetorically.

'As I always say; that's your job. I have the easy part to say how he died.

'And when,' Phil replied.

'Correct. If I was pushed for an answer, which I know you will, I'd have to say between midnight and 2am last night. As I always tell you, I'll be able to give you a more precise time, all being well, after the post-mortem.'

Phil nodded his thanks.

'Sir!' a shout came from above Phil and Mark and a member of the forensic team came running down the bank.

'We found a wallet. It looks like it was thrown from the bridge fairly recently. We had rain the night before last and this is bone dry.'

'Good work. Any ID in it?'

'A driving licence for a Michael Woods.'

Phil and Mark looked at the driving licence and at the mutilated body in front of them.

'Difficult to tell from all the swelling and mutilation, but I'd say it's him. Same colour eyes,' Phil said looking at the pathologist.

Both men stared down at the dead, lifeless, hazel eyes staring back out of the mutilated face, and back at the driving licence.

'I'd tend to agree. That was easy. You just have to find out who murdered him.' Wilton said and patted Phil on the shoulder before heading off.

'Thanks Mark, you're all heart,' Phil said. He looked at the address on the driving licence and hoped it was current. He knew many people forgot to change it when they moved; he hoped Mick Woods wasn't one of them. He'd pay the house a visit and soon find out.

Mark Wilton walked back to his car his thoughts on his latest assignment. It was going to be an interesting autopsy as there were so many factors that could've been the cause of death. Asphyxia from choking on his own shattered teeth or from the gag that had been rammed into his mouth afterwards, presumably to prevent the victim from screaming. Internal bleeding from the multiple fractures caused by being savagely beaten with what he suspected was a hammer, or from heart failure or shock. It was job he was looking forward to undertaking. It was always good to get a case that would challenge his abilities as a forensic pathologist. Often it was too easy, almost tedious, but this one was going to be quite a challenge.

To many people his passion for his profession would be seen as macabre, but to Mark, he just saw it as a medical challenge to establish a probable cause of death and time that was so important to the officer in charge of a case.

Given a choice, he'd rather be dissecting a corpse than trying to find out who turned a living person into a corpse. Mark was always curious as to why a person would murder or more precisely murder in such a brutal manner. In this current assignment the person who killed the victim had obviously done so with great relish and anger. So far he'd only given the body a cursory examination, what the full post-mortem would reveal would be interesting.

CHAPTER FOUR

Crete

The small pleasure cruiser cut through the still waters at a sedate pace. Frank had invited them all to partake in some deep sea fishing on his recently acquired new toy. He'd ordered it new and decided to name it "The Triple Whammy". Over twenty years ago, he and was involved in the robbery of three security vans, netting a cool twenty million pounds, which had enabled him to become a rich man, eventually, and be able to afford a luxury like a pleasure cruiser.

The coastline of Crete was visible in the distance and the sun beat down on the deck where John, Frank, Ed and Angel sat in a row at the stern of the boat keeping a keen eye on their fishing rods, while sipping on ice cold beers. Emily was at the helm, content to guide the boat through the Mediterranean Sea. She'd got no interest in fishing and found piloting the small craft a relaxing distraction. Her only interest in fishing was the end result that she'd cook into a gastronomic delight, assuming her team of fishermen were lucky and caught something that would be suffice to feed them all. Emily had come prepared and had some pork in the cool box that she'd make into kebabs. It wouldn't be the first time they'd gone sea fishing and not caught anything.

The evening before had been a great success once Angel had overcome being star struck at meeting the legend that was John Stone. The food was excellent and the wine and beer flowed as easily as the conversation. Emily, Frank and Ed, spent much of the time listening to John and Angel, talking about their time in the army and their subsequent careers after leaving. John did most of the talking as to a greater extent what Angel did for MI5 was mostly classified, but Angel told him as much as she felt she could without breaching the official secrets act. John was also interested in Ed's time working with Team Nemesis. Ed like Angel had told him as much as he could, as he too was bound by the official secrets act.

'Frank,' Ed said, turning and looking past Angel and John. Frank took his eye of his rod and looked across at Ed.

'I never got round to asking you last night, but how did you manage to survive twenty years inside? I did a week and it was hell on earth.' Ed asked.

'You did a stretch? I never knew that.' Frank asked surprised.

'It was a recent thing and a favour to our friend Jack Griggs. He wanted me to get information from a guy who was banged up for five years and he couldn't risk putting a bona fide agent inside in case he was found out and was either killed or it tarnished the image of MI5, so Jack tugged on my heartstrings and I agreed.'

'I take it you got what you wanted?' Frank replied.

'Of course I did, but it was bloody horrendous.'

'Within five minutes Ed was in solitary, and when he got out he stabbed a homosexual rapist in his knob and started a riot,' Angel said cheerily.

John and Frank laughed.

'Now why doesn't that surprise me? I reckon prison life must've been tough for someone like you?' John said.

'Yeah, not an easy place to be for a gobby, little bugger like you, who doesn't take shit from anyone. Tell me how you ended up in solitary? I'm guessing it was a fight,' Frank asked.

'It was on my first trip to the canteen and everyone was bashing cutlery on the table to intimidate me, which it did. When I sat down some guy swiped my tray of food off the table so I retaliated. I had to do something or I would've become a permanent victim. I bounced his head off the table and punched his lights out. I then stood up and shouted "who wants some?" and four prison officers decided they did and battered me with their batons and dragged me off to solitary.'

Frank and John laughed. Ed joined in, but at the time it'd been terrifying.

'What's the story behind the homo rapist and the riot? That sounds like it's gonna be a good one,' John asked.

'I befriended the guy who I was trying to get information from and he set me up in the showers as a test as I was pretending to play the hard man. He said I was bullshitting and I said I'm as good as I think I am, if not better; I had to keep up this persona I'd decided on playing. Anyway, I was in the shower rinsing off the soap and a guy squeezed by bum. I turned and there he was waving this enormous cock at me, and I mean enormous. I told him where to go and he pulls a shiv on me. I managed to get the shiv off him but slipped over. When he came at me again, I lunged up and stabbed it into the base of his knob.'

Frank and John laughed, but both pulled faces, imagining the pain that would've caused.

'Funny now, but at the time I can honestly say it was bloody terrifying. Anyway, I lived to fight another day. Shortly after in the exercise yard I was chatting with the guy who I was sent to get info from. I reckoned I'd got all I was going to get, which was enough. You'll not be surprised to hear it got confrontational and I chinned him. As he was the top dog in the prison it seemed to be the catalyst for all hell to break loose. Not sure if it was rival factions vying for the top spot or just an excuse to go mental and let off some steam. Whatever the cause, the riot squad arrived and subdued things. Before they did one prison officer went down and was set on by three inmates. I went to help him and fended off the three guys doing their best to kick him to death. I dragged him to safety and his mate fucking tasered me! I saved a prison officer's life and got tasered as a thank you for my efforts. That bloody hurt. I felt weird for days afterwards. Anyway, I'm sure I didn't feel as bad as the officer who tasered me just for fun. I lumped him one so hard I dislocated his jaw as soon as I could stand up and had stopped buzzing. That was more satisfying that sticking a shiv in Chester's cock. That day I managed to contact Jack, and he got me out of that hell hole. So back to my question to you; how did you survive twenty years? All that happened to me in just a week. One bloody week!'

'I feel for you Ed, but as I'd expected you to, it seems you triumphed in the face of adversity. I think I had it slightly easier than you because of who I was. As you know, I was the chief enforcer for Maurice Blair, and I was known by most of the inmates. Those that didn't were warned to stay away from me by those that did. There were a few of Maurice's crew inside so I wasn't completely friendless. Apart from my reputation, I was also bigger and more intimidating that a lot of the inmates and those that were bigger weren't as quick as I was. Once someone did have a try; I later found out it was Maurice who put him up to it so he could steal my share of the twenty million I was due. All a moot point as he killed everyone who was gonna get a share. He even persuaded my wife to divorce me and married her himself, before bumping her off. So by law what was hers he inherited. I found all this out from Haemorrhoid Harry. So I set about setting Blair up and ripped him off to the tune of twenty-five million.'

'Good for you,' Angel said.

'It was rather satisfying. I had the help of a few friends so I'd agreed to split it five ways. Anyway, to getting back to the point, it was the thought of that four or five million waiting from me when I got out that drove me on and kept me sane. Every day I'd dream of living on a tropical island, maybe running a bar and hanging out with a bunch of bikini-clad beauties. It wasn't much, but it gave me focus. Other than that I kept myself fit and by and large I was left alone. There were times when I felt that I couldn't cope and wondered if going to prison for a crime I didn't commit was worth it for the money. I just kept on telling myself I was earning a quarter of a million quid every year for doing nothing. It wasn't much to cling to, but it saw me through. Think yourself lucky you were only in for a week.'

Ed looked across at Frank and could see the unhappy memories etched into his face and made a quick apology for dragging up painful memories.

'How big was Chester?' Emily shouted at Ed.

Ed laughed.

'I didn't have much time to measure and admire it, but I reckon about ten inches, give or take a little.'

'How big was Monty's, Frank?' Emily asked.

'Just so you know and don't get any wrong ideas. I worked with a guy called Monty. It was a nickname; short for Monty Python as he as blessed with a huge penis. He showed it to us and said it was eleven inches, but the girth was off the scale,' Frank replied and made a large circle with both his hands.

Ed nodded, thinking how impressive that was and how envious he was; as did Angel, he noticed.

'Monty said it made him very popular with the ladies. He made me feel very inferior,' Frank added.

Angel's rod and reel made a racket as the line reeled out rapidly, taking everyone by surprise, and ending the conversation about Monty.

'What do I do? I've never caught a fish before,' Angel spoke urgently to anyone who was listening.

Emily immediately killed the engine and the boat drifted to a halt.

Frank took over and immediately stopped the line reeling out. The silence was almost eerie. The line snapped taut and the rod bent alarmingly; although it seemed not to faze Frank. Angel moved out of the way and Frank began to work the line. Heaving it towards him, then letting it drop and taking up the slack again, gradually drawing the fish closer to the boat.

Ed wondered how big this fish was as Frank was sweating under the exertion and he was a big strong man. The tussle with the fish seemed to be going on a long time. Ed looked at his watch and thought it'd been at least ten minutes. He knew nothing of fishing and assumed a fish took the bait and in a couple of minutes was on the deck either to be eaten or thrown back. It was another five minutes before the head broke the surface of the water and Frank flipped the rod and the fish landed on the deck with a heavy thud and flapped around. Frank reached round, grabbed a baton and gave the fish a thump on the head. The fish lay there unmoving, making Ed feel a little guilty.

'Tuna; not a massive one, but enough for a decent stir-fry for the five of us, I reckon,' Frank announced.

Ed liked tuna and was quick to forget all about this fish's unhappy demise.

John landed a sizeable bream and Angel and Emily set about cooking the fish and Frank took over as captain. Ed and John manned their rods, but had no luck. Ed was an unlucky fisherman. He'd been deep sea fishing twice, freshwater fishing only the once with a friend, and netted nothing; not even a stickleback. Both times he'd enjoyed the time with friends on a boat and was amazed at the effort it took to land their lunch, but freshwater fishing, he'd never do again. Spending all afternoon in silence so as not to frighten the fish was not for him. It must rate as the dullest hobby on earth, up there with train spotting in his opinion.

They dropped anchor to eat their late lunch. Emily had filleted and cut the bream into chunks, and pan fried it with a selection of crunchy vegetables. The tuna she'd skewered along with onion, tomato and peppers and served them with a green salad and Greek pita bread.

Ed couldn't remember a time he'd felt so relaxed and happy. Sitting on the boat, his arm around Angel, a cold beer in his hand, a full stomach and spending quality time with three great friends. The last two times they'd been together had been less than relaxing but that seemed a lifetime ago. He pushed thoughts of Kristina Kovac and Reece Greenfield aside. They belonged in the past and had no place to intrude into the present.

After their lunch and cleaning up the boat and stowing the rods, they made their way back to port in Elounda. After a quick freshen up at their hotel, Ed and Angel made their way back to Luca's for drinks and nibbles as Emily called it. They knew it'd be more than just a few nuts and crisps and were not disappointed with the spread laid on by Emily and her two cooks.

Halfway through the evening Angel's mobile phone rang. Angel looked at the caller display; it was Jack Griggs. Ed saw this too and his heart sank, knowing his and Angel's holiday was going to be disrupted. Angel answered the call and moved away to a quiet corner of the restaurant.

'This is gonna be the end of the holiday,' Ed said to the others. 'All part and parcel of the job, I know, but it's still bloody annoying when it happens.'

His three friends nodded, understanding Ed's disappointment.

Angel walked back to the table and sat down with a sigh.

'That was Jack. I've got to go back tomorrow morning as something urgent has cropped up for Team Nemesis. Sorry Ed.'

'Shit happens, but it's only a few days short of what we planned so I can't complain,' he replied trying to sound upbeat.

'Jack asked me if you were staying on or would be coming back with me.' Angel asked.

As much as Ed wanted to spend a couple more days with his

friends, he knew that going back with Angel was the right thing to do and told her so.

'I knew you'd say that so I got him to change your flight too. MI5 will pick up the admin fee for doing so,' she replied and grinned. She leaned over and kissed Ed on the cheek, appreciating him doing the gentlemanly thing and appreciating the sacrifice he was making.

'Looks like it's holiday over so let's go out with a bang,' Ed said and downed the remains of his drink.

CHAPTER FIVE

Padstow some years previous

The boy walked home from school, alone as usual. Tonight it was late as he'd been playing football with his mates, until the last light of the autumn evening brought an end to the kick-about. It wasn't so much the bad light that stopped play but more the bad sportsmanship with both sides accusing the other of cheating. One side claiming a goal and the other side claiming it hit the post; or rolled over the jumper or school bag that was acting as a goalpost. They eventually agreed on a draw before tempers became frayed and a fight broke out. It wouldn't have been the first time things got out of hand.

The boy didn't have too many friends, well not good friends like the other boys did. He was introvert and for the most part kept his own company. However, like all boys of his age, football was his passion and he was always up for a kick-about after school. He wasn't a bad player so was always welcome to join in with the other kids from school.

It was getting cold so he tucked his hands into his anorak pockets to keep them warm. He hadn't noticed the temperature drop as he'd been running around chasing every loose ball, like he was playing in a cup final, for the last couple of hours. He noticed his breath misting in the air as he approached a street light. He brought his hand up and pretended he was holding a cigarette and blew out billows of smoke, like he'd seen the older boys do after school in the garages. A sudden gust of wind hit him in the face. He let out an involuntary shudder and dug his hands deep into his pockets, suddenly forgetting his pretend cigarette, more intent on keeping warm.

He approached the pub and could hear raised voices in the car park to the side. Curious, he stood and watched. He recognised the two people arguing and his spirts dropped. The high from playing football rapidly fading and being replaced by a feeling of dread. Some days he hated life and wished he was dead. Like he wished his father was dead.

'Like him, do you? Want to fuck him, do you?' the man shouted, jabbing a finger in the chest of the woman opposite; their faces just inches apart. There was a lot of menace in his voice, which probably meant his father was drunk; again.

'It's my job to be friendly with the punters. It's what I'm paid to do; pull pints and smile,' his mother replied, doing her best to stand up to her drunken bully of a husband.

The boy knew how his father would react, but stood rooted to the spot unable to take his eyes off his parents.

His father grabbed his mother by the collar of her jumper and pushed his face forward, their noses now touching.

'I don't know why I married you. You always were a little too popular with the boys.'

'Bullshit. You're drunk and shooting your mouth off again. I've been a good wife. Only you never appreciate it because you're a jealous drunk.'

His father let go of his mother, stepped back and swung a punch into her face. His anger still unabated, he threw two more punches to the stomach, causing his mother to double up. His father pushed her over and kicked her twice more in the midriff. He spat on the ground next to her and stormed off.

The boy, knowing what the outcome was going to be, even before it'd happened, had crouched down behind a van, out of sight of his father. When he was a few paces down the road stomping off home, the boy came out of hiding and ran to his mother, who was pulling herself painfully to her feet, sniffing back her tears.

'Mum, mum,' the boy cried as he reached his mother and hugged her.

'It's OK son. You know what you're father's like when he's had a drink. Don't worry too much; he'll be asleep in the chair when we get home.'

The boy knew the drill, it wasn't the first time this had happened in his short life, and was unlikely to be the last. He followed his mother into the pub and found a quiet corner where his mother brought him over a cola. He opened his school bag and made a start on his maths homework; he hated fractions and wondered what use they had in the real world. He was convinced it was just a tool to confuse kids like him, who were a little academically challenged.

The customers knew what had just transpired, but as usual, nothing was mentioned. A couple of the customers gave her a sympathetic smile but most knew to keep out of other people's relationship issues. It wasn't the first and wouldn't be the last time Davy had given his wife a beating. He'd always been a bully, even at school and was even worse once he'd had a few pints, which was most days after work. Alas, nobody wanted to get involved as most men were scared of Davy, and so the cycle of abuse would continue.

She looked over at her son and wondered how he was coping. It was something they never really talked about. The boy, sensing his mother was looking at him, looked up and smiled at her.

One day when he was bigger he'd beat his father like he beat him and his mum. He balled his fists and dug his nails into his palms; one day he thought, one day.

The man snapped awake, the dream or memory still fresh in his mind. It was a shame he never got big enough to exact his revenge on his father, who beat him as often as he did his mother. His father after a long boozy session was staggering home and teetered off the pavement and into the path of an oncoming juggernaut. He was rushed to intensive care, but the doctors said they didn't hold out much hope that he'd pull through, but they were doing all they could to make him comfortable. He recalled visiting him with his mother. His father on his back in a hospital bed with tubes in both his arms, an oxygen mask pressed to his face, his head bandaged and his leg in a plaster cast. The boy recalled looking on, willing his father to die. His wish was granted, when less than a week later, he died of his injuries. It was one of the happiest days of his childhood.

The man shook his head and looked at his watch and wondered

why these disturbing childhood memories kept returning. They'd remained hidden for many years but had resurfaced suddenly and inexplicably. It'd given him a focus a quest for knowledge; he needed to why his father was the way he was. Why he terrorised the woman he once loved and the child he once wanted. He needed to know what made him tick.

CHAPTER SIX

Padstow present day

Any murder investigation was going to be high profile, but in Cornwall, let alone Padstow, there were very few murders, therefore it was on the watch list from Chief Superintendent Clatworthy all the way up to the chief constable for Devon and Cornwall. For Detective Inspector Phil Reynolds it was a major feather in his cap to be heading up the investigation, albeit on a temporary basis until his superior, Detective Chief Inspector Morris, returned from his training course next week. He was surprised when he was told by the chief superintendent that he'd be running the case, expecting a more experienced officer to be appointed from another area, such as Bodmin or Truro, even if only on a temporary basis. Every hour of the day he kept telling himself not to screw it up. So far he thought he'd held his own, but he was under the microscope and couldn't afford to make a mistake. A case like this could make or break a career, he prayed for a quick closure, which would help his career no end. Phil dreamed of dizzy heights, but knew if he made it to detective chief inspector before he retired, he'd be doing well. His friend and mentor, Bob Brown, only made it to DCI before retiring, but he'd been old school and was outspoken, and despite being successful was too outspoken and anti-establishment to make it any further up the career ladder. Phil had also been involved in some successful and high profile cases, but had never led a murder investigation, only under the supervision of DCI Brown. This case was a really big deal. Don't screw it up, Phil, he said to himself once again.

The post-mortem had just finished. It was particularly grizzly as the body was in such a bad way. Almost every inch of it seemed to be covered in cuts and bruises. The face was swollen and disfigured; it really was like something out of a horror movie.

Phil had attended a few post-mortems in his time but was still baffled by some of the jargon. He went to meet Mark Wilton in his office to get a verbal summary in a language he could understand, while he waited on Mark's formal report to be sent over to the station.

'Hi Mark,' Phil said as he knocked and entered his office to which the door was open.

'Hi Phil. I know you want a summary so I'll give you a quick one because as soon as I've finished my coffee I have another post-mortem to do, which your friends in Bodmin want in a hurry. Nothing related to your case, you'll be glad to know. Some guy dropped dead, but because he'd had an operation recently we need to rule out if that was the cause. I guess everyone will be clambering for compensation if it's found out to be negligence. The good news for you is that you're not looking for a serial killer; well not yet anyway,' Mark replied, grinning at Phil's discomfort.

'I bloody hope not. I'm already a little out of my comfort zone with one murder to investigate,' he replied.

'I thought you were the man that cracked the infamous Black Cockle Strangler case, earning yourself a nice little promotion to detective inspector?' Mark replied, enjoying teasing his old mate.

'Bob Brown was running that case. I just got lucky. Bent the rules a little too, which might've been the end of my career had it been picked up by the suspect's solicitor. Bob and I were convinced that due to the nature of the murders he didn't try too hard to defend him. He knew he was guilty and he had pleaded guilty. We eventually found out that when he was younger he was fixated on a popstar who did some topless photo shoots with her nipples painted black and it affected him so badly he began to murder young girls whom he'd seen topless on the beach. That's all in the past. What about the present, what can you tell me about Mick Woods' death?' Phil asked, wanting to get back to the station, anxious to keep on top of any developments and ensure the team were doing things the way he wanted.

'Death was by asphyxiation, as I suspected. We found multiple teeth, or parts of teeth to be precise, lodged in his trachea; that's windpipe to you. The initial hammer blow took out at least six teeth from the top and six from the bottom. Subsequent blows took out most of the others and broke his jaw in three places. The gag was pushed back in after that, which would've made swallowing very difficult and he would've died around seven minutes later. I suspect he knew very little, as the other blows with the hammer would've rendered him unconscious, which was fortunate for the victim.

Initially, the victim was likely rendered unconscious by a nasty blow to the back of the head. We found a gash that was consistent to the hammer blows found to the rest of the body. He was then immobilised by what I assume would've been plastic cable ties judging by the width and depth of the wounds on the victims wrists and ankles. I have fibres so can run tests on those…'

'No need. We've been to the victim's house and the ties were there, where he'd been nailed to the floor,' Phil interrupted.

'OK that's good, that'll save me some time. There were scald marks on his chest, abdomen and genitals. I've taken samples and will get them analysed but it smelt like coffee. I don't need to tell you, it was a frenzied attack, as you saw the results yourself. I had the body x-rayed and there were multiple fractures to his legs, arms, hands, ribs and skull. Some of which were inflicted when the victim was alive, but most of the fractures continued to be inflicted after he died. So time of death, I would say would've been between one and two o'clock. Oh, and your murderer is right-handed, and before you ask it could be a man or a woman; you don't need to be particularly strong to inflict those type of injuries with a heavy hammer.'

'Thanks Mark. That doesn't narrow it down a great deal. Ninety percent of the population are right-handed, fifty-one percent are women and sixty-four percent are classed as adults between the ages of fifteen and sixty-four. I'll make up a Venn diagram to see what my odds are,' Phil replied.

Mark Wilton laughed at Phil's joke, but felt sorry for his friend. He smiled and patted him on the shoulder compassionately.

'That's why I like my job. For the most part I'm dealing with science and hard facts. I couldn't do your job; there are too many variables. Right, I don't want to be rude, but I've got another post-mortem to carry out. Fortunately it's not as gruesome as your one. Then I've just about enough time for quick round of golf before the sun goes down.'

'Lucky you. I've got to go and give an update to the chief super.

Phil adjusted his tie and cufflinks, knocked and entered Chief Superintendent Clatworthy's office, dead on the appointed time.

'Good afternoon, sir,' Phil said, hoping his voice didn't show any signs of nerves.

He'd only been in his office once before when he was questioned about a facial recognition check he'd run. The man turned out to be an MI5 agent and Clatworthy had told him to forget all about the man, but then surprisingly, just before he left his office, had told him, off the record, to carry on with his investigation; it seemed he was as intrigued as Phil was to find out why an MI5 agent was operating in Padstow.

'Take a seat Reynolds,' Clatworthy instructed him and sat there appraising him.

Phil was unsure if he should wait or just give him an update on the case. He decided to wait and tried his best not to fidget while trying to keep eye contact.

'What's the latest with the murder inquiry?' he finally asked.

Phil gave him the details of the post-mortem not holding back on any of the gruesome details.

'Very nasty. How far have you got in your investigation?'

'We notified his next of kin, who was the deceased's wife. They were separated. She was living in a halfway house with her young daughter as her husband had a restraining order out on him as he was found guilty of domestic abuse.'

'Is she a suspect?'

'The pathologist told me the wounds could've been inflicted by a man or a woman, so she can't be totally ruled out. Sergeant Walsh paid her a visit to inform her of her husband's death as she's still his next of kin, despite their relationship issues. My gut feel is she didn't murder her husband. Unsurprisingly there was no remorse when she was informed, but that isn't unexpected after what her husband put her through. I'm convinced she didn't kill him based on what Sergeant Walsh told me. I shall interview her again myself and see if she's got a motive, other than revenge for domestic abuse or an alibi that rules her out.

We've asked around with friends and work colleagues and nobody knew of any enemies he had or of anyone who had a grudge against him. Most of them knew he used to beat his wife and that's why they were separated. Those who knew his wife didn't think she would've murdered her husband. Most of them said she was a very timid woman.'

'Could she have arranged for someone else to murder her husband?' Clatworthy asked.

Phil paused for thought.

'It was something I considered. However, the extent of the mutilation to the victim suggests not. I think anyone who was hired to kill Mick Woods, wouldn't go to all the trouble of torturing the victim. It doesn't fit with the profile of a professional hit and a non-professional would be nervous, and again would do it as quickly as possible to avoid being seen or caught,' Phil replied.

'I would tend to agree with you, but we can't rule out any possibilities. If we're correct in our assumptions, then it was either someone with a personal grievance with him, a random attack by some very sick individual or he was targeted for a particular reason. If it wasn't a personal grievance, I do believe there's a possibility the perpetrator of the crime may murder again.'

'That was also something I considered. Let's hope we're wrong; one murder inquiry will be difficult enough.'

'Indeed. Keep me updated of any developments, Reynolds. I'm sure you don't need me to remind you that this is very high profile and a quick result would be advantageous.'

'I'll do my best, sir,' Phil replied, hoping that his best was going to be good enough.

'Don't screw this one up, Phil,' he muttered to himself over and over as he returned to his desk.

The halfway house which was Gillian Woods' temporary accommodation, until the council found her a permanent residence, was nothing more than a single room in a converted house with a shared bathroom, living room and kitchen for Gillian and two other women. It wasn't squalid, but it had an air or neglect about it. The cheap, flat-pack furniture in any normal household would've been replaced long ago. Gillian noticed the disapproving look DI Phil Reynolds gave as he gazed around the shared living room.

'It's not exactly the Ritz I know, but perhaps now that Mick is dead, my case worker will ensure I can move back into my old place,' Gillian Woods said.

'I expect that would be the logical thing to do, but who knows how social services work,' Phil replied, trying to put Gillian at ease.

'I don't think logic is something that exists within social services. Anyway, what can I do for you? I was interviewed yesterday by your lot and your sergeant there was with the detective,' Gillian said, nodding her head towards Sergeant Fiona Walsh who Phil Reynolds had asked to accompany him.

He was always wary of interviewing a woman alone and always felt that two male detectives would be intimidating so preferred the company of a female officer, especially as Mrs. Woods' recent experience with men wasn't a happy one.

'I know you were, but we have a few more questions we'd like to ask you. I won't take up too much of your time,' Phil replied.

Gillian nodded but said nothing.

'Where were you between 11pm and 3am the night before last?' Phil asked.

'You don't beat around the bush do you?' Mrs. Woods replied.

'I prefer to be direct,' Phil replied and smiled reassuringly.

'If you must know, I was here sleeping. And no there isn't anybody who can confirm that apart from my daughter. I was here chatting with Milly until about ten-thirty and then I went to bed. Am I suddenly a suspect?' she asked him, unable to hide her amusement that she thought it possible she could kill her husband.

'We're just trying to eliminate you from our enquiries. Your husband was violent and abusive, which gives you a motive, and as such I have to be satisfied that you were not involved in your husband's murder.'

'Involved? By that you mean hired someone to murder my husband?' she replied and scoffed.

'By involved, I mean personally or indirectly through a third party. It's a possibility and as such I need to ask,' Phil replied.

'Mick gave me nothing. Any money I brought in from my part-time jobs he took, because he was paranoid if I'd got any money,

I'd go out with friends and find someone else or just get on a bus and leave him. So I couldn't have hired a hitman, even if I wanted to. I won't lie to you inspector, there were times, many times in fact, that I wished he was dead, but I kept telling myself he was ill. He used to be a nice guy, well to me that is, but, but… something changed…'

Gillian paused as she wiped a tear from her eye. Phil noticed the anger in her eyes as she recalled the good times, and the resentment towards herself for still having feelings for her husband.

'OK Gillian. Do you know of anyone who would want your husband dead? Did he have any enemies?'

'Not that I know of. He didn't have many mates. He used to go to the local a lot and chat with the lads there. He took me once or twice, but that was a long time ago. I got the impression they didn't really like Mick; he was more tolerated. One of the boys, you know how it is. I think they were scared of him. He was a bit of a bully; even at school he was. Maybe you should ask around in The Admiral's Daughter; that was where he drank most nights.'

'We will be interviewing everyone he knows in time. Was Mick a wealthy man? Perhaps he was due an inheritance from a relative?'

'No. Mick was an only child and both his parents are poor as church mice. The only thing he might inherit is their debts and his father's battered old Toyota that he somehow manages to get an MOT for each year.'

'OK, thanks for your time Mrs. Woods. We may need to speak to you again, but that's all for now,' Phil replied.

'Do you think she did it or is involved? Phil asked Fiona once they were seated inside the car.

'No chance. She's too timid for one and I think deep down she still has feelings for him. Do you?'

'Nah, very unlikely. Unless she's a good liar, but as you say, I think for some unknown reason she still loves him. Strange but it happens. Let's get back to the station and see if there have been any positive leads,' Phil replied.

CHAPTER SEVEN

The Ship had become something of a regular haunt for Ed and his good friend and business partner, Bob Brown, a former DCI with the Padstow police. Ed couldn't call it a local on account of it being in Padstow town centre, a few miles from the sleepy village where Ed's house was on the outskirts. Ed would occasionally drive in to meet Bob for a beer and take it easy with what he was drinking. However, today like most other times, he was in the mood for a good drink, so had walked in, and would catch a cab home.

Ed spotted Bob in a chair by the window facing out towards the harbour. On seeing Ed walk in, Bob downed the contents of his glass and waved it towards him, letting him know it was his round. Ed acknowledged with a nod.

Lewis, the pub landlord, saw Ed before he got to the bar and began to pull the first of two pints of Doom Bar, which he knew was Ed and Bob's preferred ale.

'Did you enjoy your holiday?' Lewis asked.

'Great thanks. Crete is a lovely island. It'd make a great place to settle down and retire to,' Ed replied, thinking of John and Frank who'd done just that.

'So why don't you?' Lewis replied.

'They haven't got Doom Bar,' Ed said with a smile, and wondered what was stopping him from living there.

'You'd miss that gorgeous girlfriend of yours, more like.'

'There's that too. Good job they haven't got Doom Bar; it'd be a difficult decision to have to make, but I'm sure Angel would understand.'

Ed grinned and shared a laugh with Lewis. He tapped his debit card on the card reader to pay for the drinks. Ed had only recently started using the contactless payments, having finally caught up with the rest of the population of the UK. He still didn't fully trust the system and thought it was open to abuse if you accidently dropped your card or some light-fingered bastard stole it from you, but he had to admit, it was very convenient. He walked over to Bob and put their drinks on the table.

'A man could die of thirst waiting for you to get a round in,' Bob greeted him.

'Drink slower then. It might also help with your weight problem too. Although… you do look a little thinner in the face. When I say thinner, I probably mean more jowly; saggy even.'

'I'm neither saggy nor jowly, you anorexic cretin. As it happens I have lost a few pounds, if you must know. Raechael is still trying to put me on a strict diet and trying to make me drink less.'

'So life isn't much fun right now?' Ed replied.

'I said trying to; I didn't say she was succeeding. I'm trying to eat more healthily, but there's no way she's going to get me to cut down on my drinking. I don't drink that much and a man has to have a few pleasures in life. Anyway, how was the holiday, shame you had to come back early.'

'Crete is a beautiful island. John and Frank send their regards. Nice set up Frank and Emily have and by all accounts it's very popular and turning a nice profit. Unsurprising really as the food she serves is delicious. Frank's bought himself a nice little boat so we did some deep sea fishing.'

'Did you catch anything? I've been fishing loads of times and never caught a bloody thing. Hardly surprising when you consider the available food in the ocean. Why would a fish be tempted by a hook with a rubber squid on it?'

'You have a point. I never caught anything, yet again. Angel caught a tuna. Only a small one, but it took Frank half hour to land it. It tasted bloody delicious.

Angel was happy to finally meet her idol, so she was very happy catching up with the legend, John Stone. It was a great holiday, just a shame it was cut short. It was only two days of the holiday we lost so I can't complain. I was half expecting her to be called back in the first week so I consider myself lucky. Just a pain in the arse it was the two days we were intending to spend hanging out with Frank and John,' Ed replied.

'I went to Crete years ago. I had a great time with a couple of mates from the Met. John and Frank made a good choice retiring there. It might be something to consider in the future,' Bob replied, his face seemed to suggest he was giving it some serious thought.

'I've just had this conversation with Lewis. You'd miss the beer so I'm pretty sure that isn't gonna be an option for you. So what's new business wise? What have I missed?' Ed asked, changing the subject. He liked having Bob on the payroll. They made a great team and it wouldn't be the same without him.

'Well, it's actually been very quiet. One guy called asking for a price to snoop on his wife to find out if she's having an affair or not. I told him the daily rate and he said he'd call back. Oh, and this morning I got a call to look into a missing person. I told her the daily rate and that you'd be back in a day or two to take the case, if the person was still missing. I sent you all her details in an email. You know I hate missing persons. As always, I'll be happy to help you and advise you, but I won't take an active part in it; unless, of course it turns out to be something big, like that Jade Wickham case.'

Bob handed Ed the SIM card Ed used for his business number in his mobile phone, which Bob had used in his own phone during Ed's absence. Ed powered his own phone down so he could put the second SIM card back into his own phone. Modern technology was a great thing, he thought.

'I'll give the lady a call in the morning to see if we can help. So basically it's been nice and quiet. Good job we don't rely on this business to make a living or we'd both be homeless,' Ed said.

'The joys of being a millionaire, eh?'

'You too, now?'

'That money we got from Griggs, added to the savings I already had, plus the twenty-five percent tax free from my pension put me in the millionaire club, but only just. I'm nowhere in your league but I have enough to see me comfortably to the end of my days.'

'OK, so we don't need it too busy, just busy enough to stop us getting bored and drinking ourselves into an early grave.'

'I'll drink to that,' Bob replied.

'Let's face it, Bob, you'd drink to anything, which is good as I do believe it's your round.'

Bob took the empties back to the bar.

Ed smiled, happy that he'd have a case to work on to take his mind off missing Angel, and worrying about what dangers she was getting herself into this time.

CHAPTER EIGHT

DI Phil Reynolds was exhausted. In between running the murder inquiry for Mick Woods, he was also doing as much as he could at home to ensure that the wallpapering was completed. There was no rush to get it completed, other than he knew Emma wanted to get it finished as soon as possible so she could get on with painting the walls and woodwork, and living in comfort again. Emma had been busy and stripped all of the walls now and had sanded them down, after filling in any holes in the plaster, ready for Phil to put up the lining paper. He knew how much Emma hated stripping and sanding but she did what she could to help; appreciating the stress her partner was under. Therefore, Phil felt obliged to do a couple of hours each evening, despite being tired and stressed himself. Emma was a great help, pasting the wallpaper so there was one ready after Phil had hung a strip. They made a great team and he appreciated her understanding of his job and the demands it made on his personal time. Sometimes striking a decent work to home life balance was difficult, but Emma was tolerant and he did his best to make up for it when it was quieter at work.

The office was already a hive of activity when Phil arrived just before eight o'clock. He made himself a strong coffee and wandered over to the whiteboard to make notes. He noted all the detectives working on the case were already hard at work and rapped on the desk in front of him to get everyone's attention.

'OK, I'll not take up too much of your time, but I have a few updates since yesterday and I want to make sure everyone on this case is kept in the loop. If we're all armed with the same facts and information, the more chance one of us might come up with a crazy idea that might just lead to finding out who killed Mick Woods.

If you haven't yet had a chance to read the post-mortem details I'll give you a quick overview. It's gory and not good reading for the squeamish. Woods died of asphyxiation from choking on his own teeth. He was severely tortured. He stomach and genitals were scalded with what we now know was black coffee no sugar. Not every black coffee drinker is a suspect or half of us might be in the frame,' Phil joked to ease the tension in the room.

'The actual murder weapon is believed to be a claw hammer. He was knocked unconscious with the same hammer and nailed to the floor using plastic cable ties. We know this from the wounds inflicted. The hammer was used to smash the victim's teeth down his throat causing him to choke on the splinters. Just about every major bone in his body was broken by the same hammer, mostly after his death, which was fortunate for the victim.

He was killed in his own home, forensics are still there going over the place with a fine tooth comb. The body was moved and thrown from the bridge on the A39 where it came to rest on the Camel Trail. Time of death is between 1am and 2am. It's a thirty minute drive from the victim's house to the bridge.

I went to see the victim's wife yesterday. She confirmed what we already knew that her husband was a wife beater and a bully. That said, his wife, Gillian, although she's got the motive, myself and Sergeant Walsh are convinced that she isn't our killer. She's a very timid lady, as perhaps you'd expect from a victim of domestic abuse. We also believe she still has strong feelings towards her now deceased husband, despite how he'd treated her.'

Phil paused noting that the chief superintendent had walked into the room. Phil suddenly felt under immense pressure.

'Carry on, DI Reynolds,' he said.

'It's also my belief his wife was not involved in hiring a professional hit or friend to kill him. If it was a professional hit, I doubt whether he would've taken the time to torture Woods. Professional hitmen get the job done quickly and efficiently to remain undetected. If it was a friend Mrs Woods hired, I think it would've been messy and possibly frenzied but, I doubt very much an inexperienced hired hit would've taken the time to nail the victim to the floor first or dump the body elsewhere.'

Phil paused and looked around the room, inviting questions but there were none at this time.

'DC Edwards, you went to the victim's place of work. What did you find?'

'Woods worked at a small engineering firm in the Trecerus Industrial Estate on the outskirts of town. It's a small firm that employs around a dozen people. They have a couple of lucrative government contracts making aircraft parts, which keeps them afloat. Woods was a CNC centre lathe turner and he'd been working there for about seven years. The boss said he was a good worker, punctual and put in a decent shift.' Shaun Edwards replied.

'What about his co-workers? Was he popular?' Phil pressed.

'I wouldn't say he was popular, but they rarely socialised with him outside of work. One guy knew him from school and said back then he was a bully and because of that kept his distance. They all knew he bullied his wife. He made no secret of that and often bragged that he'd had to "sort her out", that was the phrase one of the guys used. One thing we did find out was that most nights he could be found in The Admiral's Daughter pub, which is about a five minute walk from his home. I'll be following up with that one this morning sir.'

'Nice work Shaun. His wife told us about his local, I'll come with you this afternoon. Harris I'd like you to get all the CCTV from likely routes from Woods' home to the A39 bridge over the Camel Trail and see what you can find. I know we don't have too many cameras out that way but you never know. OK any questions?'

'Is there a possibility we might be looking for a serial killer, sir?'

The question from Detective Constable Will Pascoe threw him. He glanced nervously at Clatworthy who was standing in the corner and gave him a rare smile. It wasn't a friendly smile but one that seemed to take pleasure from seeing Phil shuffle nervously, wondering how he should answer the question.

'We only have the one victim, and as yet we don't have a motive or a suspect. It's too early to say, but something that I believe cannot be ruled out. Let's just hope we catch whoever did this and that they had an axe to grind with Woods, and he isn't the first of many. Let's park that idea for now and concentrate on the facts rather than speculating. Right then, let's get going.'

Phil walked over to Clatworthy assuming he wanted to talk to him.

'Did you want to speak to me sir?' he asked.

'Yes. I was on my way to my office and I thought I'd stop by and see what progress you've made and to tell you that your DCI, who was due back tomorrow, was taken to hospital last night and had emergency surgery to remove his appendix so he'll be off work for at least another week or perhaps longer. So you'll continue to be in charge until he returns. If the case is still ongoing,' he replied.

'Oh, I'm sorry to hear that. I'll stop by and see him this evening. As for the case, I think if we can confirm he was in the boozer the night he died it'll be a big help. The post-mortem report did state he'd been drinking. I'll go with Edwards later this afternoon, sir. He's a good detective, but hasn't had much experience of a murder case. None of us have to be honest, sir. We don't get too many round here fortunately.'

'Let's hope it continues to be the case. Keep me abreast of any further developments; the local press are getting excited and we will need to give them a formal statement. I'll arrange for something via the press office. So no need to worry about that one, Reynolds; I think you've got enough on your plate,' Clatworthy replied.

'Of course, sir, and thank you.'

Clatworthy turned around and left. Phil breathed a sigh of relief and went to see Edwards.

CHAPTER NINE

The house was at the end of a terrace on a steep hill on a road called High Street, not far from the church. Ed and Bob were both a little out of breath after the steep walk up to the house where Mrs. Moore lived. Ed knocked and waited. The door was finally opened by a woman Ed guessed to be a few years past middle age, with blonde hair scraped back into a short ponytail, greying at the temples.

Ed held his private investigator licence so Mrs. Moore could read it.

'Ed Case, private investigator, and this is my business partner, Bob Brown, who you spoke to when you called.'

'I was only expecting you. He told me he didn't get involved with missing person cases,' Mrs. Moore told him,

'He doesn't as a rule, but I wanted him here today as he's something of an expert on missing person cases from his years in the police force. Bob was a DCI here in Padstow until he took early retirement.'

Bob's experience wasn't a lie, but his reasons for being there were. Ed wanted him to come along to ensure he was asking the right questions to get the investigation off to a good start, but Mrs. Moore didn't need to know that.

'I know who he is. I remember seeing him on telly a few years ago. He was being interviewed on the local news channel about that serial killer we had around here.'

'You're famous, Bob,' Ed replied and received a frown in return.

'Well, you'd better both come in then,' she replied and turned and headed down the corridor.

Bob and Ed followed, Ed closing the front door behind him.

They entered the small living room and took seats on the sofa, which was as lumpy and uncomfortable as it looked. In fact all the furniture looked well-lived in apart from the TV, which appeared to be brand new and was enormous. Mrs. Moore left them and could be heard in the kitchen rattling a teapot and crockery. She entered a few minutes later with a pot of tea on a tray with a plate of rich tea biscuits.

'Can't stand tea without a biscuit to dunk,' Mrs. Moore informed them as she placed the tray on the coffee table.

'Quite right and proper,' Bob replied.

Ed had never been a fan of dunking anything in a cup of tea. Many a time he recalled his grandmother dunking rich tea biscuits and then spending ages trying myopically to fish out a disintegrated biscuit from her brew with her arthritic fingers. Still each to their own, he thought.

'Who is it you want us to find, Mrs. Moore?' Ed asked.

'I want you to find my son,' she replied.

Ed wondered how old her son was as she looked to be in her mid-to-late fifties, but perhaps she'd had a hard life or started a family late in life.

'What's your son's name and how old is he?' Ed asked.

'He'll be thirty-eight next birthday and his name's Owen.'

Ed made a note in his phone. While mentally calculating that Mrs. Moore must be at least fifty-four years old, assuming she conceived her son at a legal age, also making his initial guess of her age about right.

'And how long has Owen been missing?'

'About six weeks, I think. I'd spent a few days with my friend in Camborne and when I came back, Owen wasn't here. I can get my diary and get an exact date, if you want.'

'Later will be fine,' Ed replied holding his hand up as Mrs. Moore began to rise from her armchair opposite them. 'Six weeks is a long time. Have you notified the police?' Ed asked a little perplexed. He wasn't sure if Mrs. Moore was playing with a full deck.

'The police wouldn't help me. Bloody useless the lot of 'em.'

Ed glanced at Bob who raised his eyebrows to the ceiling.

'I don't understand.' Ed replied. 'Normally the police would be happy to log someone as missing if they were notified and especially after being missing for so long.'

'Well not that lot in town. They told me not to worry and that he'd turn up sooner or later.'

'That doesn't sound right?' Ed replied and turned to Bob and gave him a nod, letting him know he needed his help.

'Mrs. Moore, has your son done anything like this before?' Bob asked.

'Never. We have a very good relationship and have always been a close family, ever since his father left us.'

'I hate to ask, but does Owen have any mental health issues?' Bob asked, thinking that the mother was clearly a little unhinged and might've passed the crazy genes on to her son.

'No, of course he doesn't. Owen is in perfect health, both physically and mentally.'

Ed frowned. Something wasn't quite right. If someone had been missing for six weeks and the police had refused to help, he'd expect the person reporting it to be at their wits end. Mrs. Moore seemed far from troubled.

'Have you contacted his place of work or his friends?' Ed quickly asked, before Bob could ask his next question.

'Yes. He worked for his friend who runs a building maintenance service company. He told me Owen had resigned six weeks ago,'

'Mrs. Moore, did your son take his belongings with him when he went missing?' Ed asked.

'Yes, of course he did. What a strange question. Why wouldn't he?'

'So technically speaking, Owen isn't really missing... it's more a case of he's moved out. Is that correct?' Ed pressed.

'Yes, of course it is, but that's beside the point. He's still missing and I would like him found. You deal with missing persons and I'd like to hire you to find my son. Money isn't an issue, I just want him found. Will you help me or not; or do I have to look for another private investigator who will?'

Ed looked at Bob. His body language told him he was having difficulty in keeping his temper and his laughter at bay. Ed scratched his chin and thought about telling Mrs. Moore that he was unable to help, but the compassionate side of his nature kicked in. He felt sorry for the woman who clearly doted on her son. It'd be an easy case to solve and he'd got nothing else on the go right now and it'd be a nice distraction until Angel finished her assignment; whatever and wherever that was.

'It's a little strange, but as you say, missing is missing. I'm not sure if this makes it more difficult or easier. I'll take the case, Mrs Moore. So to make a start, I'd like you to find me the most recent photo you have of Owen and let me know the exact date he left home,' Ed told her.

Mrs. Moore left the room to find the photo of her precious son.

'You're not seriously gonna take this one on are you?' Bob asked.

'I don't have any other cases and this one shouldn't be more than a couple of days work. I feel sorry for her too. Call it me being a soft touch. I know that's what you think,' Ed replied.

'You're way too bloody soft. But it's up to you; it's your time and effort not mine.'

Mrs. Moore came back into the room smiling. Ed smiled back as she handed him a photo of her son. Ed took a photo of it, before slipping it into his jacket pocket.

He was a handsome man with the same pale-blue eyes with a darker blue circle around the iris as his mother. He had a full head of blond hair, not unlike the colour his mother's probably was when she was a few years younger. It was parted on the left and was off the ears and collar. Ed's first impression was that he was a smart and intelligent man.

Ed asked a few details about his height and weight, which might help with jogging people's memory if Ed was describing Owen Moore to someone. Moore was quite a common surname and he hoped it wasn't going to make his task any more difficult.

'Is Owen in a relationship?' Ed asked.

'No. He did have a nice young lady a couple of years ago but that ended when she moved away because of her job. They tried to stay together but they drifted apart. Since then he's not found the right girl, he tells me.'

Another door shut.

'Does Owen have any places he's goes to on a regular basis?' he asked.

'Like what?' Mrs. Moore asked.

'Coffee shops, tea shops, internet cafes or pubs? If I went missing Bob would probably go straight to The Ship in town to look for me. It just makes it quicker for me to find your son, if I know where he goes. I can speak to the people who work there who might know where he is,' Ed replied.

'I don't know. I'm sure he must go to pubs and other places but he never mentioned anywhere specific.'

'Does he have any hobbies? Is he a keen golfer for example? If he is I can check out golf clubs. If he liked to work out, I can try the gyms that sort of thing,' Ed asked.

'No. He kept himself in shape, but that was through diet and not over-indulging, but he wasn't a keen sportsman. He liked to watch football; he was a big Liverpool fan, but only on the telly. He never went to watch a game. I don't think he had any hobbies or not in a long time. He used to like chess when he was little.'

'OK thanks, that's very useful. Would you mind letting me see your son's room?' Ed asked.

'Of course not. Up the stairs and it's the first door on the left,' she replied

The two men left the room and entered the bedroom. Both Bob and Ed looked around, but it seemed anything of importance had been taken. There were no photos, paintings or posters on the walls and nothing on the bedside unit or dressing table. The drawers were empty, bar a few old pieces of clothing that her son clearly didn't think were worth taking. The wardrobe was a similar story, just a couple of old and worn out shirts. The shelf at the top had a few old board games, such as monopoly and a chess set and a couple of old books. Disappointingly, there were no documents that might've suggested where they'd find him.

'Still think you'll find him in a couple of days?' Bob said unable to hide his sarcasm.

'I reckon so. Everyone leaves a trail. Nobody just disappears off the face of the Earth.'

'Earth is a big place, he could be anywhere,' Bob replied.

'Or he could be round the corner or anywhere in between, I know. Right then, I reckon we're done here. I fancy a massive Cornish pasty and after that I reckon I'll be a little bit thirsty. I'll start looking for Owen Moore tomorrow.'

'I'm glad you haven't lost all your common sense,' Bob replied and pushed Ed towards the door.

Mrs. Moore was waiting for them in the living room.

'There was nothing in his room that gave us any indication as to where he might be. I'll make a start on the internet searches, social media that type of thing to see if that gives me any clues as to Owen's whereabouts. If that yields little in the way of results, I'll start the footwork tomorrow, asking around with friends and work colleagues and a door to door of likely places people might've seen him. I'll provide you with an update in a day or so,' Ed told her. He deliberately didn't mention hospitals and police, so as not to alarm her.

'Thank you, Mr. Case. I know you'll find him,' she replied.

'No pressure then,' Bob muttered as they walked down the short hallway to the front door and clapped him on the back.

CHAPTER TEN

The landlord of The Admiral's Daughter, Jim Pengelly, was standing at the end of the bar talking with one of the regulars. Phil recognised Jim as he knew him through a mutual friend; Padstow wasn't a big town. He looked up as DI Reynolds and DC Shaun Edwards entered the bar, cut his conversation short and walked towards the two detectives.

'Hi Phil, good to see you again.' Jim said and nodded an acknowledgement to Edwards.

'Likewise, Jim. This is DC Shaun Edwards, we're here to ask you a few questions about Mick Woods; we were told this was his local.'

'I thought you might be. I know you're on duty, but can I get you a drink, on the house of course.'

Phil looked at the clock on the wall then the length of the bar to see what beers were on offer. He nodded in appreciation of the good selection the pub had to offer.

'I shouldn't really, but by the time we finish here it'll technically be knocking off time so I will. Not that I ever seem to be off duty these days, even more so when there's a murder investigation to run, but sod the rules. I'll have a pint of Tribute. Shaun what do you want?'

'I'll have a Korev. Thanks Jim.'

Jim shouted the order over to Penny the barmaid, asked her to bring them over and ushered Phil and Shaun to a table in a quiet corner of the room.

'Nice pub you have; great selection of ales too. Too many pubs these days only have one or two ales and all the rest are lagers.'

'That's because I'm a free house and can sell what I like. A lot of the others are owned by the brewery or part of a chain and sell whatever the brewery or chain tells them to. I sell five times as many ales as I do lagers so I try and keep a good selection and always have guest ale each month.'

Penny placed three pints on the table. The three men took an appreciative gulp.

'Shaun, I'll leave you to ask the questions,' Phil said.

In truth he wanted to get an idea of how good a detective Edwards was and also be in a position to ask any questions he felt he'd missed his old boss and mentor, Bob Brown, operated in the same fashion.

'No pressure then, boss,' he replied and turned towards Pengelly.

'We understand Mick Woods was here the night he was murdered. That's the fourteenth, if you need a reminder. Is that correct?' Edwards asked.

'I can confirm Mick was in here the night he was murdered as he was in here just about every night; that night was no exception. He arrived about six o'clock as he used to come here straight from work. I remember that night well, because he'd gotten into an argument with Steve Trethowall about women's football of all things. I had to break them up as it looked like it was going to come to blows. Mick could be a bit short-tempered and it wasn't the first time he's gone toe-to-toe with one of the customers. As it was Steve finished his drink and left.'

'What time was that?' Edwards asked.

'It was about ten-thirty. Mick carried on like nothing had happened and stayed until about eleven-fifteen.'

'Did Mick lose his temper a lot? I know he was something of a bully,' Edwards asked.

'No. Like I said, he'd had one or two fights, handbags at dawn really; nothing serious. He was opinionated and wound a lot of people up. He seemed to relish the confrontation, especially after a few pints of ale. He wasn't one of the most popular customers I have, and for the most part, people would steer clear of him. They all knew he was a wife beater and that made him unpopular. He usually sat at the bar and would talk to anyone who sat next to him or stood next to him waiting to be served, but he'd no close friends he could hang out with.'

'What about Steve Trethowall?'

'They're not friends. Both men have been coming to my pub for years. Steve was probably waiting for a beer and they got talking. They were talking about women's football as an advert had been on the sports channel plugging an England international game at the weekend. I know this as I was standing behind Steve, talking to another punter, but didn't take too much notice at first. Steve said something about wanting to see the match and Mick replied, telling him that women belong in the kitchen and should leave the sport to the men. Steve told him he'd be happy if his wife was a professional footballer and would happily be a househusband as it'd mean his wife would be fit and earning a lot more than he did. Mick then said something along the lines of his wife not being fit and rich. I reckon Steve thought Mick was saying his wife was fat, which to be fair, she is a bit on the chubby side, but you don't insult a man's wife to his face and expect him to leave it at that. Anyway, it got heated and I pulled them apart and as I told you Steve knocked back what was left of his pint and left.' Jim shrugged as if it was nothing.

'Do you think Steve would've waited outside and taken it further?' Edwards pressed.

'No. Steve's normally an easy going guy. He's certainly not a violent man. Mick just hit a nerve; that's all.'

'Apart from that, did you notice anything out of the ordinary? Was anyone acting strangely or were there any new faces in the pub that night?

'Nothing at all. It wasn't a busy night; it never really is on a weekday, unless there's a decent football match on. I would've recalled any new faces. It tends to be regulars and locals in here as it's a little too far out of town for tourists and there are no hotels or caravan parks this side of town.

I have CCTV and can give you a copy of the recordings if you like. I have two cameras inside and two in the car park. It's all digital so I can put it on a thumb drive if you have one. If not I think I have an old one you can have somewhere.'

Phil looked at Edwards and told him he didn't have one. Edwards smiled and pulled one from his trouser pocket.

'Always keep one with me,' he replied and grinned.

Phil liked him, he was easy going and resourceful. He'd acquitted himself well today.

Jim returned a few minutes later and handed the drive back to Edwards. By this time the two detectives had finished their beer. They thanked Jim for his time and for the drinks and returned to their car.

A five minute drive from The Admiral's Daughter was Steve Trethowall's house. It was a nice semi-detached cottage on the outskirts of the town. Phil thought it was probably an inheritance, much like his own, as property prices in Padstow were out of reach for many people. Steve was an assistant manager at a bank in the town and he didn't think even an assistant manager's salary would stretch to a lovely cottage like his.

The door was answered by Steve's wife an attractive woman and as Jim had suggested, she was a little overweight. Phil showed her his ID and asked to speak to her husband. She looked at her watch and said it'd be another five minutes or so before he arrived home from work, and invited them in to wait.

'Nice cottage you have Mrs. Trethowall,' Phil said trying to put her at ease, as she seemed very nervous of the police presence.

'It was an inheritance from my mother. She died of cancer a few years back and I was her only child. Otherwise we'd never be able to afford a place here. Steve's not in any trouble is he?' she asked

'No we just need to speak to him in regard to an ongoing investigation,' Phil replied again, trying to put her at ease.

'It's about that Mick Woods, isn't it?'

'What makes you think that Mrs. Trethowall?' Phil replied trying to keep his tone neutral.

'Steve said he'd gotten into an argument with him the night the poor man was killed. He said the police would try and pin it on him if they could.'

'What time did your husband come home that night?'

'It must've been about a quarter to eleven as the local news had just finished and I was ready to go to bed. You can ask him yourself, he's just walked up the front path.'

'Didn't take you too long, did it?' Steve Trethowall said when he entered to room, immediately knowing they were police.

'DI Reynolds and DC Edwards,' Phil said, introducing themselves.

'I didn't kill him,' Trethowall said. His voice was tinged with anger.

'We're not accusing you of killing him, Mr. Trethowall. At the moment we're just trying to piece together Mr. Woods's movements leading up to his death. Care to tell us what happened in the pub that night?' Phil asked.

Trethowall looked across at his wife then turned to Phil and spoke.

'I was waiting to be served and was standing next to Mick. On the TV they were plugging the England ladies next match against the USA. As a passing comment to Mick, I said it might be worth a watch. He said something like a woman's place is in the kitchen. I expected as much from a sexist pig like him. I then told him I'd be quite happy if my wife was a famous footballer as she would be making pots of money. He said that's never likely because your missus is short and fat. I told him to watch his mouth and squared up to him. Jim pulled us apart before punches were thrown. I finished the last mouthful of my pint and left and came straight home because I didn't want to get into any bother with Woods. The man's a bully and always up for a fight. If I'd stayed, I'm pretty sure he would've tried to provoke me into a fight and that bastard's not worth it.'

'What time was this?'

'Jean was still up. She likes to watch the ten o'clock news before turning in for the night. The local weather was on so I reckon about ten forty-five. It's about a fifteen minute walk, so would've meant I left the pub about ten thirty.'

'Then what did you do?'

'I went to bed of course. What d'you think I did?'

'I don't know, Steve, that's why I'm asking. Maybe you were still annoyed with Mick for insulting your wife and decided to pay Mick a home visit?' Phil suggested to see what the reaction was.

'I knew it'd come to this, you coppers are all the bloody same. I went to bed and slept and got up for work the next day. I didn't go anywhere near Mick Woods's house. The man is a violent bully. I'd made my point with him and that was that. I should never have spoken to the bastard in the first place. I don't even like the guy.'

'And you can vouch for your husband, can you?' Phil asked.

'Of course I can. He kept me awake all night snoring. He always snores when he's had a drink.'

'Did you notice anyone suspicious in the pub that night or maybe outside the pub?' Phil asked.

'No. I was angry and stormed out and didn't pay any attention to anything. I didn't calm down until I reached home.'

'I see,' Phil replied.

'What's that supposed to mean?' Trethowall asked.

Phil ignored him.

'So you saw nobody on your way home?'

'It was pushing on for eleven o'clock I reckon most people would be in bed.'

'You weren't and Mick's murderer wasn't.'

'Very funny detective, but I didn't kill him. We had an argument in the pub and I went home because I didn't feel like staying after that. I have my job to think about and getting into a scrap with that arsehole would be seen as tarnishing the bank's reputation and I might get fired or overlooked for promotion, if there was any.'

'OK, Mr. Trethowall, thanks for your time. That's it for now.' Phil replied and stood.

'For now; what's that supposed to mean?' Trethowall said the anger back in his voice.

'Just a figure of speech, but if any new evidence comes up we may need to speak to you again.'

'I won't be able to tell you any more than I have. You'll be wasting your time.'

Phil shrugged and made his way out to the hallway. 'That'll be my call to make,' Phil turned and replied as he pulled the front door behind him.

'Get your coat, Jean. I need a drink.' Steve said to his wife.

CHAPTER ELEVEN

The pint after a Cornish pasty turned out to be anything but a quick drink. Ed had moved his car from the car park at the top of the town and parked it in the yard behind his friend Chris's shop where she had three parking spaces. The other two spaces were occupied by her car and her fiancé's Harley Davidson, which was padlocked with two heavy chains. Ed wondered if one of them was the one her fiancé had tried to take his head off with, before they became friends. Chris allowed Ed to use one of the spaces whenever he was in town. Ed, not wanting to feel like he was abusing the privilege, only parked there on the odd occasion when a quick pint was likely to turn into anything but a quick pint. He went inside the shop and had asked Chris and her fiancé, soon to be husband, if they wanted to join him and Bob for a beer but they already had plans and had a table booked at a restaurant.

After it looked like it would be a long session, Ed suggested Bob gave his wife Raechael a call to see if she wanted to join them for dinner, which she did. As they were looking at the menus, Phil Reynolds and his fiancée Emma walked in. They spotted Ed and made their way over.

'I guess a quiet night and a romantic meal for two aren't on the cards,' Phil said and gave Emma a look of apology.

'You can sit over there, if you like. We won't be offended,' Ed replied.

'That's OK. We haven't seen you for ages. We've been really busy with the house,' Emma said.

'You'll soon be settled and you can get back to painting and making jewellery,' Ed said.

'The only painting I'm doing is walls, ceilings and skirting boards. Even that's slow going, as Phil's hanging the lining paper and is too busy looking for murderers and too tired when he gets home.' Emma said it jokingly, but Phil knew there was some truth in what she said.

Phil shook his head. He knew Emma wanted to get the house finished, but his hours were often long when there was a high profile investigation going on, and he'd very little spare time. Today, for the first time, he'd managed to finish at a reasonable hour and suggested a date night, which now looked more like a lad's night.

'I'll tell you what. I just have a missing person case that I think will be very quickly solved, so I can come round and do the papering if Phil hasn't finished it. I quite enjoy papering and find it strangely therapeutic. Hanging lining paper is a piece of piss as there's no patterns to match up or worrying if it's the right way up or not,' Ed told her.

'I'm not so sure it'll be a couple of days.' Bob informed her, and proceeded to tell everyone about the case, much to everyone's amusement.

'So the guy just moved out and didn't tell his mother?' Phil asked.

'Yeah, it took me long enough to drag it out of the mother, but that's how it is. I just need to ask everyone he knows. I'm sure one of them will know where he went. Three days max, I reckon.' Ed replied confidently.

Phil's phone rang. He pulled it from his pocket, looked at the caller display and gave it an unhappy look before answering.

'Hi, Will. Please don't tell me we have another body.'

'No. I'm just phoning to let you know I found the car used to dump the body over the bridge. I got CCTV of the A39 and caught the guy in the act. The lighting wasn't great, but the car was a dark coloured Toyota. I managed to zoom in enough to get the registration. Turns out it was Mick Woods's own car.'

'Clever bugger. Tell me you got some decent shots of the murderer.'

'He was wearing a mask and well covered up. I'd say average height and build, which isn't very helpful. I did my best to clean up the images, but I've sent it over to the experts at HQ in the hope that they can do a better job, and get us something that'll help. I tried to track the car using the traffic cameras but he turned down a back road and there are no cameras along those so it's anyone guess where he went.

'Great work, Pascoe, and thanks for letting me know,' Phil replied.

Phil was about to hang up.

'Hang on, boss.... uniform just got a report of an abandoned car and it's Mick Woods's. A farmer found it blocking one of his gates and called it in. They've sent a patrol to secure the vehicle and have called out the forensic team. Do you want me to attend?'

'Yes and take DS Walsh with you, she's on call tonight.'

Phil ended the call and smiled.

'You're smiling. I take it you've had a breakthrough?' Bob asked Phil.

'We got traffic camera footage of Mick Woods's body being dropped over the bridge. Turns out our murderer was using the victim's own car and that's just been found abandoned down a lane, blocking a farmer's gate. We've got a forensic team on the way out there, but as with Woods's house, I doubt there'll be anything to find. Whoever killed him seems to be very careful.'

'Aren't they all? I'm free to help in an advisory capacity as Ed is gonna be tied up for weeks chasing shadows,' Bob offered and grinned at Ed.

'Oh ye of little faith. It'll take a week at tops,' Ed replied.

Bob laughed.

'It's gone from a couple of days to three days to a week in less than five minutes. He could be anywhere in the world and you reckon a week. I've worked more missing person cases than you've had hot dinners. You'll be lucky to find your man in a month.'

'Lucky is my middle name, watch and learn, grandad, watch and learn,' Ed replied cheerily.

The truth was he didn't have a clue how to go about this and was concerned Bob was right; nothing irked him more than Bob being right. That was enough to spur him on in finding Owen Moore within a week. Seeing the look on Bob's face would be more satisfactory than actually solving the mystery of his man's whereabouts.

Ed finished his drink and went back to looking at the menu, pushing thoughts of taking a month to solve the case to the back of his mind and concentrated on having a great night out with friends; Owen Moore could remain invisible for another day. As Bob once said to him, if he was alive today, he's likely to be alive tomorrow, and if he's dead, he'll still be dead in the morning. Ed loved Bob's black and white approach to life, or death as the case may be.

CHAPTER TWELVE

Padstow some years earlier

The boy walked home alone. He couldn't remember if his mother was working this evening or not. When he arrived at the pub he paused. If his mother was working she'd be behind the bar or walking around collecting empty glasses and bottles and emptying overflowing ashtrays. The boy pressed his face against the dirty glass and scanned the interior. He couldn't see his mother, but that could mean she was in the cellar, getting bottles and cans to replenish the shelves.

Two strong hands grabbed his shoulders. The boy almost cried out.

'Looking for your mum?' a friendly voice from behind him asked.

The boy nodded still too shaken to reply. He'd nearly wet himself in shock, thinking it might be his father.

'It's her night off tonight,' the voice said and gave the boy's shoulder a friendly squeeze. 'Frightened the life out of you, didn't I?'

The boy looked through the window, seeing the other barmaid was working tonight. He turned and looked at the man behind him for the first time.

'Thanks, mister,' the boy replied, recognising the man from the pub as he and his mum were friendly.

'Just John is fine. Mister makes me feel like an old man. Go on, get going, or your dinner will be getting cold and your mum will give you a cuff round the head.'

The boy smiled and jogged off towards his house. He liked John. He wished his father was more like him. His father was a bastard. He just hoped he wasn't home when he got in. Life at home was nice when he wasn't there. When he was there, it was always a constant worry; would he be drunk and abusive, physically and mentally or would he be too drunk to care about him and his mother. He'd find out soon enough.

The boy entered the house though the back door which led to the kitchen. He peered in and saw his mother, immediately relieved his father was nowhere to be seen. His mother gave him a warm smile and invited him to come in with a jerk of her head. She rose from her chair and gave her son a hug, which he returned. He loved his mother as much as he hated his father. His mother kissed him on the cheek and turned her attention to the cooker. A few minutes later his dinner was warmed and placed in front of him. It was a stew made with tinned meat that was so soft it flaked into pieces when he touched it with his fork. It was served with boiled potatoes and carrots. It was his favourite dinner and his mother knew that and made it often. He wiped his plate clean with a slice of the cheap, sliced loaf his mother brought from the supermarket. The boy had no concept of rich or poor, it was just how his life was and he got on with it. It was only many years later he looked back and realised they were extremely poor, and every day was a struggle to survive financially.

The front door banged open, making both boy and mother flinch. The boy looked at his mother, who gave him a smile that said everything would be OK. The boy hoped that was true. The boy rose and took his plate over to the sink and began to wash it in the now lukewarm dishwater with trembling hands. As he placed it into the drainer it almost slipped through his fingers. The kitchen had two doors; one to the hallway the other to the living room. He was in a quandary as to which door to leave by to avoid his father. He opted for the living room, thinking his father would go directly to the kitchen to eat.

'Going somewhere, boy?' he father boomed as he pushed through the door he was about to exit from.

His father gave him a shove and he had to take a number of steps backwards to avoid falling over. His mother was there to stop him falling. She stood behind him, her protective arms around his shoulders crossed over his middle, pulling him in closer. He could feel his heart beating hard, thumping against his ribs. He was sure he could feel his mother's own heart thumping into his back, or was that his imagination?

His father strode into the room, stinking of stale beer and cigarettes, a smell he'd never forget and hate even as an adult.

'You're turning that lad into a bloody sissy,' he bellowed and cuffed him round the ear.

The boy saw stars and his ears were ringing such was the force of the blow. Tears prickled his eyes, but he didn't want to give his father the satisfaction of seeing him cry again, but he always cried; he couldn't help it. It wasn't the pain; he was used to that, but feeling impotent and not being able to fight back. His father was so much bigger and stronger.

'One day when I'm big and strong like you, I'm gonna kill you!' The boy blurted out.

His father laughed mockingly. He felt his mother stiffen and pull him tighter to her body.

'You will, will you? I'll tell you what you ungrateful, snivelling little shit. I'll save you the trouble and kill you long before you get big enough and strong enough,' his father taunted.

The boy screamed in rage and tore himself from his mother's grip. He flew at his father, his fists balled. Alas the boy had never had a proper fight in his life. He didn't know how to fight, but he battered futilely at his father's chest and stomach with every ounce of strength he possessed. Spittle flew from his mouth as he screamed at his father, telling him he hated him and would kill him. His father laughed and looked on impassively as his son beat impotently at his chest. The father became bored and slammed a meaty fist into his son's stomach. The boy doubled over, barely able to draw breath and crumpled into a heap onto his knees. His father kneed him in the side of the head sending him onto his side.

His mother ran to him to protect him from further punishment, knowing what the consequences would be, but her motherly instinct for her son overriding any concerns over her own safety.

The man grabbed his wife by the hair and pulled her away from her son. Her face contorted as he twisted the handful of hair he was holding her by, threatening to tear it bodily from her scalp.

'By god you're an ugly woman. What happened to that pretty

girl I married. The girl who made all the other men envious of me eh? What the fuck happened? You don't even try to look half decent. You disgust me!' he screamed, his face just inches from his wife's

The boy looked at his terrified mother as he fought to catch his breath. He knew she was pretty. The man called John from the pub had told him once that his mum was a beautiful woman and he couldn't understand why she'd married his father. She could've been mine, he told the boy, but for some reason she fell in love with your father. He remembered that sad look on his face as he told him. Even he thought his mother was beautiful. When she was in the pub working, she was happy and smiled and he knew she was the best mum in the world, but only until she got home.

His father slammed a fist into his wife's stomach and carried on doing so until she cried out for him to stop, but he wouldn't stop. Right now the boy wondered if it would ever stop. Life was miserable and he didn't know if he could take any more. He sobbed impotently on the floor as his father continued to beat his mother. He put his hands over his ears and pressed them as tight as he could, but he still failed to drown out the sound of his mother's sobs and his father's punches beating out a steady rhythm on his mother's face and body.

CHAPTER THIRTEEN

Padstow present day

Brandon Taylor came round and entered a world of pain. He felt like he had the worst hangover in his life. He tried to recall the night before and didn't remember having drank that much, well not by his standards. The police presence where he lived was minimal, but he still took it easy when having a meal and a few drinks at the golf club after work. So why was his mouth bone dry and his head pounding like he'd been on a heavy session? He opened his eyes and stared at the ceiling. Panic set in; it wasn't his familiar bedroom ceiling. He tried to sit up but his arms and legs wouldn't move. He felt the nylon cable ties bite into his wrists and ankles and hissed in pain. He was also as naked as the day he was born.

'What the fuck?' he mumbled.

Out of the corner of his eye he saw a silhouetted figure in the doorway that led to the kitchen. It was a man, that much he could tell as the lounge where he was pinned to the floor was in relative darkness making it difficult to make out any features.

'Who the fuck are you?' he said his voice angry.

The figure laughed and returned to the kitchen. Brandon wasn't a stupid man and knew that shouting and screaming in his current position would end badly for him. He'd have to bide his time looking for an escape or talking himself out of trouble. He looked across at his wrist. The thick heavy-duty ties were fastened to the floor by large masonry nails. The nail was so close to his wrist it allowed hardly any movement. As soon as he tried, the tie bit into the flesh. It was the same for his other wrist and he assumed, as he was unable to see and by the lack of movement, his ankles.

What seemed a very long time to Brandon, but was in fact only a couple of minutes, the figure returned to the doorway and looked down on him.

'I'm a wealthy man, you know. Name your price to let me go. I swear I'll never tell anyone about this, never. Just let me go, please.'

The man walked over and sat down on the sofa and peered down at him and spoke in a cold, even tone.

'People with money always assume they can buy anything they want. Well, it might buy you flashy cars and expensive, designer clothes, but somethings cannot be bought; like me. I really don't care much for worldly goods. Therefore any amount of money you offer me to buy your freedom or your life are wasted on me. So shut your fucking mouth,' he said his voice full of menace.

'What do you want from me? If you don't want money, I, I... don't understand,'

'Just a friendly chat. I want to find out what makes a man like you do the things you do. What makes you tick, Brandon Taylor?'

'Who are you?'

'My name is John' I would shake your hand but it appears you're a little tied up, if you'd excuse the pun.'

'Good one,' Brandon replied clearly not appreciating his captors' sense of humour.

'Where is your wife, Mr. Taylor?' John asked.

The question seemed to throw him and he paused before answering.

'How the hell would I know? Probably somewhere thinking of ways to spend the money her and her money-grabbing solicitor are planning to screw me for when we get a divorce.'

The bitterness in Brandon's voice was clear despite the dire predicament he was in. John shook his head and almost laughed. Taylor was facing death, and was likely to be aware that was a possibility, but the hatred for his wife was greater than the fear of an imminent death.

'Why are you getting a divorce, Brandon?' John asked, despite already knowing the answer. It was always good to hear both sides of the story.

'Why is that any of your business?' he replied angrily.

John leaned forward and tipped his recently made black coffee over Brandon's genitals. Brandon screamed as the piping hot liquid scalded his genitals. Brandon didn't need to look to know that the thin skin on his penis and scrotum, would be red raw and that blistering was sure to follow. John didn't care how much noise the man made, Brandon's house was a large, detached home in Rock and some distance from the nearest neighbour. Nobody would hear his scream, or those that might be near enough to hear were second homes for the wealthy and mostly unoccupied this time of year.

'Here's how it works, Brandon. I ask the questions, you provide me with the answers. You think the coffee was painful? The next time you fail to answer or lie to me, the coffee will seem like a mere pin prick. Now, I'm off to make another coffee. While I'm doing that maybe you'd like to think about that?'

Brandon nodded and sniffed back the snot in his nostrils. He could do nothing about the tears that welled up in the corner of his eyes and rolled down the side of his face to tickle his ears.

John came back, nursing a new cup of coffee. Brandon gave John a furtive glance and noted the steam rising from the cup. His genitals were now on fire. He couldn't rid his mind of images of his red and blistered penis and swollen testicles. He closed his eyes and swallowed.

'You were going to tell me why you got divorced.'

'She was having an affair,' Brandon replied, his voice full of anger, or was it hatred, John wondered.

'How did you know?' John asked.

'I didn't for sure, but she was on her phone more often, always texting and being secretive.'

'Perhaps she was texting a friend, discussing you or plotting to leave you? Maybe she was just telling her friend what a bad husband you were?'

'I gave Liz everything. I paid for her lavish lifestyle and she repaid me by having an affair.'

'What did you do? If I'm not mistaken, it's she who's divorcing you. Now that would suggest you were in the wrong not her or it would be you divorcing her.'

'How the hell do you know?' Brandon spat back.

John picked up the claw hammer by the side of the chair and tapped it lightly on Brandon's thighs and worked his way up to his forehead. He enjoyed watching Brandon flinch with every tap.

'I won't tell you again, Brandon. Just answer the questions or things will be even more unpleasant for you. He leaned forward and splashed his steaming coffee on his left nipple. Brandon hissed in pain once again but managed to stifle the scream. John nodded for him to continue.

'We had a row and I told her to leave.'

John smashed the hammer down into Brandon's ribs.

'I want the truth, you piece of shit. Tell me the fucking truth!'

John waited until Brandon had stopped swearing and sobbing.

'OK. Please put the hammer down and I'll tell you everything. Just put the hammer down, please.'

John placed the hammer on the floor but in reach for when he needed it.

'We had a fight and after that she left me,' Taylor continued.

'A fight that ended up with your wife covered in bruises and needing twelve stitches over her eye, because you hit her repeatedly. It sounds like she didn't put up much resistance.'

Brandon shook his head

'Things got a little out of control. I…I lost my temper.'

'Not for the first time,' John replied finding it difficult to hide his disgust.

'What do you know?' Brandon said defiantly.

John swiftly picked up the hammer and slammed it down into the other side of his ribs, this time hard enough to be rewarded with the sound of at least one rib snapping.

Brandon screamed and shortly afterwards passed out.

John waited but soon became agitated, wanting to get on with his questioning. Emptying the rest of his coffee over Brandon's right nipple had the desired effect. He came round and started sobbing.

'I'm sure your wife cried when you beat her, but unlike me, I bet you didn't stop, did you?'

Brandon shook his head.

'Why, Brandon? Tell me why?'

'Liz married me for my money. I'm no fool. She was way out of my league. She was as vivacious as she was beautiful. She could've had any man she wanted but I got her. I know it was so she could live a wonderful life and never want for anything. She grew up in relative poverty and saw me as a meal ticket. But I was infatuated and wanted her at any cost. Soon she was unable to hide her contempt for me. She grew to hate me because I was jealous and thought she was sleeping with everyone she met. It consumed me. She denied any affairs and I got angry and beat her. There happy now?'

'Not really. Why did you beat her?'

'I thought that it might get her to tell me the truth about her affairs. I also thought that if she'd got a few bruises, she might be afraid to go out in public. If any of the men she was sleeping with saw the bruises they'd see me as a man to fear, because I'd do the same to them or worse.'

'How very sad and stupid of you. I'm not sure if I feel sorry for you or contempt for you. Liz wasn't seeing any other men. She married you for your money, of course, any fool can see that. You even admit it yourself, but she didn't hate you. In her own way she loved you, at first; until the abuse started. You may be a successful businessman, but you're not a smart man, are you, Brandon?' John said.

John shook his head, mockingly.

'How…. how the fuck do you know? Just how the fuck do you know so much about my life, eh? You're bullshitting.'

'How I know is not relevant to this conversation. I know, Brandon, I know and that's all that matters. Now say goodbye. This conversation is over. I think I know what makes a man like you tick.'

The hammer came down with such force onto Brandon's forehead the bone shattered leaving a bloody crater in the centre of his skull. John wrenched the hammer out the hole he'd just put in Brandon's head; it came away with a sucking noise as if his pulverised brain was trying to hold on to the hammer as evidence. It was swiftly followed by a crunching sound as the hammer grated on the shattered bone. He was dead within seconds, but John wasn't finished; he was only just beginning.

CHAPTER FOURTEEN

Missing person cases were often as dull as dishwater. Ed knew why Bob never got actively involved in them. He was happy to advise Ed, but left the drudgery of finding someone who didn't want to be found alive or otherwise to Ed. Fortunately, Ed had yet to be involved in a missing person case, where the person he was looking for had been murdered or fallen into a life of drugs and prostitution to fund their habit. Ed was very grateful for that. Bob had told him of the horrors he might find. Having to report that back to the person who'd hired him, telling them of the demise of their loved one and then presenting them with a bill for doing so was something Ed hoped he'd never have to do.

Ed was on his way to meet Owen Moore's ex-boss who would hopefully shed some light on why Owen had disappeared, and with any luck where he went to.

His car was still parked in the yard behind Chris's shop. He knocked on the back door as the shop was yet to open and he wanted to ask if she minded if he left it there all day. He knew what the answer would be, but he didn't like to just assume. Her fiancé, Lionel, opened the door, his huge frame almost completely filling the doorway and insisted he come up for coffee and breakfast that Chris was preparing. Ed couldn't believe his good fortune. Ed spent most of his time alone, rattling around like a pea in a bucket in a house way too large for one person and had no heart in making meals for one. Breakfast was invariably a cup of instant coffee, black no sugar, after his morning run and workout in the gym. Lunch was invariably a sandwich, if he'd got any bread in the house that was edible and not covered in green mould.

Dinner was something simple and quick, that didn't make a mountain of washing up, like a pasta dish, a chilli con carne or a curry he'd cooked in bulk and frozen. Getting a decent homemade fry-up accompanied by Blue Mountain filter coffee was a real treat. He'd got the same filter coffee at home but a spoon of instant coffee was quicker and good enough. He really needed to sort out his laziness in the kitchen when Angel wasn't there, which unfortunately was most of the time.

Breakfast was over all too quickly, and he promised he'd come round for dinner with Angel once she'd finished her latest assignment. He didn't know the details, but it was somewhere in Europe. He knew not to ask too many questions.

Ed walked to a town house that served as the offices of several local businesses. He looked at the list and noted that Lawry Property Management Services was on the first floor. Ed stepped into the building and took the stairs to the first floor that were directly in front of him. At the top of the stairs there were two doors, one to a solicitors and the other to LPMS. He knocked and entered.

'Mr. Lawry? Ed Case, we spoke on the phone yesterday,' Ed said and smiled congenially.

'Oh yes, the P.I.,' the middle-aged man behind the desk replied.

Ed wasn't sure what to make of him. His tone was flat, but the words on their own could easily be interpreted as either derisory or mocking.

'Thanks for agreeing to see me. I wanted to have a few words about Owen Moore who I understand worked for you for a number of years.'

'He did until he quit about a month ago, perhaps a little longer. I can check if it's important.' Lawry replied.

Ed Lawry's tone was one of boredom. He wasn't sure if it was just his natural speaking tone or if he was trying to belittle Ed in some way. He got the feeling this was going to be a difficult interview but smiled again, despite already deciding he wanted to punch the man in the face.

'That's OK; it ties in to the time he went missing. Did he give you notice or did he just not turn up one day?'

'He gave me a month's notice as per his contract.'

'OK. Did he tell you why, like he'd got another job, better

money; that sort of thing?'

'No, he didn't, and to be honest it's none of my business. He left and he was replaced.'

Ed checked his anger, for now at least. He needed information not to make an enemy.

'Didn't Owen's new employer request a reference?' Ed asked.

'Owen asked me for a reference personally and I typed one up and he came in and collected it the next day. I'm a small company and don't have the luxury of a human resources department.'

Ed had never heard of that. He assumed all new employers wanted to speak directly to the previous employer or send them a reference request directly. What did he know? Ed hadn't had a real job in ten years.

'Were you and Owen not close or did you have a falling out? I was given the impression that you were old friends,' Ed asked a little perplexed at Lawry's lack or interest or compassion.

'Now I'm a suspect, am I?'

'Perhaps if he was dead Mr. Lawry, and for all I know he could be, but that's no concern of mine as that's a police matter. Anyway, as far as I know he's alive and well. I'm a private investigator, not a policeman. I look for people, not motives and suspects. All I'm trying to do is find an ex-employee of yours on behalf of a distraught mother. I hope that if you have children and one goes missing, the people who might have vital information on their whereabouts are more forthcoming than you are. At this point in time, I believe Owen is alive and well, but his whereabouts is unknown, so nobody is a suspect. Additionally, as a private investigator, I really don't care about any criminal activities he may or may not have been involved in. I don't care if he's a mass murderer or robbed a bank. I just need to find him and try to get him to get in contact with his mother,' Ed replied doing his best to keep his voice as emotionless as Lawry's.

'Mr. Case, I keep myself distanced from my employees. You can't be a leader and run with the pack at the same time. I like to think I'm a fair boss. I pay the going rate and offer a good benefits package, for a small company. I don't befriend my employees as it makes business decisions much easier. It's difficult enough firing an employee should the need arise, but if that person is a friend or someone you like, it makes the decision all that much harder.

Friendship can cloud many business decisions that have to be made. You probably think that makes me a bit of a cold fish, but business and pleasure should be kept apart in my view. To answer your question I was friendlier with his mother. I've known her for years and wanted to help her son out, but I never told him that was the reason I gave him a job. As it turned out he was a great worker. I wish some of my other staff were as good as he was.'

Ed nodded and understood, but did think he was a cold fish all the same.

'I understand your perspective. If you don't know anything about Owen, would it be possible to speak to any of Owen's colleagues he may have associated with outside of work or even worked together?'

'Most of the team work alone. Occasionally, there may be a job that requires two or three people to be involved, but not often. Some of my staff are CORGI registered and some not, so if I have a problem that involves gas, such as changing a boiler, I send one of those men to another site to help the engineer there. But as you say, if one of my kids went missing, I would like to think everyone would help as much as possible. I only have a team of nine so it'll be a very short list.'

Ed nodded and waited until Lawry had scribbled down first names and mobile numbers for his nine employees after consulting the contact list on his own phone.

Ed thanked him and walked out into the street rather disappointed. He'd hoped he'd find out if Owen Moore had left town or where he was now employed. Finding a missing person was like a game of snakes and ladders Bob had once told him. Some days you got lucky and shot up a few ladders. Other days it was just a slow laborious trudge towards the end, one square at a time, and others you seem to land on all the snakes and go back to the beginning. Right now, Ed felt like he was waiting to throw a six on the dice so he could actually join in the game.

Ed pulled out his mobile, took it off mute and looked at missed calls and messages. He'd received a text message from Angel from a number that was withheld. She was still alive and missed him. It was tedious work, not a single gunfight and she thought she'd be at least another week. Great, Ed thought; another week alone; not what he wanted to hear. His day was just getting better and better.

He strolled back down the hill towards the town centre, ordered himself a coffee and found a spare bench facing out into the harbour. No time like the present he thought and pulled out the list given to him by Lawry. He dialled the first name on the list, a few minutes later the call was over and he was still no further forward. The man he'd spoken to said he wasn't close to Owen and never saw him outside of the office as he lived in Wadebridge and only ever ventured into Padstow if he was called in by the boss. It was a similar story with all eight of the other employees of Lawry Property Management Services. Only one man claimed to have worked with him in the last six months as Owen was the only other available employee who could work on a broken boiler as he himself wasn't CORGI registered yet. Either someone was lying to him or Owen wasn't a very sociable person or perhaps not a popular person, which he'd find out, well find out eventually.

Normally, if Ed wanted police help he'd give Phil a call but he knew his back was up against the wall trying to find a murder suspect. Ed was grateful to be looking for a missing person not a deranged killer. He walked to the police station and recognised Kelvin Mortimer behind the desk. He'd been kind enough to give him a lift back to Padstow when his car mysteriously exploded after being stopped and breathalysed by the police.

'Hi Kelvin, or should I say, Sergeant Mortimer?' Ed replied seeing the recently gained three stripes on his epaulets.

'Kelvin is fine. What can I do for you, Ed?'

'I was after a favour. I've got a missing person case and I just wanted to check my man isn't in police custody or reported dead in a car accident,' Ed replied.

'I can do that. What's his name?'

'Owen Moore spelt with two O's and with an E on the end. He's a local man from Padstow and went missing six weeks ago, if that helps?'

Kelvin turned to his computer screen and typed in a few commands.

'Nothing. He's not been arrested and in case you want to know he doesn't have a criminal record either.'

Kelvin typed in a few more commands.

'No reports of him being in a road accident and admitted to hospital either. That doesn't mean he isn't in hospital. It just means the police weren't involved.'

'Terrific. I didn't think I'd be that lucky. Thanks for your help. I owe you a beer or two,' Ed replied.

'Thanks and good luck,' Kelvin replied as Ed turned towards the door.

Ed made a few Google searches on his phone and called all the hospitals in the region. Each time he had to explain who he was, and as he'd done with Lawry earlier, laid it on thick about finding a loved one. Each call proved to be negative and nobody by the name of Owen Moore had been checked in or out of hospital in the area. He'd look at hospitals further afield later as his gut feel was that he'd not gone that far away. Mrs. Moore's missing son was either alive and well and didn't care about his mother or he was dead and waiting for some dog walker to find him. Ed hoped it was he who found him and not a dog walker.

With nothing better to do, he called Bob to see if he'd got any words of wisdom for him. He told him he had a few ideas and said to meet him in The Ship in fifteen minutes. It was a little early for a drink, but if Bob had an idea it was worth starting early and Ed was fresh out of ideas.

Bob was in a good mood and was already waiting for Ed at their table of choice by the bay window, a freshly poured pint waiting for him, which made a nice change. Bob made a point of looking at his watch as Ed pulled out a chair and sat down. He didn't really want a drink, but made an effort as it'd only be met with a barrage of derisory comments about his sexuality from Bob if he declined.

Bob lifted his glass and they clinked them together. Bob drained half the contents and smacked his lips appreciatively. Ed took a couple of gulps, feeling nothing positive about the cold ale when it reached his taste buds.

'You've got a face like a slapped arse. What's the problem?' Bob asked.

'Nothing much, just this Owen Moore case. I went to see his old boss and he was a bit of a git, but having said that, he did give me the numbers of all his employees. As I told you earlier they all said they rarely worked together as each team member managed their own place of work or portfolio of premises. Basically they're glorified caretakers. Some work at schools, some at business facilities, and others at private properties. When something goes wrong they fix it or in the case of something big, call in specialist. They all live in different areas so never socialise; not even a Christmas do. It feels like a wasted morning really.'

Bob grinned.

'Now you know why I don't get involved in these cases; they're bloody frustrating. You might go a few days without a sniff of a clue to his whereabouts and then you make a breakthrough. I hated them with a passion back in the day when I was a lowly constable in London. I've had plenty of missing person cases. When I was in C.I.D. as it was called back then, most of the missing cases turned out to be murder cases. But that was London for you. This is Padstow, where you hardly ever see a murder by comparison. So I think you'll most likely find him alive. Unless he's moved to London,' Bob replied and punched Ed on the arm, making Ed laugh.

'I'm fairly confident Owen isn't a murder victim. He handed in his notice as per his contract. Like I said, the boss was very hands off with his staff and never asked why he was leaving or where he was going. So I reckon he's just gone to ground for some reason.'

'What about mates? I thought his mother said the guy he worked for was a mate.'

'Lawry never said he was friendly with Owen. His attitude was he was the boss and he employed people but never got close. He told me it made making business decisions easier; I guess he has a point. Apart from Lawry his mother never mentioned anything about mates when we were there. Either he's a loner or not a great conversationalist or everyone thinks he's a bastard and therefore don't socialise with him,' Ed said.

'Everyone has mates,' Bob replied.

'That's true. Even you've got mates,' Ed replied.

Bob shook his head; clearly not in the mood for some mindless banter today.

'I'll start with some door to door stuff around Padstow. Flash his photo around the local shops; that kind of thing.'

'Along the lines I was thinking of, but I was going to suggest targeting more specific establishments,' Bob said and smiled.

Ed raised his eye to the ceiling, knowing exactly what kind of establishments Bob had in mind.

'And by specific, I can assume you mean pubs?' Ed replied and shook his head knowingly.

'It's a great starting point. Everyone likes a drink and goes to the pub.'

'I think you're basing that assumption on your own standards. Not everyone is a borderline alcoholic like you. If Owen is a man with no mates or someone who isn't very chatty, I reckon a pub would be a nightmare for someone like him. I reckon the library would be a better place. But if you want to go on a pub crawl in the name of duty and put it on company expenses, then drink up.'

'Good man, you know it makes sense.'

'I recall the last time we went to pubs looking for our old mate Paul Faulkner. You ended the evening getting into a brawl with four of the locals.'

'Well that's not gonna happen as everyone round here knows me.'

'Just because someone knows you, it doesn't mean they actually like you,' Ed replied.

'And just what do you mean by that?' Bob said indignantly.

Ed picked up the empty glasses to take back to the bar.

'Come on, let's go, before I change my mind,' he said to Bob.

CHAPTER FIFTEEN

Having left school with barely a qualification to her name and with a string of minor offences for shoplifting and possession of cannabis under her belt, it was always going to make finding employment a challenge for Stacey Abbot. After several years of claiming benefits, short-lived jobs as a barmaid and waitressing, a friend's mother managed to persuade Brandon Taylor to take her on as a cleaner at the clothing factory he owned. Primarily she was cleaning the factory floor and toilets, but twice a week she cleaned the small number of offices belonging to the administrative staff and senior managers on the upper floor.

Stacey may not have been blessed academically, but she was by no means stupid, and used her youthful good looks and curvaceous figure to curry favour with the office staff, many who worked late in the evening, which was how she came to the attention of Brandon Taylor.

One evening Brandon Taylor was working late. Stacey assumed the office was empty and walked in without knocking to vacuum the carpet. She apologised and smiled at the boss, who told her to carry on and that he was just finishing anyway. Stacey always wore leggings and a baggy T-shirt when cleaning as it was hot work. A number of times she caught Brandon admiring her shapely backside in the panes of glass that made up the office wall as she pushed the vacuum cleaner back and forth, and also when she turned around, catching him staring at her cleavage down the deep V of her T-shirt.

Brandon asked her why a good-looking, young girl like her was cleaning offices. She replied honestly that she got off to a bad start in life and screwed up at school and was grateful for any employment. Over the course of a couple of weeks she and

Brandon spoke many times. It was obvious by some of his double entendres and the way he leered at her that he fancied her. One evening she made a point of accidentally brushing the back of her hand across the front of Brandon's trousers while running the hoover around the desk he was standing by. It wasn't long afterwards that the blinds were pulled and the door was locked and Brandon was taking her over the desk.

Shortly after, Brandon told her he needed a cleaner at his large house. Brandon doubled her salary and effectively halved her working hours and hired her to clean his mansion in Rock, across the Camel Estuary from Padstow, three times a week, when his wife was at the local nature reserve doing voluntary work. There was very little cleaning involved as most of the time was spent making love. She'd give it a quick flick over with the duster, sweep the tiled floors and give the bathrooms a quick once over.

This morning she drove to the house on the moped bought by Brandon and let herself in with the key provided by her employer. Usually, he was around the pool drinking a cocktail when she arrived. She'd make a show of cleaning the pool area, which really amounted to Stacey striking a few poses with a broom or mop and letting Brandon ogle her, while she bent over in front of him so he could look at her backside or her breasts. After that she'd strip off and swim a few lengths naked, breast stroke and back stroke. By this time Brandon would be fully titillated and beside himself with anticipation of what was to come. She'd then get out of the pool and drape herself seductively over the sunbed next to Brandon where they'd make love for an hour or so before she gave the house a cursory clean, which also involved sex in one of the bedrooms, or Brandon's particular favourite, over the snooker table in his games room.

Brandon was a good and attentive lover as well as being a very wealthy man, but to Stacey it was an arrangement more than a relationship. In her mind it was her letting Brandon screw her, and in return she was regaled with expensive gifts such as perfumes, lingerie and dresses and the greatest gift of all, money. She arrived this morning wondering what Brandon would give her today. She hoped it was money, money was always preferred. Often she gave his expensive gifts away or sold them online. There were only so many bottles of perfume a girl needed.

As was the norm, Stacey went straight to the pool but today Brandon wasn't there. It wasn't that unusual as often he was in a meeting or tied up with business affairs. His car was in the drive so he was definitely at home. Stacey stripped off and swam a few lengths naked anyway. After lounging around the pool for twenty minutes or so she wondered where Brandon was. Business always came first, but he was a randy old sod and sex was almost as important. Stacey slipped on the dress she arrived in, which Brandon had bought for her on her last visit and insisted she wore it today. She left her skimpy, lace underwear, also purchased by Brandon, on the sun lounger and went in search of Brandon or as she referred to him, her sponsor.

His office was empty. His laptop was closed, which was unusual as it was only ever closed at night time. Stacey mentally shrugged and wandered through the house smiling, wondering where her sugar daddy was. Stacey wrinkled her nose up. The smell was awful. It reminded her of the smell of meat that made her want to vomit when she needed to cut it up to cook; only this was stronger, much stronger. Stacey put her hand over her mouth, wondering if the drains had backed up. The smell was getting stronger the further she walked down the hallway. She wondered what the hell it was; it was almost making her gag. She finally entered the living room and recoiled at the stench. She tilted her head trying to make out what she saw in the middle of the large room.

'Oh my god, no,' she mumbled, 'no…no…no…,' when the realisation hit her. She screamed and staggered to the kitchen, her legs turning to jelly, where she managed to reach the sink before throwing up. A few seconds later gasping for breath, her legs gave out and she slid down onto the tiled floor, where she passed out.

She came round with the gory vision of Brandon Taylor spread eagled, naked on the floor, blood splashed over the floor, walls and furniture, imprinted into her memory as if written in an indelible marker. Tears flooded down her cheeks as she tried to come to terms with what she'd seen. Her head was a mess, wondering what to do. Eventually, she made up her mind to run away and pretend she'd never been there, but knew she couldn't do that. Her moral compass kicked in and she decided on doing the right thing. She staggered and crawled to the telephone in his study and dialled the emergency services and waited.

Why Mark Wilton was always at the murder scene before he was would probably always remain a mystery to DI Phil Reynolds. He parked his car on the spacious drive, alongside the ambulance, its lights flashing. He thought it ironic that the person they'd be taking away was long dead and that the flashing lights were very much surplus to requirements.

Phil nodded a greeting to the constable at the front door. He looked a little green around the gills.

'Is everything alright, Damian?' Phil asked.

'Not really. It's a mess sir. I mean a real bloody mess. I've never seen anything so bad in my life. A couple of us were throwing up in the sink.'

'Thanks for the warning,' Phil replied and walked into the living room, dreading what he was going to find.

The smell was the worst thing he'd smelt in a long time. He pulled out a handkerchief and placed it over his nose and mouth. DC Edwards did the same. The body was spread-eagled. The head was just a misshaped lump on top of a body that was covered in angry cuts, gashes and welts. As with the last body it had been smashed repeatedly with what Phil assumed was the same hammer. The face had taken the brunt of the assailant's anger. Once again, there would be no identifying the body by dental records. Something was protruding from the victim's mouth. Phil peered at it but it was just a bloody mass. He was struggling to keep his breakfast down and had to look away several times and try to detach himself from the horrific scene in front of him, and the smell that was easily permeating his handkerchief.

'I can see you're wondering what's in his mouth and I can confirm it's his penis and testicles,' Mark Wilton said casually.

'Jesus Christ! What kind of sick, twisted individual would do that?' Phil replied rhetorically, looking at the cavernous bloody gore between the man's legs.

'As I always tell you, Phil, that's for you to find out. All I can provide you with are the facts,' Mark replied.

'Yeah, don't I know it? So what are the facts?' Phil asked, trying to breathe as shallowly as possible through his mouth. It didn't seem to be helping and he was desperate to get out of the room to breathe some clean air.

'I'll take a guess at the time of death being around midnight, give or take an hour. The body has been heavily mutilated as you can see, but I think most of that was post-mortem. I think it likely that death was caused by a blow to the temple. It was a particularly heavy blow, as you can see by the indentation and splinters of bone protruding through the skin. Unless, of course, that was inflicted after something else had been the cause of death, but my money is on the blow to the temple. I'd say the weapon was the same one used in the murder of Mick Woods, which I can confirm after I've carried out the post-mortem' Mark told him and smiled ironically.

'I was afraid of that. A serial killer, just what I need. Thanks Mark. When will you do the post-mortem?'

'I'll do that first thing tomorrow. You'll have the results by lunchtime. You've been lucky this week, it's been a quiet few days in the office for me.'

'Lucky? Are you sure about that? Thanks, Mark,' Phil didn't feel at all lucky. As if one murder wasn't enough to deal with he now likely had a potential serial killer to deal with. 'Tomorrow is great and I appreciate that. Right then, where's the person who called it in?' Phil said to DC Edwards who was standing to one side, really wanting to leave the carnage of the living room.

It never ceased to amaze him how so little blood inside a human could make such a mess. The living room looked like it was bleeding to death; blood had splattered and dripped from every surface and piece of furniture. The police photographer was in his element.

'The cleaner did, a young girl called Stacey Abbot. She's with one of the paramedics. She's been given a mild sedative as she's pretty shaken up as you'd imagine.' Edwards replied.

DC Edwards led Phil through to the kitchen where Stacey was sitting holding a cup of coffee; a blanket was draped over her shoulders. Phil wondered why her hair was wet.

The paramedic explained she'd been given something to calm her down but would be OK to answer a few questions, but told Phil to take it slowly and go easy on her. Phil acknowledged that and introduced himself to Stacey, who in return barely acknowledged him.

'I understand you found the body, Stacey. Can you tell me what time this was?'

'I'm not sure. I arrived at the house at around eleven as I do every morning I come to clean for Brandon. He wasn't by the pool so I went for a swim. When he didn't come after about a quarter of an hour, I went to find him and...'

'You don't need to tell me about that, I've seen it for myself,' Phil replied.

'The call was made at eleven thirty-five, boss,' Edwards added to confirm Stacey was about right with her estimation.

'Do you always go for a swim when you arrive,' Phil continued, now knowing why the girl's hair was wet.

'Most days I do. I have a key and let myself in and we swim then hang out and after I clean.'

Phil gave Shaun Edwards a look and wondered how to phrase the next question.

'Are you and Mr Taylor... romantically involved?' he asked.

Stacey nodded.

'I used to clean at the factory and we flirted with each other and he got me to work here. It started before his wife left him, but her leaving was nothing to do with me. It was more an arrangement really than a relationship. He paid me a good wage, way too much for what the job was worth. He also gave me extra money and gifts. In return I had sex with him. It suited both of us.'

'Thanks for being so honest, Stacey. Did you notice anything different or out of place when you arrived?'

Stacey took a moment to think then shook her head.

'No. Everything was normal apart from the smell as I got nearer the living room. Oh god... that...that smell' she replied.

It was as if she could actually smell that awful stench. Stacey gagged and put her hand over her mouth. She leapt from her chair and just managed to get to the sink before she threw up once more. When her gagging and retching had subsided, Stacey took a deep breath and spat into the sink. The paramedic was at hand and offered her a glass of water, which Stacey took and swilled around her mouth and spat it out into the sink before taking her seat. Phil decided he didn't need to ask any more questions at this point, and more importantly the girl needed to rest.

'OK thanks, Stacey. We'll probably need to ask you a few more questions later, but for now, we'll leave it and let you get some rest. We'll arrange for one of the officers to give you a lift home.'

'I have my scooter outside,' she replied.

'You've had a sedative so you can't drive. We'll make sure someone takes it back for you.'

Stacey nodded.

'Right then Shaun, let's go and see what the forensic team have found, if anything, before we get back to the station. I'm sure Clatworthy will be calling within minutes of finding out we likely have a serial killer on the loose.'

'Sir, there's something I think you should see,' one of the forensic team said urgently.

Phil and Shaun followed him out to the kitchen. There under a coffee cup was a note. It was unremarkable, the type of sticky, yellow note found in homes and offices up and down the country. This one had a short message on it, which read "SAY THANK YOU JOHN' written in capital letters. Shaun Edwards took a quick photo of it before the forensic officer placed it inside an evidence bag and began dusting the coffee cup for prints.

'What the hell is that all about?' Phil asked rhetorically. 'Was that something written by Brandon Taylor or a message from the man that murdered him?'

'No idea, boss. There was nothing in the evidence from Mick Woods' house,' Shaun replied.

'Right then, after, we've finished here, we'll go back to Woods's house and check. Perhaps a draft blew it under the sofa or something, if indeed there was a note at Woods's home,' Phil said urgently, feeling a little more positive about the case.

'Before we go, let me check on something.'

Shaun left and returned shortly with a copy of the Telegraph newspaper in his hand and began flicking through the pages, finally finding what he was looking for. He left the newspaper open on the kitchen table at the crossword page and then checked the handwriting against the note he'd photographed. He put the phone down next to the almost completed crossword and moved aside so Phil could look.

'I don't think it was Brandon Taylor's handwriting on the note. If you notice the crossbar on the "T", Brandon's slant upwards, whereas the one on the note is perfectly horizontal. Also in the crossword you can see that Taylor doesn't put a crossbar above his

"J" whereas the note has,' Shaun said.

'I'm no handwriting expert but I tend to agree with you. Also the "I", Taylor just uses a straight line but the note has the crossbars both top and bottom. Nice work Shaun. Bring that newspaper with you; it might be useful if we get any handwriting experts involved in the case.'

The forensic team continued to dust for prints and scour the room for fibres or clues left behind by the killer. After analysis later in the lab, the only prints they had found were those belonging to Brandon Taylor. No stray hairs other than the victim's. Even the coffee cup had been washed to remove any traces of saliva. The killer had been meticulously careful, as they were at Mick Woods's house. Phil and Shaun Edwards did their own search but it seemed nothing had been missed by the forensic team. They left to go to search Mick Woods's house to see if they'd somehow missed a similar note to the one they'd just found.

CHAPTER SIXTEEN

Ed was on another pub crawl with Bob. Ed knew it was a worthwhile exercise and what Bob said actually made sense. Bob had taught Ed that in any case they took on, they had to explore every possibility and nothing could be ruled out until it'd been checked out. Ed didn't know many men who didn't like a visit to the pub once in a while; even if they were adverse to crowds or people and not particularly inclined to chat to strangers, if that was the case with Owen or not. A pub was an easy place to be a stranger in a crowd. Ed had spent a few years drinking alone very often after the disaster of his first marriage and would find the background noise of others enjoying themselves a nice distraction. Often chatting to a relative stranger was a nice release from the anger and hatred he felt at being cheated on and humiliated by his deceased wife. Perhaps Owen Moore was no different. Maybe this was just an excuse to join Bob for a few pints and put the frustration of not being any closer to finding their client's son aside and getting drunk in working hours, who knew?

Bob, he knew would have a beer in every pub. Ed could handle the alcoholic content within reason, but not the volume of liquid and knew he'd be blown up like a balloon with all that beer sloshing around inside him so he would opt for a gin and tonic or perhaps a bottled beer or even a soft drink. Bob would rib him and call him a lightweight, but it was better than the alternative.

The first pub they chose was one very close to the Moore's house. Bob seemed to have a map of Padstow imprinted into his memory; especially the pubs unsurprisingly. Ed guessed being a copper for so many years he'd likely know the town and surrounding area like the back of his hand. The Salty Dog was open, but the customers inside were few. Ed expected it to be busier as it was still lunchtime for many people, but a quick look around the interior of the pub seemed to suggest that unless lunch was going to be anything more than a pint and a packet of dry roasted nuts, it wasn't the place for you.

Ed approached the woman behind the bar and smiled.

'What can I get you?' she asked.

Bob was about to order, but Ed gave his ankle a tap with the toecap of his shoe, silencing him. He pulled out his phone and pulled up the photo of Owen Moore and showed it to the woman.

'We're just after some information. I'm a private investigator and looking for this man. He lives nearby and was wondering if this pub was his local.'

The woman peered at the photo.

'That looks a little like Carol Moore's son, Owen.'

'You know him?' Ed replied, excited that at least she knew him.

'No, not exactly, but I'm friends with Carol; we used to go to school together.

'Did Owen use this pub?'

'No, never. I run this place with my husband and I'm here just about every waking hour; or it seems that way. I'm pretty sure he never came here, or if he did, I don't recall seeing him.'

'So you wouldn't know where he drank or if he drank?' Ed pressed.

'No idea, I'm sorry. I'll go and see Carol later, she never told me her son was missing. She must be worried sick.'

'Technically he's not missing. He just left home and didn't tell her. I guess that amounts to the same thing. I'm sure he's got his reasons. Anyway, I have a lot of other calls to make so I won't take up any more of your time.'

'Why didn't we stop for a pint? Some pub crawl this is turning out to be!'

'Because it was a shithole, that's why. We'll have a pint in the next pub. Wherever that one is,' Ed replied.

'The Dog and Whistle; follow me.'

The Dog and Whistle wasn't exactly palatial, although it was a step up from the Salty Dog, but still not a pub Ed would drink in through choice. The customers looked a grim bunch. After a quick glance round, Ed reckoned there were a few alcoholics and the others thugs out binge drinking. A bigoted opinion perhaps, but after a second furtive glance around, he decided was probably a fairly accurate assessment.

Bob ordered a couple of pints and Ed pulled out the photo of Owen Moore and pushed it under the barman's nose. He shrugged and said nothing.

'Does he drink here? Have you seen him lately?' Ed asked slightly annoyed.

'No to both and a word of warning, the customers in here don't like the police so drink up,' the barman said quietly.

'We're not police. I'm a private investigator and I've been hired to find this guy. His name's Owen Moore and he lives nearby.'

'You might not be, but he is,' the barman said jabbing a finger in Bob's direction.

'Was, but now retired,' Bob said defensively.

'Once a copper always a copper; a leopard doesn't change its spots,' the barman replied and gave them an unfriendly smile.

'I nicked him for receiving stolen goods a few years back. He's obviously a man who holds a grudge,' Bob said and smiled at the barman.

The barman ignored him.

'Bob the bastard fucking Brown.'

Both men turned and faced a big man who from his appearance Ed assumed was a farmer or farmhand.

'A friend of yours, Bob? He sounds like he knows you very well. He even knows both your middle names,' Ed asked Bob and sniggered.

Bob narrowed his eyes and stared hard at the man walking towards him.

'John Talbot what a pleasure to see you again,' Bob replied sarcastically.

'You've got a nerve showing your face in here. You killed my fucking father,' Talbot said pointing a finger at Bob menacingly.

One thing that was sure to raise Bob's hackles was being pointed at. Talbot was lucky he was far enough away not to prod Bob or he'd be in trouble. Ed stifled a smirk. This was only going to end one way.

'I put him away for manslaughter and having a barn full of cannabis plants. You can't pin his death on me,' Bob said his anger level rising.

Ed smiled, this was getting interesting.

'Prison killed him. He wasn't a well man. He should've been in hospital.'

'He should've thought about that before he punched Tommy Lanyon's lights out. Anyway, he wasn't exactly father of the year, was he? He used to beat your poor old mum senseless and didn't treat you too much better, if I remember rightly,' Bob replied with a sneer.

Ed knew Bob was enjoying antagonising John and braced himself for the inevitable.

'You were an arsehole when you were a copper and nothing's changed.'

John lashed out with a haymaker, taking Bob completely by surprise and Ed for that matter. It caught Bob off-balance and he staggered and landed heavily on the flagstone floor. Bob seemed stunned as John came forward to take advantage.

When he drew level with Ed, Ed took a step back and slammed his fist into John's ribs and kidney, severely winding him and checking his progress. John doubled over but Ed grabbed Talbot's hair, jerked his face up and raised his fist to smash it down into Talbot's upturned face. His fist was grabbed from behind. Ed turned and a fist flew at his face. Ed's reactions were lightning fast but even he was unable to evade the punch that glanced off his cheekbone. It stung like hell but Ed didn't have time to dwell on the pain as another blow was heading towards him. Ed threw his arm up to block the punch that never came. The man about to punch him crumpled as Bob, still on the floor, but his senses returning, slammed a foot into his balls. Ed took full advantage and punched him in the temple. He hit the flagstones, where he remained; dazed, but not out for the count.

Bob was now on his feet and squared up to John who was still holding his side, his breathing laboured. Bob moved in but John held his hand aloft, letting Bob know he'd had enough. Bob grinned and kneed him in the stomach twice, letting him fall to the ground.

Bob turned towards the bar, picked up his beer and drank half the glass in a couple of swallows. Ed picked his own up and did the same.

'You two are barred for life,' the barman informed them.

'No skin off my nose,' Ed replied 'This place is an absolute shit hole. You should be fucking ashamed of yourself.'

He left a tenner on the bar, finished what remained of his pint in a few large swallows, tugged Bob by the sleeve and made his way to the exit.

'I do believe you got your arse kicked,' Ed said to Bob and chuckled.

'I was distracted. I know John has a temper on him. He's no different from his father, Rod; just a thug and a farmer. I've no idea why he was sticking up for him. He was a bloody awful father and husband. Always full of anger and pent up hatred for the world. Rob Talbot was distributing cannabis; had a barn stuffed to the gunnels with big bushy plants. Him and his mate Tommy Lanyon were in business together and had a falling out about money. Talbot's father, lost his temper, and as usual, lashed out. Knocked Tommy clean off his feet and he hit the deck catching a fatal blow on the temple on the way down, when his head bounced off the ploughing attachment on Rod's tractor. It was just bad luck really, but the huge cannabis farm was his undoing. He got ten years in total, I think, and died in prison from ill-health. He'd got a dodgy ticker or something. John seems to hold me responsible. Guess he just needs someone to blame for having a shit dad.'

The words "shit dad" hit Ed like a sledgehammer. The last words he spoke to his daughter when he found her murdered was "sorry for being a shit dad" he turned and looked away from Bob. He took a deep breath and pushed the painful memory to the back of his mind.

Bob knew something was wrong and put a hand on Ed's shoulder.

'What's up, mate?' he asked.

'The last words I said to Anna were along the lines of "sorry for being a shit dad". If it wasn't for me creating a shit storm with Kristina Kovac, Reece Greenfield and Anthony Brown-Smith, I wouldn't have been targeted by The Messenger, and she and TJ would still both be alive.'

'The old butterfly effect again. I thought you were over that?

You were a great dad to Anna. I know you didn't get to spend too long with her but in the time she was with you and TJ she wanted for nothing. If you hadn't saved her at Aldbury House, she would've died in the flames that night. If that night had never happened, she would've had a god awful life, probably very short, being used and abused by the sick bastards that used the place.

Don't be hard on yourself, Ed. What happened was a tragedy, but I know you loved her and gave her a great life. She couldn't have wanted for a better dad than you. Come on, let's get to the next pub and see if we can keep out of mischief.'

Ed smiled slapped the older man on the back, mumbled his thanks, and tried to think of things other than his dead wife and daughter.

'Keep out of mischief? That's rich coming from you. You need to heed your own advice and don't get into any more fights, you're too old and too slow for brawling in pubs,' Ed replied, knowing full well that Bob would rise to the bait. Not so much about his age, but a slur on his fighting ability would.

'I can't dispute I'm not getting any younger but I'm still a match for anyone in a punch up.'

'Apart from John Talbot, it seems,' Ed replied his face deadpan

'His mate got the better of you too, if I recall correctly. If I hadn't kicked him the knackers, he would've taken you to the cleaners.'

'You might have a point. I guess neither of us are getting any younger. Let's just say we both had a bad day at the office and move on,' Ed replied.

'I'm still not too old to give you a run for your money.'

'Is that a challenge, granddad?'

'If you think you're good enough. Me and you one on one down in your gym. It'll be interesting to see if you're as good as you think you are.' Bob replied.

Ed grinned. They'd both often wondered, so it might be a good time to find out before they really did get too old.

'You're on. I'm probably better than I think I am. Anyway, I've got some protective headgear and boxing gloves that me and Angel use sometimes because there's no point in killing each other is there?'

'Pussy,' Bob said.

'Over-confidence is often the cause of failure,'
'You're still a pussy.'
'Whatever you say, granddad.'

CHAPTER SEVENTEEN

The uniformed officer was waiting for them when they reached Mick Woods's house. He opened the door and let them inside and stood guard outside. Phil thanked him, explained he'd only be a few minutes and then he could lock up and get back to the station, and walked into the narrow hallway. Phil looked for a telephone table but the corridor was too small to have one.

'Shaun, take the living room and I'll search the kitchen,' Phil said.

When they opened the door to the living room the smell of blood still lingered in the air and the carpet was thick with congealed blood; he pitied the poor sod tasked with cleaning it all up. Phil took a deep breath and went through to the kitchen. Every surface looked to have been dusted for prints so he was sure that if there was a note forensics would've found it. The dustbin had also been removed so there was very little else to check. To be thorough he got down on his knees and shone the flashlight from his mobile phone down the sides and underneath the fridge and cooker, but found nothing other than the expected accumulation of detritus. He went back to the living room to see how Edwards was getting along.

Edwards was staring at a note pad he'd picked up, presumably from the unit the telephone was on.

'Do you have a pencil on you, boss?' he asked.

Phil fished one out of his pocket and passed it to him. Edwards began to lightly run the pencil backwards and forwards over the notepad. His face broke into a smile and he handed the notepad to Phil.

Phil studied it and could just faintly make out where the pencil had revealed the indentation from the pen that had written the previous note that had been torn off. The words "SAY THANK YOU JOHN" were just about clear enough to make out.

'Great work Shaun, I mean really great,' Phil said clapping him on the back. 'All we've gotta work out now is what it means,' Phil paused for thought. 'Let's go and see if we can find the original before we head back to the station. I reckon it must've been dumped with the body. It's not rained in a couple of days and it's not been particularly windy so we might have a chance of finding it near where the body was dumped.

They thanked the uniformed officer, leaving him to lock up and sped away to the bridge over the Camel Estuary where the body was dumped. They managed to find a spot where it was fairly easy to climb over the wall without breaking a leg or worse. Both men were fit and agile and landed on their feet. They split up both looking for the original note, which might hold a vital fingerprint or be of use to a graphologist or forensic handwriting expert. It was slow work as the spot seemed to be a popular place for tossing away fast food wrappers and containers out of car windows. Phil hated litterbugs with a passion. Phil knew the piece of paper he was looking for was only a few inches in size and it was a proverbial needle in a haystack despite it being bright yellow. Halfway down the slope Shaun once again proved his worth and found the original. It was a little damp and covered in a little dirt as well as lot of blood from the victim, but he bagged it in an evidence bag. Phil was ecstatic as any clue no matter how small might be a vital piece of the jigsaw and lead to an arrest.

The two men got into the car and returned to the police station. Phil wondering who John had to say thanks to and what linked John to the two victims?

It was too early to say if Phil was looking for a serial killer or two separate murderers. The mutilation of the bodies was similar and both had been pinned to their living room floors with cable ties. However, until the post-mortem had been completed Phil had to keep an open mind. It was a difficult thing to do when everything was leaning towards a single murderer. What the motive was for the murders was perplexing. Whatever it was must've been something that the killer was passionate about, hence the frenzied mutilation. Mick Woods had been a working class man. He was something of a bully and not popular. Brandon Taylor was a successful businessman and well-known in the local community. It'd be just Phil's luck if he was in the same masonic lodge as Chief Superintendent Clatworthy or moved in the same social circles, which would put extra pressure on Phil he could well do without. He sat down at his desk and sighed.

'Having a bad day, boss?' Fiona Walsh asked.

'You could say that. There's a possibility that we have a serial killer on our hands. Brandon Taylor was killed in much the same way as Mick Woods.'

'I'll run some checks on Taylor and see what comes up. If it's a serial killer they usually target specific groups of people and don't just select people at random; although it's not been unknown.'

'Thanks Fiona. Also can you look into any common friends and acquaintances by the name of John' Phil replied.

'Sure. Is there a reason for that?'

Phil was unable to reply because his mobile vibrated as he opened his mouth to speak. He looked at the message and sighed for a second time. Fiona indicated with her head to the upper levels of the building. Phil nodded back.

'Good luck,' she said and grinned.

Phil took the stairs wanting to delay the inevitable and give him time to think about the second murder and have answers to the questions Clatworthy was bound to throw his way. He was nervous, as right now he didn't have any answers; only his own questions.

He adjusted his tie and pulled his cuffs down and straightened his cufflinks. It was another delaying factor he knew, but it was something he always did before entering the chief super's office on the few occasions he'd been summoned there.

He knocked and entered and took the seat opposite when Clatworthy indicated he should with a subtle hand gesture.

Phil waited for Clatworthy to speak. The silence seemed to drag out forever as it always did in these high-pressure situations.

'Your thoughts on Brandon Taylor's murder, DI Reynolds?' he asked when he finally spoke.

'I don't want to jump to any conclusions, sir, but at face value it appears that he was murdered by the same person who killed Mick Woods,' he replied, being vague with details.

'I see and what brings you to that conclusion?'

'Both men were killed in much the same way; nailed to the floor by cable ties and bludgeoned to death with a hammer. Taylor's death seemed much more brutal. His penis was hacked off and stuffed into his mouth.'

Phil paused and swallowed, doing his best to push the images he saw earlier out of his mind.

'Good god!' Clatworthy said. 'What kind of monster are we dealing with?'

'I'm sure the post-mortem will give us full details of the atrocities inflicted on Mr. Taylor and confirm the murder weapon was similar. What the motive was isn't known, but we're on the case trying to find what ties Mr. Woods and Taylor together. It's very unlikely they moved in the same social circles, but perhaps they were involved in some other activity together. Forensics found a note at Taylor's house it read "Say thank you John" in capital letters. Thinking we might've missed something DC Edwards and I went back to Woods' house and we, well, by we, I mean, Edwards, found the indentation of a similar note on a notepad by the phone. We went back to where the body was found and in amongst the litter we found the actual note,' Phil said feeling quite proud of their find.

'That's interesting and good work. It seems to indicate the same person killed them both.'

'We're looking into any common friends called John. To see if we can work out why he has to say thank you.'

Clatworthy was silent for a few seconds and looked at a point in the distance. Phil didn't like to interrupt his thoughts.

'It could be John is the murderer. Did the sentence have a comma before John? If it did, it would indeed suggest John should say thank you. On the other hand without a comma would suggest John has to be thanked. Personally I'd put inverted commas round the "say thank you" part of the sentence if it was my intention to suggest John should say thank you. Conversely, I'd put inverted commas around the "thank you John" if it was John who should be thanked,' Clatworthy finally spoke.

'I hadn't thought of that,' Phil replied honestly. 'I don't recall seeing a comma. We're assuming the person who wrote the note also knows the difference in meaning of having a comma or not. I'm sure a lot of people wouldn't know, therefore we can't jump to any conclusions,' Phil said.

'The lowering of standards in the education system has a lot to answer for,' Clatworthy replied.

'So we could be looking for a mutual friend or acquaintance that would benefit from Woods and Taylor's murders or someone called John who has a grudge against both men.'

'It seems so. I'm sure the press will be all over this; both the local and national. As I did with Mick Woods's murder, I'll arrange for another press conference when the need arises, via the area press officer based in Bodmin. I won't burden you with that task. I'll also review staffing levels.'

'Will you still want me running the investigation or will you draft in a more senior officer?' Phil asked.

Part of him wanted to impress and perhaps take a step nearer promotion. Another part of him wanted to take a back seat and leave the responsibility to a more experienced detective and avoid any career damaging repercussions should he not solve the crime.

Clatworthy seemed to be appraising Phil and smiled before he spoke.

'I think you're quite an experienced officer and did rather well with our last serial killer, the infamous Black Cockle Strangler and can easily cope with this investigation. We are rather short staffed as are most of the forces round here. For now, I'd like you to carry on leading the investigation, liaising closely with me. If at any time you feel you can't cope or it's out of your depth, let me know and I'll review your position.'

'OK. Thank you, sir.'

'One last thing before you go. Brandon Taylor was a friend of the assistant chief constable so he'll be keeping a close eye on proceedings. No pressure, DI Reynolds,' Clatworthy said barely suppressing a smirk.

'None at all, sir,' Phil replied, his voice betraying his confidence.

Phil closed the office door behind him muttered "fuck" three times and made his way back to the office. He looked at his watch. He really needed a beer.

The Ship was quite busy. Ed and Bob had visited every pub in reasonable walking distance from the town centre and nobody had seen or remembered seeing Owen Moore. Ed was thinking that perhaps he was teetotal and would be better off looking in coffee shops or tearooms. He'd be doing that on his own; he couldn't see Bob showing the same enthusiasm for drinking tea or coffee and eating a slice of sponge cake; he was definitely a beer and peanut man. Bob had a pint in every pub and showed no signs of being drunk. Ed on the other hand, being a lightweight compared to Bob, just had a lime and soda in a few, knowing he'd be a complete mess by the end of the night, if he'd tried to keep up with Bob.

'So what's next, boss?' Bob asked.

Ed could tell that Bob was testing him, probably assuming he was at a loss as to what to try next to find his man. In part he was right but Ed wasn't about to confess that.

'Coffee shops, tearooms and internet cafes. Start local and then widen the search, and include pubs,' Ed replied confidently.

'When you go outside of Padstow, I can help with the pubs and you concentrate on the tearooms,' Bob volunteered.

'I thought you might suddenly have an appetite for a missing person case if it involved beer,' Ed replied and shook his head.

Bob opened his arms wide and laughed softly.

'I am merely offering my services to save you any unnecessary work.'

Ed raised his eyebrows and shook his head,

'He may've gone much further afield,' Bob said.

'I know and he could be anywhere in the world, but I have to start somewhere. No point in going to Timbuktu when he might be in Wadebridge, is there?'

Bob shrugged and looked distracted.

'Now there's a man who looks like he's had a rough day,' Bob said and grinned.

Ed looked towards the bar where Bob was staring and saw Phil. Even from some distance, Phil looked like a troubled man. Bob waved and caught his eye and he walked over and sat down heavily on the chair next to Ed.

'A tough day at the office, Phil?' Bob asked.

He knew from experience what that job could do to you,

especially on a murder case. Part of him pitied him and another part of him envied him. He used to love a good murder case.

'Not one of the best. We've had a second murder. Looks like the same guy killed him, but we can't confirm until the post-mortem is complete tomorrow. I thought the first one was gruesome but this one was far worse,' Phil replied and took a few hefty swigs of his pint.

'Are you going to embellish us with any details?' Bob asked.

'I shouldn't do, but I can trust you two to keep your mouths closed. Please not a word to anyone. We don't want this information made public,' Phil replied, taking a hard look at both men.

'There's nobody for me to tell, and even if there was, I respect your position,' Ed replied.

'You don't need to remind me. I've been there before and know how it works,' Bob replied.

'OK, good. Same as the first one, the victim was nailed to the floor using cable ties. There was an element of torture both before and after death although I suspect mostly after. This time death was caused by a massive blow to the forehead with what we believe was a hammer. It caved half his skull in. Then, presumably with the claw end of the hammer his genitals were ripped off and stuffed into his mouth,' Phil told them.

'Jesus. No wonder you look like shit and need a beer,' Bob replied.

'Clatworthy wants me to continue to head up the investigation and gave me some old flannel about being experienced blah, blah, blah, but we all know it's because there isn't the manpower. If that isn't bad enough, the worst part is the victim was a friend of the assistant chief constable so even more pressure,' Phil said and took a few more hefty swigs of his beer before continuing and telling them of the note they found at both crime scenes.

'Sounds like John has all the answers, either as the maniac with the hammer or the person who should be grateful to the maniac with the hammer,' Ed replied.

Bob frowned trying to work out why there were two scenarios. Phil helped him out with the gramma conundrum, also pointing out that the person who wrote the note also, like Bob, may not know the difference the missing comma made.

'You must've thrown a sickie on punctuation day at school,' Ed replied and grinned at Bob, who gave him the middle finger.

'Well, if you need any help or advice, I have time. Magnum here is on a missing person case and it's going nowhere fast. We carried out a preliminary check of all the local pubs and nobody has seen him. Someone may have lied to us but it's unlikely. So next up its coffee shops and that's not really my scene,' Bob replied.

'He won't be much use with any gramma problems though, but if it involves beer, he's definitely the right man for the job. He was happy to go on a pub crawl at my expense but won't help out further as there isn't any alcohol involved. Just as well really, I can't be doing with Bob getting into punch ups in every cake shop we go to visit; I've a reputation to keep up.'

'Oh, who did you upset?' Phil asked.

'Local farmer called John Talbot. Seems he blames me for his father dying in prison. I put him away for manslaughter and having a massive cannabis farm in one of his barns.'

'I recall his father. Nasty bastard used to beat his wife and kids. Not sure why his son would stick up for him after all he went through. Guess it takes all sorts. Anyway, I might take you up on your offer if it gets a little messy. I'm good for now though. My round, who's up for another?' Phil asked.

Two empty glasses were pushed towards him.

CHAPTER EIGHTEEN

Hangovers didn't get any more pleasant with age. Ed recalled the rest of the evening and couldn't remember drinking too many, but then he did have a few during the afternoon in his attempt to find the elusive Owen Moore, which would've been enough to ensure a rough start to the day.

Ed dragged himself out of bed and made his way downstairs to the kitchen where he willed the kettle to boil. He knew the best cure for a hangover was a jog, but he wasn't going anywhere without first having a strong coffee. He put two heaped spoons of instant coffee in the mug and flicked the kettle off, deciding it'd be hot enough. He usually put a drop of cold water in it anyway so he didn't have to wait for it to cool down.

The coffee hit the spot and working in conjunction with the ibuprofen he began to feel a little more human. His car was still in town so he decided to forfeit his run and to shower and walk into town to start the next phase of looking for Mrs. Moore's errant son, and to collect his car and begin looking a little further afield if need be.

It was a bracing walk along the undulating clifftops to Padstow, the strong sea breeze blowing away the remnants of his hangover. By the time he arrived and had eaten a hearty fry-up in the cafe facing out onto the harbour, his hangover was a distant memory. He vowed never again, but knew that was a promise he'd never be able to keep. While he was in the cafe, he showed the waitress the photo of Owen.

'Have you seen this guy in here?' he asked optimistically.

The waitress looked at it and for one minute he thought he was going to get a positive answer, alas it wasn't to be.

'He looks familiar and might've been in here,' she replied.

'Recently?' he pressed.

'I couldn't say. We get so many people in here every day and I honestly can't remember, but he does look familiar. Sorry.'

'No problem. If you do remember him, give me a call,' he replied and passed her his business card and left to find other likely establishments.

The incident room was a hive of activity when DI Reynolds returned from the post-mortem with DC Edwards, who despite the Vicks vapour rub smeared copiously around his nostrils had to leave at one point. Edwards now had a little more colour back in his cheeks, Phil was happy to note.

The result of the post-mortem concluded that the massive blow to the centre of Brandon Taylor's forehead was the cause of death and would've been a very quick death. The mutilation, in addition to having his penis and testicles ripped out and inserted into his mouth, which had also been hit hard several times with a hammer, breaking most of his teeth and dislocating the jaw, was carried out after death.

The injuries were horrific. The victim, like Mick Woods before him, had almost every bone in the body broken. There was also some damage to the internal organs caused by shards of shattered ribs that had been driven deep into the organs, when the murderer bludgeoned his ribcage to oblivion.

It was even more brutal than the attack on Mick Woods and Phil wondered what state they'd find the next victim, if there was one, which seemed to be very likely if they didn't find the perpetrator of these heinous crimes soon.

Phil got everyone's attention and informed them there would be a quick briefing in five minutes, which would give him a few minutes to get himself a coffee and eat the sandwich he'd purchased from the bakery. He didn't have much of an appetite but knew he had to eat and to eat while he could. Often something would come up that meant he'd end up going all day without food, leaving him tired and irritable and not at his best. He needed to be on top of his game at all times or a vital clue might slip by unnoticed. Edwards abstained from any solids and nursed a bottle of water.

Phil banged on the table to get everyone's attention once again.

'I've just attended the post-mortem of Brandon Taylor and can confirm that both men were killed by the same person, be that a man or a woman, Mark Wilton said the wounds could equally be inflicted by a very strong right-handed woman as it could a man. We also found notes at both crime scenes, as I'm sure you all know by now, that read "SAY THANK YOU JOHN" in capital letters. Now we don't know if the killer is called John and wants thanking or if he's killing for the benefit of John whom he wants to thank him. For those of you like me who aren't gramma gurus it depends on if there's a comma before John. There isn't, but maybe he's also unaware of the ambiguity of his note, or perhaps does and is doing it to throw us off the scent. Equally, John might be a complete red herring for the same reason. You could also argue that if he wanted to be thanked the sentence would benefit from inverted commas to make it clearer; that's speech marks to you Pascoe.'

There was a ripple of laughter at Will Pascoe's expense.

'Fiona, did you dig anything up on John?' Phil asked

'No. The tech guys have been through both men's laptops and contacts as well as address books etc. on their phones and there are John's known by both men, as you'd expect being a common name, but no mutual contacts. I'll contact each of them individually after this meeting.'

'OK, thanks. I'm sure that'll be an interesting conversation. Moving on, what do we know about Brandon Taylor that may link him to Mick Woods?' Phil asked.

The question was met with silence.

'Fiona, when this meeting is over, I want you to do some digging on Brandon Taylor, what he was into business wise and what he did in his free time, apart from seducing his young cleaner. Shaun, you and I will go to Taylor's clothing factory and get a list of all current and former employees and while we're there we'll interview everyone.

'Will, I want you to go through all the CCTV we have in the area. Whoever murdered Brandon Taylor had to get there somehow and he might be on camera. We have quite a few in the Rock area as it's an affluent area so we might get lucky.'

Will Pascoe nodded but didn't relish the task of viewing hours of traffic cameras, but it had to be done and someone had to do it. It wouldn't be the first time and wouldn't be the last that he picked up that unenviable task. Being the rookie in the department sucked sometimes. He sighed and picked up the phone to request everything he thought would be useful based on Brandon Taylor's address. Fortunately most cameras were now digital so obtaining the footage he required was simple and quick and could be viewed from his own computer.

Phil and Shaun were shown up to the offices away from the factory floor, where the clothing was being made. The offices overlooked the factory floor. Phil looked down to see staff busy at sewing machines, while other machines were being fed material which was cut and handed out to the people sewing. Phil assumed most of the staff sewing would be women, but there were a handful of men at the sewing machines, which surprised him.

The receptionist who took them to the offices, knocked and explained to the man sitting behind the desk that the police were here to see him.

'Trevor Vaughn, finance director and assistant company director to Mr. Taylor, or was until this morning; terrible news, we're all devastated,' the man said, introducing himself.

'DI Reynolds and DC Edwards,' Phil said taking an instant dislike to the man, who he tagged as being officious and over-zealous. Phil trusted his instincts and was a good judge of character.

'When was the last time you saw Mr. Taylor?' Phil asked wanting to get the interview over and done with and to speak to as many other employees as he could.

'Last night at about six o'clock. He came to see me before he left for home to ask me to get him some financial details. I ran them off on the computer and left them on his desk. I left shortly after that at about six-twenty.'

'Did he seem different or pre-occupied?'

'Not at all, He seemed his usual self.'

'Do you know if Mr. Taylor went straight home or did he have an engagement?'

'He sometimes goes to the golf club in St. Enodoc. But I know he didn't have any business meetings yesterday evening. I know that as all employees diaries are online and can be accessed by anyone in the company. It makes arranging meetings that much easier.

'OK, we know he was murdered much later so we'll check that out. Thank you. If you don't mind me asking, is the company in a good financial, position? No debts or cash flow issues?' Phil asked.

'None at all, quite the opposite in fact. The last quarter financial statement showed a very healthy profit. As a business we're in an excellent position and have new orders coming in every day,' Vaughn said proudly.

'Did Mr. Taylor have any enemies or anyone who would benefit from his death, like a rival business perhaps?'

'Not that I'm aware of. There are very few clothing factories in this part of the country. In fact a lot of clothing is made overseas in sweatshops where the labour is cheaper. Our customers are generally smaller designers, who care about the environment and use of slave labour. I guess now he's dead, the business will go to his wife as they haven't finalised the divorce, unless of course Brandon changed his will when they separated.'

'I see. How long have Mr. and Mrs. Taylor been separated?'

'I'm not sure exactly, but think about six months or so. Brandon was a…bit of a ladies man, should we say, and his wife, Louise, got fed up with his string of affairs and left him. I don't know any details, Brandon kept that part of his life very quiet, but he confided in me over a drink after work one evening.'

'I see. Do you know if he had any business associates or friends by the name of John?'

'It's a very common name. I'm sure he must have friends or family by that name but I can't think of any business associates. Certainly none of the staff here are called John. We're a small friendly business and I know all the staff by name.'

'What about ex-employees, any of those called John?' Phil pushed.

'No, I don't recall there ever being a John here, which is surprising, considering it's such a common name.'

'Are there any current or ex-employees who might hold a grudge or have been sacked and wanted revenge?'

'I don't recall anyone ever having been sacked. People have moved on for better money, less hours and such, but nobody who would bear a grudge against the company or Brandon. The same can be said for current employees.'

'OK, thank you, Mr. Vaughn. If possible I'd like to see the files you have on your staff and I'll want to interview everyone. I'll try to be as quick as I can so I don't disrupt your output.'

'We do have a human resource manager but both Brandon and I have access to all company files so it's just as easy for me to do that to save you time. All our records, past and present, have now been digitised. If you have a thumb drive I can download everything for you.

Phil looked across at Edwards who fished one out of his trouser pocket. Phil had been meaning to buy a couple, but just hadn't seemed to have the time, what with the workload in the office and his decorating when he got the chance to do any, to appease Emma.

As promised the download was just a couple of minutes. Phil handed the drive back to Edwards who put it in his pocket.

'Right then Mr. Vaughn, we'll start up here and then interview your workforce on the factory floor.'

Vaughn didn't look happy, but stood and led them to the next office along.

It only took a couple of hours in all and Phil thought that for the most part it had been a waste of time, but it was something that was necessary and he always prided himself on being thorough. All the staff said they left before Mr. Taylor and hadn't noticed anyone or anything suspicious in the last week. Nobody knew anyone past or present called John or knew of anyone who might have a personal issue with Mr. Taylor. It appeared at face value to be a small close knit community and everyone was shocked by Taylor's murder.

They headed back to the station. Phil looked at his watch and decided he'd spend an hour or so looking through the staff records and then head off home, where he hoped to get an hour or so wallpapering before relaxing with Emma.

CHAPTER NINETEEN

It'd been an unproductive day, just like the day before but thankfully without beer involved. Ed knew that there would be a lot of unproductive days but buoyed himself with the thought that he'd get a breakthrough soon. His only one positive from the day was that a waitress knew Owen Moore as he used to stop by after work for a cup of tea and a slice of cheesecake twice a week. Ed was getting his hopes up, but alas she hadn't seen him for at least a month and although they were on talking terms, she never got into any personal conversations with him. It was part of her job to be polite to the customers, but she'd only ever have a conversation if the customer initiated it. A lot of her customers came in to relax and unwind over lunch or after a hard day in the office and she didn't want to lose her boss any customers by annoying them. Ed thanked her and made a mental note to check out anywhere in the area that sold cheesecake. It wasn't a lot to go on.

He arrived at the yard to pick up his car and bumped into Chris who was taking the rubbish out. She invited him in for a coffee but Ed just laughed and told her he never wanted to see another cup of coffee for a long time. He did however take her up on the offer of something stronger, and joined her and Lionel for a glass of wine and a chat. He stopped at one glass as he really wanted to get home, shower and rest his feet that were aching from walking in and around Padstow for the best part of a day.

Ed arrived home, scooped up the mail and put it on the coffee table where he'd pick it up and read it later. Most of it'd be junk mail. Periodically he opted out of receiving junk mail, but inevitably it'd start to trickle back and he'd go through the process again when it got to annoying levels. He wished he could do the same for leaflets and flyers.

Ed showered and made himself a sandwich and after eating it began to feel refreshed and decided a gin and tonic would be in order. He sat down and wondered what his next steps should be. He thought about widening his search area but as Bob had told him, Owen could be anywhere, even overseas. Ed decided he'd check out a few of the villages in and around Padstow and then the major towns nearby such as Wadebridge and Bodmin. If that failed, he'd have to have a rethink. He wouldn't admit defeat and give Bob the satisfaction of telling him, he told him so; he wasn't sure he could cope with that level of smugness.

He went to his study and retrieved his laptop and began looking at Facebook, Instagram and even TikTok. There were plenty of entries for Owen Moore but none were his Owen Moore. Either he was one of the few social media averse people on the planet or he went by an alias. Ed broadened his search to a Google search. Again there were plenty of listings but none were the man he was looking for. It was the same with Twitter and all the many other social media sites he reviewed, which Ed only had for reference. Ed was surprised at drawing a blank, as he'd typed in his own name once and after trawling through the records had managed to find out a lot about himself. How Owen Moore remained so invisible on the internet in this day and age baffled him. He wondered what his old mate Data would do. Ed grinned and thought, rather than guess, he could give his old mate a call and ask him.

Ed picked up his phone and made the call.

'Hi Ed. You usually only call when you need something. I'm guessing this isn't a social call,' Data said when he picked up.

Fortunately, Ed could tell he was only joking, despite it being the truth.

'You know me too well. I'm guessing you're pretty busy with the team being away on another mission.'

'It's had its moments, but it's been relatively quiet for me. It's a lot easier working from HQ, rather than going out in the field with the team. I might be out with the guys on the next mission depending on the outcome of this one. I haven't actually been out in the field with the team since we bagged The Messenger so it'll make a nice change,' Data replied.

'Sounds like you're onto something big. I know not to ask too many questions. Hopefully whatever it is it's a short mission and not a dangerous one. It's very lonely in this old house of mine without Angel. Any ideas when she'll be back?' Ed asked hopefully.

'In a few days with any luck, obviously I can't tell you too much as it's classified.'

'Just like my file, I guess; that's the one that the whole team have seen that I'm not allowed to see,' Ed replied.

It still irked him that his file was off limits to himself. However, as Angel had pointed out it was full of the shit that he'd done in his life, so for the most part, he knew exactly what was in it.

Data laughed. 'Correct. It's an interesting read Ed, very interesting.'

'If you're trying to wind me up, you've succeeded,' Ed replied light-heartedly.

'I'll let Angel know you're missing her next time I'm in contact with the team. Anyway, what do you want from me?' he asked.

'I've got a missing person case and I've hit a brick wall. Nobody has seen the guy for weeks, unless someone has been lying to me, which is always a possibility. He quit his job and left home without informing his mother who he lived with. He's not on social media or if he is, he's not using his real name. I've been round every pub, cafe, tearoom, coffee shop and internet cafe in Padstow and it's like he's disappeared off the face of the earth. I was thinking of broadening my search, but as Bob happily informed me, he could be anywhere in the world.

Anyway, I was sitting here wondering what you'd do as you're pretty adept at finding people and thought I'd call and ask.'

'I see. Well, it's a lot easier for me as I have access to a lot more databases than you do, with me being MI5 and also a master hacker of course. If it was me, I'd run one of the many programs I've generated for just such purposes. It doesn't work every time as often the people I'm looking for are very shrewd and use sophisticated encryption to hide behind and do their best not to leave behind a digital footprint, but I'm guessing your man has very little to hide, only away from his mother it seems.

My programs search for credit and debit card usage, mobile

phone records, utility bills, electoral roll and so forth, which is pretty successful with pinning a person down to a location and then I can run other searches to pinpoint them exactly. Most of those will unfortunately be off limits to you and use facial recognition from CCTV and such. Even the police have to get a warrant to be able to search for bank details and phone details. So, I hate to be the bearer of bad news, but you're up against the proverbial brick wall.'

Ed paused to think.

'Of course, a nice person like myself would be able to do this for you as I'm sure that's what you're really asking, if I'm not mistaken. You didn't call to ask what The Great Data would do, more a case of hoping, what I will do for you. Am I correct? Data added and laughed softly down the phone.

'As your lovely boss would say "you're a smart man; that's what I like about you" or something like that,' Ed replied.

'OK, give me his details and I'll run the programs and get back to you. It won't be until at least the morning as I'm going into a meeting with Jack very shortly and then going home; if I'm not given another load of urgent work to do for the team.'

'You're a star. I was hoping you'd oblige, but I don't like to ask and take too many liberties,' Ed replied.

'We both know that's bullshit; just give me his details, Ed.'

Ed laughed, slightly embarrassed at being found out so easily.

'Do you want it verbally or in an email?' he asked.

'Send it in an email as I need to get to my meeting and my desk is littered with paperwork and I might lose it. How far back do you need to go?' Data asked.

'He's been missing for about six weeks so a couple of months would be great.'

'OK, leave it with me and I'll get it to you as soon as I can. Good luck.'

Ed thanked Data and ended the call. He then set about typing in the very few details he knew about Owen Moore and pressed send, full of renewed optimism that he could have the case wrapped up in a couple of days. That'd be something to wind Bob up with.

Ed smiled at the thought of annoying Bob and turned his attention to the pile of mail he'd picked up off the doormat when he returned home. The first letter was his electric bill. He opened it and frowned; prices were going up and up. Ed was financially set up for life, but it still irked him that the utility companies were making billions in profit, and yet still felt the need to increase prices. The second letter was also from the electricity company, this time informing him his direct debit would be increasing as of next month. Ed swore. The rest of the crap that had besieged his doormat was an unwanted pile of flyers, one informing him of a pizza company's buy one get one free offer, yet another menu from the Indian restaurant in town and another from a double glazing company. The final one was a blank sheet of paper, or what Ed thought was a blank sheet of paper until he turned it over.

Ed read it and was shocked. He stared at the typed message and read it again. It read "I know you're looking for me. Don't. You have been warned". It was obviously from Owen Moore as he was the only person Ed was currently looking for. Ed was more concerned that he knew he was looking for him than where he lived, which meant that someone he'd spoken to had lied to him. Unless it was a chance meeting with Owen and whoever it was had told him a private investigator was asking about him. Not that it really mattered; Data would hopefully come up with enough information on him for Ed to find him. He couldn't make him see his mother, but he could at least inform Mrs. Moore that Owen was alive and well, but for reasons unknown didn't want to come back to the family home. He'd take a selfie with him to show Mrs. Moore that she wasn't being bullshitted to, just so that Ed could get paid.

Ed shrugged and headed to the kitchen to fix himself another gin and tonic. He'd call Bob in the morning and give him an update. He knew if he called him now, he'd try and persuade him to meet him in the pub to talk about developments and he was tired of pubs and wanted a little alone time.

CHAPTER TWENTY

Padstow some years previous

It would've been a Thursday night as Top of the Pops was on the television. The boy was sitting on the floor finishing off a drawing that had to be handed into the art teacher in the morning. The boy wasn't much of an artist. He could copy things quite well, but wasn't creative like some of his classmates. He recalled a girl called Trudy, but not her surname. She was a great artist and very creative. Everyone in his class wanted to be able to draw as well as Trudy. She came from a poor family and her clothes always looked well-worn and a little grubby. He himself wasn't from a rich family, but his mum always made sure his clothes were washed and ironed, even if they were old, he never felt like he was from a poor family. At the time he didn't know just how poor they were. His father had a good job, so his mother told him, but he drank away whatever he earnt and his mother, a proud woman, did her best for herself and her son with whatever she kept hidden from her husband from the housekeeping money he gave her and received from her family allowance. The boy always looked half presentable as his mother knew that anyone deemed poor or different would be bullied; he had more than enough bullying from his father to contend with. She knew that more bullying at school would be just too much for the young boy to deal with.

The front door slammed shut and he could hear his father staggering down the corridor, cursing something, as he always did, as he put his coat on the newel of the banister. His mother was in the kitchen and shouted through the door to her husband to sit down and she'd get his dinner out the oven where it had been keeping warm. The boy concentrated on the television to take his mind of the shouting in the kitchen. His father was drunk again and that was never a good thing.

After a short pause, presumably while his father ate his lukewarm dinner, there was an almighty crash as his half-eaten dinner was hurled at his mother, who managed to duck and avoid the plate smashing into her face. The plate flew past her head and shattered against the kitchen wall. Chicken casserole splattered the cooker the rest slid slowly down the wall along with her hopes of seeing the day out without a beating. She prayed it'd be a short outburst. On a good day she'd get away with a vicious verbal onslaught meant to belittle her, to scare her and humiliate her. The other extreme was a severe beating, which would go on for as long as her husband wanted it to go on, until he was exhausted or his anger sated. The boy's mother cowered in front of her husband, like a dog when threatened by its master. To show any defiance would only make him angrier and prolong whatever was in store for her; servility was her only defence.

'I've worked all fucking day and the best you can do is a cold stew! Useless fucking bitch,' his father shouted.

'I'm sorry. I expected you sooner...' his mother said in barely a whisper, not looking her husband in the eye.

'Sorry are you? I wouldn't give that plate of shit to a stray dog. Is that all I am to you? Is that all I'm worth, to be treated like a flea-bitten mutt?' his father screamed at his mother.

Whatever his mother was going to say went unsaid. The only sounds from the kitchen were his father's slaps and punches followed by his mother's sobbing. Today his mother was lucky; the assault had been brutal but thankfully short-lived.

The kitchen door flew back on its hinges as his father stormed into the living room.

'Turn that shit off you little bastard,' his father roared.

The boy rose quickly to his feet but not quick enough to avoid the heavy cuff round the head from his father. He fell to the floor and curled into a ball to protect himself from his father. The inevitable kicks that followed felt as real today as they had all those unhappy years ago.

The boy, now a man, awoke with a start. He looked at his watch. It was time to get to work again.

CHAPTER TWENTY-ONE

Padstow present day

The caravan was old and dirty but it was home for Pete Quigley and had been since his divorce. It was all he could afford in the area and he had no car, his money grabbing bitch of an ex-wife had taken that along with everything else of value. As a result, he needed to be near enough to Padstow to get to the harbour each day where he was employed as a trawlerman on his friend's small trawler. The caravan was sited in a field on a farm some way from the main farmhouse. The small toilet was plumbed into a septic tank. The lighting was from small gaslights and water was from two large jerry cans that he filled up each morning from the outside tap at the farmhouse, where the farmer allowed him to shower in an old outhouse that had a water heater. The water was never more than tepid, but it was better than nothing; only just. In winter it was perishing cold, but beggars can't be choosers he reminded himself on a regular basis. The field was sometimes used for cows or sheep but for the most part was free of livestock. When it was used for grazing he had to watch his step as the field would be strewn with cow pats or sheep droppings. The sheep were timid and kept away from the caravan when Pete was home, but the bloody cows were different. On a moonlit night, Pete would be kept awake by their constant grazing, especially around the caravan where the grass was lush. Fortunately there weren't too many moonlit nights, in part due to the lunar cycle and also because of the cloud cover.

It was late evening by the time Pete arrived home, having stopped off to have a couple of jars with the boys. Pete wasn't a big drinker, well not now, as he used to drink far too much and that got him into all manner of trouble. He liked a drink; but the drink didn't like him. Now a couple of pints would be his limit if he was out in company. Occasionally, if he wanted a good drink he'd buy a bottle of cheap supermarket branded vodka and drink until he passed out at home, alone, where he couldn't get into any trouble. He'd finally learnt his lesson; better late than never.

Tonight he recalled putting the key in the lock and nothing else. He opened his eyes and tried to move but couldn't. His head was hurting and his vision was swimming in and out of focus. It took him a short time to realise his arms and legs were somehow pinned to the floor. Worse still; he was naked. There was movement. Someone else was in the small caravan with him. He could hear and feel the heavy footsteps on the worn out lino that covered the floor of the caravan. He tried to speak but his mouth had been gagged.

'I'll take the gag out if you promise not to shout or scream. If you do, I won't hesitate to kill you. Do I make myself clear Pete?'

Pete nodded and the man leaned forward and pulled at the gag, which when it was removed, Pete saw it was his own sock.

'What do you want?' Pete rasped, his mouth was parched from having his thick woolly sock in his mouth and he could taste seawater and the odour of fish.

'Right now, I'd like to finish making my coffee.'

The man rose on hearing the kettle whistle on the gas hob. A few seconds later he sat down and peered down at Pete Quigley.

'You didn't break in and tie me up just to steal my coffee. What do you want, whoever you are?' Pete asked.

'You can call me John. I want to find out, what makes you tick. What makes you the man you are?'

'I'm a trawlerman, have been all my working life,' Quigley said gruffly, not fully understanding the question.

'I know that. I know a lot about you, Pete Quigley. Tell me about your wife.'

'Is that what this is all about? Has that bitch sent you? If so you can tell that sour-faced bitch, she's already got everything; the money, the car, everything. I've nothing more to give her.'

John shook his head.

'Open wide Pete. I want to put the gag back in. I don't want to hear you bad mouthing your wife.'

Quigley kept his mouth firmly shut.

'I'm not a patient man Mr. Quigley. Either you open your mouth voluntarily or I'll smash your teeth in with this hammer and then put the gag in. Unfortunately for you, that would probably result in you choking to death on your own broken teeth and that just won't do, because as I told you earlier, I want to find out what makes you tick,' John said and smiled.

Quigley opened his mouth and John pushed the makeshift gag in as far as he could; he stopped pushing when Pete began to retch; he didn't want him choking on his vomit either. John smiled, reached down beside him and picked up the claw hammer, which he'd come to regard as an old friend. He smiled and brought it down viciously onto Quigley's left hand breaking two fingers in several places. Quigley roared in pain and began to say something that was muffled by the gag.

John sat patiently sipping his coffee until Quigley's sobbing abated.

'Can I remove the gag now?' he asked. 'If you scream, you die; it's as simple as that. Do you understand?'

Quigley nodded and John pulled the gag free.

'Tell me about your wife, Pete,' he asked.

'Her,' he replied and gave a derisory snort. 'We married when we were too young. We both had affairs and grew to hate each other. We divorced about a year and a half ago.'

'I think you're being a little economical with the truth, Pete. If you lie to me, I'll punish you.'

'I heard you regularly assaulted your wife, even after you were divorced. That's why the judge put a restraining order out on you, gave you a rather large fine and by all accounts you were lucky not to get a prison sentence.'

'You seem to know a lot about me,' Quigley replied, his voice tinged with anger despite his predicament.

'I make it my business to know. Just answer the questions or the gag goes back in and well, you can guess what will happen next.'

John sloshed his coffee cup over Quigley's abdomen. The scalding liquid quickly headed south burning a path to his groin and testicles. Fortunately for him, he managed to stifle the scream and the string of abuse he wanted to shout at his tormentor.

'We married young, like I said, and we weren't right for each other. Sandra had an affair and I got angry with her and hit her. To get even, I had a one night stand with her sister, and she found out. She hit me and I hit her,' Quigley said with no remorse in his voice.

'Once again, I think you're being very economical with the truth. You beat her quite regularly I think.'

'I used to drink heavily and when I was drunk, I got angry. When she went out, I always envisaged her with another man. I was jealous and couldn't trust her after she'd had the affair.'

'Why did you rape her?' John asked with a wide smile.

Quigley looked back in fear and surprise.

'How… how do you know about that?' he asked

'I know everything. You can't hide your sordid secrets from me.'

Pete remained quiet as he thought about how to answer the question. John finally broke the silence.

'Tell me, Pete. Why did you feel the need to rape your wife? I won't ask you again.'

'We argued. It got heated. She taunted me by saying something along the lines of she'd only had the affair for sex. She laughed at me and then told me it was great sex and that she'd had multiple orgasms because her lover was a real man. She knew how to push the right buttons. I was fucking angry. I said to her if she wanted sex, I'd give her sex. She just laughed and told me I was a lousy lover and had never been able to satisfy her. I got so angry that I beat and raped her. It was stupid, I know it was, but I was angry and upset.'

John shook his head.

'Why are you being so economical with the truth? I know you raped her on a regular basis. Making love to a woman is normally something you do out of love, not hate or spite.'

'I don't know. I used to like a drink. I did some stupid things when I drank. Back then I was a mess. I couldn't think straight. I was always angry and wanted to punish my wife for telling me I wasn't any good in bed. I wanted to show her I was just as good as any man in bed. I was fucked up. I loved her in my own way.'

'You loved her? Are you serious, Pete? You're right you really are fucked up. You're a sad excuse of a man, Pete. You know, my father used to beat me and my mother, but he never raped her. I'm not saying he was a better man than you. Maybe he was, maybe he was just as bad but in a different way. Maybe he was worse in some ways. He's dead now so what does it matter. All that matters is that I think I know what makes you tick and you're of no use to me now. Thank you for your time, Pete.'

'You mean this is it? I'm free to go?' Quigley asked his voice full of hope.

'Oh no, Pete, for you this is just the start. Open wide Pete.'

John inserted the gag and the mutilation began.

CHAPTER TWENTY-TWO

Being a detective inspector was for the most part very dull, in that there were very few big cases in a relatively sleepy seaside town like Padstow. Phil recalled his friend and superior officer, Bob Brown, bemoaning the lack of action in Padstow compared to being over-worked and inundated with murder cases and other serious crimes when he was in the Met Police in London. This week had been the exception to the rule with two murders to investigate. The added pressure of being in charge weighed heavily on his shoulders. He was happy to be given the opportunity to lead the investigation and make a name for himself, but it was a poisoned chalice. If he failed it'd mar his otherwise exemplary career and DI would likely be the highest level he'd achieve. Phil wasn't overly ambitious, but detective chief inspector wasn't out of the question, at least he thought not. He was still young and had a good few years ahead of him before he contemplated retirement.

As soon as he walked into the office DC Shaun Edwards made a beeline towards him. He really needed a coffee to ensure he was firing on all four cylinders. He smiled politely and told him to give him a minute as he needed coffee, after which he got everyone's attention for an update.

'Right, judging by the urgency DC Edwards showed when I arrived, I assume he's got an update for us.' Phil said and was met with a round of laughter.

'Sorry about that boss. I'll let Sergeant Walsh tell you herself.' Edwards replied.

Fiona smiled appreciating Shaun's diplomacy.

'First of all, I contacted all the 'John's' in our two victim's email and smartphones and nothing suspicious came up. They were either surprised or knew nothing, and they all stated pretty much the same that they'd nothing to gain by their deaths. I'm fairly certain they were honest answers and weren't hiding anything. DC Edwards and I began some more background checks on our victims and both had recently divorced or separated. Not much of a coincidence in itself, but we also found out that both had restraining orders placed on them and were fined for domestic violence,' Fiona Walsh said excitedly.

'Are you suggesting that our murderer is targeting men who abuse their wives?' Phil asked, thinking it was probably not the case, but something that couldn't be dismissed outright at this stage.

'We worked all day and late into the night on this angle. Both men moved in very different social circles. One was affluent and the other was almost penniless. The only thing they'd got in common was separation and restraining orders for common assault on their partners,' Edwards replied, unable to hide his disappointment that the team's findings were not being taken too seriously.

'It's something to consider, but seems a little thin. Both murders were horrific and violent. Why would a person go to such lengths to avenge two disgruntled wives? Perhaps we should re-interview the ex-wives. Perhaps they might know who John is?' Phil said thinking out loud.

Edwards nodded but was still a little dejected. Phil took his jacket off and put it on the back of the chair.

'Fiona, I want you to call both ex-wives after this meeting and arrange interviews them again; later today preferably and take DC Pascoe with you,' he said.

Shaun Edwards was keen to pursue the wife beating angle and wasn't about to give up without a fight.

'Sir, both victims had court cases at the Magistrates' courts in Bodmin in the last two months. Anyone can access court records in person or online and also court hearing schedules are readily available. What if our man or woman is finding out about domestic abuse cases this way?'

'We don't know anything about the killer. They could be male or female; the "thank you John" notes might be a red herring, and apart from being violent they're also very smart. No DNA from the crime scenes and so far, no likely suspects have appeared on any CCTV footage. As you pointed out, anyone can attend a court hearing. You probably don't even need to sign in. I suggest that you find out the dates of the victims hearings and check CCTV footage for those days, but right now it's not a priority.'

Phil's phone rang. He pulled it from his pocket and took the call. He listened for a few moments, muttered 'shit' and ended the call.

'Meeting over. We have another murder. Nailed to the floor with cable ties, so looks like our man has claimed his third victim. Shaun get your coat. Fiona, find out everything you can about a Peter Quigley.'

There was a collective murmur and then everyone rushed back to their desks.

Phil pulled up outside the farmhouse and opened the boot of the car so that both men could change into their wellington boots. Phil always carried his in the car and Shaun had thrown his own in before they left the station. A uniformed officer approached them and pointed them in the direction of the small caravan at the end of the next field. There was no need to have done so as they could see the lights of the ambulance flashing in the distance.

'Who found the body?' Phil asked.

'Mr. Wilkes. He's the owner of the land. He's in the kitchen right now drinking a strong tea. He's a little shaken up. The body was a bit of a mess, sir.'

Phil nodded his thanks and entered the farmhouse where Mr. Wilkes, looking very pale, had his hands wrapped around a mug of steaming tea. A uniformed constable was keeping him company.

'Mr. Wilkes, Detective Inspector Reynolds and this is Detective Constable Edwards. I believe you found the body?' Phil said by way of introduction.

Mr. Wilkes looked up from his mug of tea and shook his head. 'I've never seen anything like it in my life. He looked like he'd been mauled by a pack of wild dogs,' he replied and quickly gulped some more tea.

'Can you tell us anything about the victim?'

'His name was Pete Quigley. He's been staying in my caravan a few months or perhaps a little longer. He split from his wife and couldn't afford to pay the rent for anything half decent. A friend told him I had the caravan and he was happy to pay a few quid for a roof over his head. It's not great, but it's better than sleeping rough.'

'What time did you discover the body?' Phil asked.

'It would've been about nine-thirty. I normally see Pete early as he works on one of the fishing boats in the harbour. Always gives the dog a biscuit and makes a fuss of her when he comes to fill his jerry cans up before work. There's no running water in the old van. Anyway, I hadn't seen him and then noticed the caravan door was ajar so went to take a look, and there he was...'

Wilkes didn't finish what he was going to say as he leapt from the table and rushed across to the sink and vomited. He drank from the tap and swilled his mouth and returned to the table.

'Sorry about that. You'll understand why when you go and see him yourself, it's horrific. I've seen sheep that've been attacked by stray dogs, but whoever done that to poor old Pete isn't human,' Wilkes said. His hands wrapped around the mug of tea were visibly shaking.

'When was the last time you saw Mr. Quigley alive?' Phil asked.

'Yesterday morning when he was filling his jerry cans up. I don't know him well and tend to leave him to it. He pays the rent every week and we see each other most mornings, but we don't socialise. I finish work when the sun goes down and make myself some dinner. Then I might have a couple of whiskies and go to bed as I have to get up early. I normally get the cows milked then come back between nine-thirty and ten o'clock, and have a late breakfast.'

'Did you hear or see anything suspicious last night?'

'Nothing. Sometimes I see Pete, if he's home early, but some nights he stops off for a drink in town so gets back after sundown, so I don't see him until the next day.'

'Did you notice anything different about Mr. Quigley the last few days?'

'No, nothing at all. He seemed his usual self. He seems a pleasant enough guy. Always makes a fuss of Bessy and gives her a snack, but I can't say that he was any different to normal.'

'Thanks for your time, Mr. Wilkes. We'll take a formal statement later, but that'll be it for now.'

Phil and Shaun left the farmhouse, wondering what they were going to find in the caravan. What they saw shocked them to the core.

CHAPTER TWENTY-THREE

The smartphone vibrating on the bedside unit woke Ed with a start. He looked at the caller ID but it displayed "caller withheld" so it was just a number and not a friend. It was too early to be a cold caller, unless it was from India, but he decided to accept the call as he was awake, albeit barely.

'Ed Case, who is it?' he said, his voice still full of sleep.

'That's a nice way to greet your girlfriend,' Angel said, her voice immediately dispersing the last remnants of sleep.

'Angel,' he replied with enthusiasm. 'Sorry, I didn't recognise the number.'

'That's because it's a satellite phone and it's also encrypted. You know how it is? You can never be too careful. I just called to let you know the mission is just about complete and I should be home in a day or so after we've tied up a few loose ends. I'll have to attend a debrief at HQ, then I'll hopefully get a few days off.'

'Great. Data said you might have to go on another mission quite soon.'

'No, not this time or it's unlikely, but you know how the job is, situations change very quickly. We achieved our primary objective, but it hasn't led to anything new. Better luck next time,' Angel replied.

'Good luck for me though. I can come to London if you like or you're more than welcome to come here,' Ed replied, cheered by the thought of seeing Angel.

'I'll come down to you. My place isn't exactly the Ritz, as you know.'

'Why not come here and when you go back to London, I'll

come with you and we can book a decent hotel until you get sent on another mission.'

'Are you that horny?' Angel replied jokingly.

'Only for you my love,' Ed replied playing along.

'It better be only me or I'll rip your tackle off and ram it down your throat.'

Ed chuckled.

'You weren't down here a few days ago, were you?'

'You know the answer to that, why d'you ask?'

'Phil seems to have a serial killer on the loose and his last victim he mutilated, ripped his meat and two veg off and stuffed them in his mouth for the cops to find,' Ed informed her.

'Lovely. How's the hunt for Owen Moore?' she replied.

'I'm assuming you spoke to Data?'

'Yeah, he said you called him. Asking him for another favour and said you missed me, so I thought I'd call and let you know I'll see you in a few days.'

'OK. I'm looking forward to it. I really am missing you.'

'Good. If it's any consolation I miss you too. Now get your lazy arse out of bed and find your man so we can have some fun together without you having to worry about work.'

'OK, boss,' Ed replied happily.

Angel ended the call and Ed got out of bed and made his way to the kitchen for a caffeine fix. Feeling invigorated by Angel's call he made an effort and cracked open a fresh packet of Blue Mountain and spooned it into the coffee machine. The smell was making his mouth water. It was going to be a good day of that he was sure.

Conversely the smell that assailed Phil Reynolds and Shaun Edwards, before either man had even stepped foot inside the small caravan, was horrendous. Phil gave Shaun a look of concern and put a hand on his shoulder.

'We don't both need to go in. As the senior officer here, I'm happy to take one for the team,' Phil said and flashed a quick smile.

'I'll have to face these kind of atrocities at some point in my career so I might as well start now,' Shaun replied, knowing it was the truth, but still not relishing the prospect. Mr Wilkes' words "mauled by a pack of wild dogs" were still resonating around his thoughts.

'Your choice,' Phil said and pulled a handkerchief from his pocket and placed it over his mouth and nose. Shaun did likewise.

They walked in, the handkerchiefs doing very little to mask the pungent odour of blood, meat and excrement. Blood was everywhere, splashes of it adorned every surface and the floor was sticky underfoot with congealing blood. It was a charnel house, like something out of a horror movie.

Pathologist Mark Wilton stood up and turned to face the two detectives. Both men caught a glimpse of the offal that used to be a human being called Pete Quigley. Shaun turned and left immediately, racing out into the fresh air. He gagged a few times but managed to keep his last meal inside. Phil quickly looked away and took a few deep breaths to regain his composure and block the gory images from his memory.

Mark Wilton as usual was unfazed by the carnage and grinned back at Phil.

'Maybe it'd be better if we talked outside, as you can see it's a little messy.'

'No shit,' Phil replied.

Phil wasn't going to argue and turned quickly and joined Edwards outside. He looked at him and nodded. Shaun shuddered and nodded back, letting Phil know he was shaken but otherwise he was fine.

'It's difficult to know where to begin?' Wilton said.

Neither Phil nor Shaun could find an answer for that and looked back blankly, both men shocked and badly shaken at what they'd just seen.

'Even I was a little taken aback by this one. Firstly, I can tell you it was the same MO as the last two. The body was stripped naked and pinned to the floor with nylon ties, which would indicate the same person killed all three men. I say person as I still believe the injuries could've been carried out by a man or a strong woman. If pushed, I'd say a man, but that's your area of expertise. A claw hammer is a particularly devastating weapon and doesn't require a huge amount of effort to inflict a great deal of damage as you've just seen.

You couldn't have failed to notice the blood. It was a

particularly frenzied attack and he was most certainly alive when his ordeal began. The splashes are from where one or more main arteries were severed. Had he been dead the heart wouldn't be beating and we wouldn't get those types of blood spatter patterns. I'm unable to determine the exact cause of death right now. I'll take a good look when I'm back in the lab. All I can say is that the victim has been practically disembowelled. Most of his intestines and vital organs are outside of the body cavity and were thrown with some rage around the caravan. His head has also been beaten heavily. The face and cranium are severely misshapen by repetitive blows from the hammer.'

Wilton looked between both men, who said nothing.

'What's your guess at a time of death?' Phil eventually asked.

'That's a difficult one. I usually go by body temperature. After death a body cools roughly one degree Fahrenheit each hour. However, with the body ripped open like this one the body will cool a lot quicker. I'd guess right now at between ten and twelve hours.

'Surely someone would've heard something. I'd guess that his death wasn't quick and he would surely have screamed out in pain,' Shaun Edwards said.

'Good point. However, the victim like the other two was gagged and he may well have passed out or been knocked unconscious by one of the initial blows. I'll know more once the post-mortem is complete.'

'Thanks Mark. The pressure is mounting as technically this makes the perpetrator of these crimes a serial killer so a quick post-mortem would be appreciated,' Phil told him.

'I'll try and shuffle things around and get on to it this afternoon and have the report with you by the morning. I assume you'll attend and I can give you a verbal update.'

'I think I'll certainly have that dubious pleasure,' Phil replied, not relishing the sight of seeing what was once Pete Quigley again.

Wilton left and the body was taken out of the caravan into the waiting ambulance. The senior forensic officer handed Phil an evidence bag. In it was a blood splattered note. As expected it read "SAY THANK YOU JOHN". Who the hell was John? Phil wanted to know.

'Shaun, call into the office and see what they've managed to find out about Quigley. Get them to check out if he was a wife beater; you may be right, and as of now we have nothing else to go on.'

Shaun beamed broadly.' Yes, sir,' he replied, happy that his and Fiona Walsh's findings were now being taken seriously.

CHAPTER TWENTY-FOUR

Feeling in a great mood after his chat with Angel and two cups of Blue Mountain filter coffee, Ed opened up his laptop and checked for any updates from Data. Disappointingly there was no email from Data, which meant Jack Griggs had likely given him a bunch of urgent requests to work on. Unfortunately, Ed knew he was busy so couldn't really chase him up as he was only doing him a favour. Ed decided he'd drive into Padstow, meet Bob to give him an update and talk about developments and see if he'd got any new ideas. A chat over a Cornish pasty and a coffee on a bench overlooking the harbour was a regular thing, during the summer months. It wasn't quite summer, but it was still warm enough to sit outside with a jacket on.

Ed gave Bob a call, who as usual was up for a pasty. Ed agreed to meet him in a couple of hours as he wanted to go for a quick run and then workout in the gym for a while. He wasn't a fitness fanatic, but took a keen interest in keeping in shape; more so since meeting Angel as she was extremely fit. There wasn't an ounce of fat on her athletic body. She could out-run Ed easily over both long distances and sprints. She was also adept at all forms of armed and unarmed combat. Ed always thought he was pretty useful in a fight. He was fast with lightning reflexes and packed a punch that was as hard as it was fast. Angel put Ed in the shade. Occasionally, they sparred together and Angel taught him new techniques, and he learnt from her army and secret service training, but he was still well-below her standards. Although they sparred together Ed always held back, not wanting to cause pain or injure the woman he loved. Angel had pushed and pushed for Ed to fight her like she'd seen him fight several times before, but knew Ed was principled and stuck to his guns about never hitting a woman. There was one exception to this but she was now dead; John Stone's very own nemesis, Kristina Kovac. Ed had killed her by stabbing her with her own knife and felt no remorse; she was a monster and the world was a better place for her being the other side of the grass.

Bob was waiting for him, staring out across the harbour, watching the seagulls and few tourists boarding the ferry to take them across to Rock and the beautiful beaches and sand dunes. Ed recalled a memory of fighting for his life in those sand dunes, which now seemed a long time ago. It was a close call but Ed had come out on top, despite needing his eye stitched up along with a huge gash in his leg from a knife wound. Not a fond memory.

Ed sat down next to Bob and handed him a large coffee and an even larger Cornish pasty from the bag he carried.

'Thanks Ed. You took your time,' Bob told him.

'Ran and did a little row and cycle in the gym. I got a call from Angel. She'll be down in a few days and I don't want her nagging me that I've let myself go. I like to keep in shape, but she takes it to another level.'

'I guess she's got to be on top of her game in her job. You're a lucky man Ed. Not many people have beautiful girlfriends, who don't have an ounce of fat on them and can kick most men's arses,' Bob replied and grinned.

'I know. Don't know what she sees in me. I'm short, a bit on the skinny side and just about average all round. Reckon it must be my money,' Ed joked.

Bob shook his head. It was a conversation they'd had before. He recalled a night out with his wife Raechael, Phil Reynolds and Emma. Ed came up in conversation and Emma told a story about Ed saying Raechael's daughter was too good for him. Emma pressed Ed on how a girl in a wheelchair, albeit a beautiful girl, could be out of his league. Ed said she was beautiful whereas everything about himself was average. When she recovered and was walking on her own two feet again, she could have the pick of any man. Why, he asked, would she choose mister average? Raechael said she'd had much the same conversation. It was now a moot point as her daughter, Laura, had died after the operation that was meant to restore her mobility. They both agreed Ed was a good catch, not only for his money, but he was one of the kindest, most caring and generous man they'd met and was handsome with lovely green eyes. Raechael even went on to say she wished she was ten years younger, much to Bob's disgust. He never told Ed about that conversation, he'd be unbearable.

'So what's new, Magnum? Bob asked, ignoring Ed's previous comments.

Ed told him about the note he received from Owen Moore and the conversation with Data.

'That's interesting. What do you make of that?' Bob asked.

'Someone lied to us and told Owen Moore. Why he doesn't want to be found is anyone's guess. Hopefully, Data will give us something to narrow him down and I can chat to him in person.'

'It's useful having contacts like that. Without Data you'd be stuffed. A bit like you were with Paul Faulkner.'

'Agreed. He's always useful in a tight spot, but I don't like to use the team too often. I know Jack Griggs uses me, but I don't want to use all my trump cards too soon. I reckon about now we're even.'

'I'd say after helping him track down The Messenger and finding our old buddy Agent Offord, you're probably in credit. From what you told me about your escapade with The Messenger, the mission would've failed, and you killed dozens of his mercenaries. Don't forget you did a week in prison for him too. Without the information you found out, he'd have struggled to find Offord, and you helped him out after that in Corfu. Apart from using the team to find Faulkner and sort out the mess with that godforsaken box, you haven't asked for much apart from a few favours from Data. I reckon you're well in credit.'

'You're probably right. It'll be interesting to see what Data has come up with and how much it'll help finding Owen Moore. Hope he doesn't get too pissed off when I do,' Ed replied and shrugged to suggest he couldn't care less what Owen Moore felt.

'Worst case he gets pissed off and you can punch his lights out. Best scenario he contacts his mum and you send her the invoice. If not take a selfie with Owen and that days newspaper and send her the invoice,' Bob replied.

Ed liked Bob's approach to life. Everything was black and

white, no grey areas.

'You two look like your plotting something.'

Bob and Ed looked up to see Phil Reynolds with a large takeaway coffee in his hand.

'You look like shit, Phil,' Bob told him with a great deal of enthusiasm.

'Thanks Bob. It's been one hell of a week. We had our third victim today. It was fucking horrific. I mean really fucking horrific. It made the Texas Chainsaw Massacre seem like a Disney movie. I won't tell you the details or you'll be bringing up your pasties. The body was practically disembowelled,' Phil told them and shook his head as if to clear the gory memory.

Both men nodded and took another bite of their pasties, seemingly unconcerned by the victim's gruesome demise.

'So what's the motive, any clues? They must all have something in common, unless the man or woman committing these murders just hates men,' Bob replied.

'All three victims were separated and the first two both had injunctions out and heavy fines for assaulting their wives. Shaun Edwards seems to think it could be someone who's got a grudge against wife beaters,' Phil replied.

'Did he leave his note?' Ed asked.

'He did. Although it was difficult to read as it was caked in blood.'

'So, we're looking for a John who bears a grudge against wife beaters and is violent?' Bob asked.

'If Shaun Edwards is correct and indeed the motive is that simple,' Phil replied a little sceptical.

'John Talbot,' Bob replied.

'The farmer guy you had a run in with the other day?' Phil asked.

'Sure, why not? His father beat him and his mother senseless most days. That might give him a grudge against wife beaters. He's certainly violent and has a nasty temper and his name's John. Well worth a look into I think,' Bob said.

'You sure this isn't just a grudge cos he kicked your arse?' Ed teased.

'He got a lucky punch in, and no, it isn't. He ticks all the boxes, well worth bringing in for questioning. I would if it was my case,'

Bob replied defensively.

Ed shrugged and looked at Phil.

'I'll check him out and anyone else called John who might have an issue with domestic abuse. Remember it could be John or being done for John, which leaves it wide open,' Phil said.

'Could also be a red herring so you look for John and not Tom, Dick or Harry,' Ed said and grinned.

'Yeah thanks for the reminder, Ed. You certainly know how to stomp on a dream. Right, I need to get back and see what the team have come up with. I'll catch up with you both another time.'

They said their goodbyes.

'What's next for you?' Bob asked Ed.

'I think I'll just wait to see what Data comes up with. No point wasting time and effort chasing shadows, is there?'

'Good. So you've got time for a pint? That pasty has given me a raging thirst.'

'OK. I'll come, but I've gotta take it easy as I'm driving,' Ed replied.

'We'll see.' Bob replied.

CHAPTER TWENTY-FIVE

Being in a police cell wasn't a new experience for John Talbot. He'd been arrested twice before. The first time was for being drunk and disorderly and the second for assault, neither occasion had been his fault, at least not in his eyes. This time however, it was entirely of his own doing and he'd got nobody to blame for his predicament than himself. DI Reynolds and DC Edwards had come to interview him and he'd refused, telling them he was too busy. What he'd actually told them, was to fuck off, he didn't have any spare time to talk to the pigs, which resulted in the cuffs coming out and being dragged down to Padstow nick and thrown in a cell. On account of this, DI Reynolds had left him to stew in the cell for an hour, before having him taken to the interview room, where he'd been kept waiting a further fifteen minutes.

'You took your bloody time,' John Talbot said angrily to DI Reynolds and DC Edwards when they entered the interview room, both carrying steaming hot cups of coffee. Talbot would dearly have liked a cup himself but that wasn't to be and he was too proud to ask.

'I do apologise, I'm a very busy man' much like you told us you were earlier, which is why we're here and not having a friendly chat over a cup of tea in your farmhouse. You want to waste my time, I'll waste yours,' Phil replied and smiled condescendingly.

Talbot sneered back, tempted to vent his feelings but checked himself, knowing what the consequences would be; he hated all coppers.

'Can you tell us where you were last night, John?'

'I finished milking the cows about six-thirty. Had dinner and went down the pub about an hour later.'

'Which pub was that?' Phil asked.

'The Dog and Whistle.'

'And what time did you leave the pub?'

'About half past eleven.'

'I assume the landlord will be able to verify that?'

Talbot nodded, raised his eyes to the ceiling and sighed, letting Phil know he was bored.

'We'll check that. What time did you arrive home?'

'I live about fifteen minutes away so fifteen minutes later.'

'Was anyone awake who can verify that?' Phil pressed, keeping up his quick fire questions.

'Yes, my wife can. I got home and was feeling horny and we had a shag. Maybe you can verify that by getting some DNA off the sheets. What's this all about anyway? You drag me down here asking where I was, but don't tell me what it's all about,' Talbot said his temper rising.

'Let's hope that won't be necessary,' Phil replied, trying to keep images of the Talbot's stained bed linen out of his mind.

'C'mon, what's this all about? Why've you dragged me away from my work and kept me hanging around in a cell all afternoon?'

Phil ignored the question for a second time.

'Where were you on the night of the fourteenth and the night of the eighteenth? Phil continued trying to get Talbot to feel pressured.

'I probably did the same as last night. I guess I would've milked the cows and went to the pub. I can barely remember what I did yesterday let alone a week ago. I'm a farmer so most of what I do, I do day in, day out. I get up milk the cows, clean up the milking sheds, put the cows back in the fields and last thing I do is milk the cows again and clean up. What's this all about anyway?' Talbot asked again, his temper rising.

He was definitely feeling the pressure, Phil was pleased to see. When pressured, suspects were more likely to make a mistake. Maybe a small contradiction or an outright lie. Phil didn't let up on his questioning.

'Do you know, Mick Woods, Brandon Taylor or Pete Quigley?' Phil asked, ignoring the question.

'No. I don't... hold on, wait a minute. Mick Woods and

Brandon Taylor were both murdered, I read about that in the papers. Are you trying to pin their murders on me? I want a solicitor,' Talbot's anger rising another level.

'The fact that you think you need a solicitor, would suggest you have something to hide,' Phil said, pushing Talbot a little further.

'I've got nothing to hide, but you bastard's are always quick to find a scapegoat. Why me?' he asked. His hands were balled into fists and both detectives were ready for the worst. It was why one of the bigger uniformed officers was standing watch behind John Talbot, ready to subdue him if needed.

'OK, John. I'll tell you exactly why you're here. We're looking for a man called John. A strong man with a history of violence who might have reason to hold a grudge against a man who beats his wife. I know that your own father was a bit of thug, much like you, and he also beat you and your mother. So you tick quite a few of the boxes,' Phil replied and waited.

Talbot was silent for a few seconds before he spoke

'Brown, fucking DCI Brown or that skinny prick of a PI he hangs around with put you up to this. I know he did so don't fucking lie to me,' Talbot shouted.

'And why would Mr. Brown do that, John?' Phil asked.

'Cos he was in the pub the other day asking questions and we had a falling out and a bit of a punch up. I put Brown on his arse and now he's trying to get you to fit me up. Am I under arrest?'

'No. You're just helping us with our inquiries,' Phil replied.

'So I don't have to say anything and I'm free to go?' Talbot asked.

'No, you don't have to say anything if you don't want to, but it won't look good if you walk out now. We might have to bring you back in for further questioning and we might do that under caution. If we're still not satisfied with what you tell us, that could be very awkward for you.'

'Is that so? I'll take my chances. I've done nothing wrong and have nothing to hide. I'm out of here. I've got cows that ain't gonna milk themselves.'

Talbot stood and looked at the door and the burly police officer guarding it. The officer looked at DI Reynolds waiting for instructions. Phil nodded and the officer opened the door and let Talbot out. He stormed out the door and made his way into the street still fuming, he stomped up the road.

CHAPTER TWENTY-SIX

Ed's phone vibrated. He removed it from his pocket and looked at the notification; it was an email from Data. Ed read it and muttered 'sarcastic twat' and smiled. Data had apologised profusely for the lateness of his email but he'd been inconveniently tied up in some MI5 tasks. There were three files enclosed, which Data explained were credit card, debit card and mobile phone locations. Due to lack of time, he was unable to provide details of his mobile phone usage or check any CCTV at the times of the card transactions. Ed was happy that the files would most likely give him a pretty good idea where to look. He decided to go home and view the files on his laptop, which was much easier than the small screen on his smartphone.

'Is that the email you've been waiting for from your mate, Data?' Bob asked.

'He's sent me three files with information on where he's used his debit and credit cards and another with his mobile phone location. No call data, but I only want to know where he is, not who he's been in touch with,' Ed replied.

'Where is he then?' Bob asked, leaning forward across the table.

'I haven't opened the files to be honest. I'm sure there's a lot of details on them and it's too much to view on a small phone screen. I'll open the email at home on the laptop and have a good look,' Ed said.

Bob nodded, but seemed a little disappointed not knowing.

'You'll be the first to know when I've worked out where he is,' Ed told him.

Bob seemed a little happier.

'OK, make sure you do. It's always good to know where you are, just in case anything happens. I know what you're like when it comes to finding trouble,' Bob replied.

'More a case of trouble finding me, but I take your point and will be sure to check in.'

Ed finished his beer and Bob looked at the empty glass in his own hand. Ed knew he was deciding if he should go home or stay for one or maybe a few more. Ed knew his limit and knew if he stayed for one more, his resolve would be broken and he'd been in for the night and waking up with an almighty hangover and having to go through the files Data provided, nursing a sore head. Bob seemed to make his mind up and the two men walked outside, much to Ed's relief.

Ed had only drunk two pints and decided he'd collect his car from the yard and drive home. For Bob it was just a ten minute walk home. Ed promised to call him later once he'd reviewed Data's email and they said their goodbyes.

In the yard, Bulldog was washing down his Harley, his pride and joy and one part of his past as a Hells Angel member he couldn't let go of. Ed had never been a fan of motorbikes, much preferring the comfort of a car and the feeling of safety being surrounded by a metal cage. He did however appreciate the craftsmanship of some of the classic bikes and the feeling of freedom you'd get riding a big bike. However, having to don leathers and a helmet to go anywhere was a disadvantage especially in the summer. A conversation he'd had with Bulldog many a time. He still called him Bulldog and was always being admonished by Chris to call him Lionel. To Ed he looked more like a Bulldog than a Lionel and recently learnt the name was given to him by his mother who had a crush on Lionel Blair, some or other, seventies entertainer that he had to look up on Google to find out who he was.

They chatted for a few minutes. Lionel suggesting they should meet up for dinner or drinks as he'd promised the last time. Ed agreed and reminded him that Angel would be around in the next few days or so and maybe he'd try and arrange a meal with all the usual suspects. Ed made his excuses, telling him he'd got a lot of work to do for his ongoing case and pulled out of the yard to go home.

He hadn't gone far when he had to slow down as an ambulance, with its lights flashing, was parked at the side of the road and traffic was coming in the opposite direction. Ed moved the car out to peer past the ambulance and put his foot down once there was a gap in the oncoming traffic. He tapped impatiently on the steering wheel, eager to get home and look at the files Data had sent him.

The stretcher was wheeled to the rear of the ambulance. The two paramedics were fussing over the occupant before they lifted him into the back. Ed did a double take. Surely he was mistaken, he thought, as his heart leapt into his throat. Ignoring the blare of horns from the cars behind him, Ed released his seatbelt and threw the car door open, almost blocking both sides of the road.

Ed ran the few steps to the stretcher and looked down at the battered and bruised face of Bob. He looked like he'd been hit by a bus. One eye was closed, his lips were split and he sported a nasty cut across his cheekbone. A blanket was draped across him so he could only wonder at what the rest of his body was like.

'What happened?' He asked, placing a hand on his shoulder.

'I'm getting too old for this shit,' he replied in a hoarse whisper.

'That makes two of us,' Ed replied and gave his old friend a smile.

The paramedic placed a hand on Ed's forearm.

'We really need to get him to hospital, sir,' he said softly but with authority.

Ed ignored him

Ed knew Bob hadn't been in a car accident. He recognised the signs that he'd been beaten and quite severely. He'd inflicted the same on many others in self-defence and wanted to know who did this to Bob.

'Who was it, Bob?' he asked.

'Talbot,' He croaked in reply.

'We really do need to get him to hospital and now. Please move away,' the paramedic said firmly.

'Yeah, yeah, I understand. Take good care of him. I'll inform his wife,' Ed replied and watched as Bob was put inside the ambulance and the doors closed.

Ed turned towards his car, his face dark and angry.

The driver of the car behind him tooted his horn and leaned out of the window gesturing that Ed should get back in his car.

'Shift your fucking arse mate, some of us have homes to go to,' he shouted at Ed.

Ed was in no mood to be messed with and strode up to the car. The driver's window slid shut and he heard the central locking being engaged. Ed punched through the window and grabbed the driver, hauling his head and shoulders through the gap.

'That was my best mate being loaded into the back of that ambulance. Now, unless you want to be joining him in intensive care, then I'd suggest you shut the fuck up and wait for me to get in my car. Do I make myself clear or do you want me to drag you through this window and make myself a little clearer?'

Ed's eyes blazed into the terrified driver's face. He nodded and Ed let go of the man, muttering an apology as he did so.

'Anyone else got a problem?' he shouted down the line of traffic behind him, his arms held wide, inviting anyone willing to try to take their chances.

Nobody did so Ed got into his car and pulled the car into the bus stop a short distance in front. He dialled Raechael and waited for her to answer. Ed explained that Bob was on his way to hospital having been mugged. He didn't tell her the truth as he didn't want to alarm her any more than necessary.

'You never were a great liar, Ed Case,' she replied.

'You know me too well. Guess not being a good liar is a good thing. The truthful answer is that he was beaten up by someone with a grudge against him,' he replied honestly.

'Why didn't you go with him?' she asked.

'I wasn't with him and I'm driving. It was just luck that the ambulance was blocking the road and I noticed them wheeling Bob along. I have something to take care of then I'll go to the hospital and see you both there.'

'Ed, I recognise that tone. Don't do anything stupid and end up being arrested,' she admonished.

'As I said before, you know me too well. See you at the hospital; hopefully not in the bed next to him,' Ed replied.

'That's not even remotely funny, Ed. See you soon.'

Ed drove up to The Dog and Whistle, and parked the car. He sat there for a few moments to compose himself. Going into a confrontation angry was never a good idea. Always fight with the head and not the heart was his mantra. Sometimes that was difficult but after a few minutes Ed got out of the car and walked into the pub hoping to find the man he was looking for. If he wasn't there, he'd ask where his farm was and confront him there. He took a look around and saw John Talbot sitting at a table with three mates, laughing and joking. Probably bragging about how he beat up an old man. Ed bit his lip thinking how unfair it was that Bob was getting patched up in casualty and Talbot was enjoying himself. Ed told himself to keep calm repeatedly as he walked over to where Talbot and his cronies were sitting.

Talbot looked up at Ed and sneered.

'Didn't think it'd take you long to come and find me when you found out I gave your dad a good kicking,' Talbot said and gave Ed an unfriendly smile.

'You went a bit over the top, just because he got the better of you in here the other day,' Ed replied.

'He grassed me up to the cops. Now I'm number one suspect for three murders. He deserved what he got and more.'

'It must've felt good winning a fight against an old man. I heard your dad meted out a few good hidings on you, only you didn't put up much of a fight. Too much of a pussy I suppose,' Ed replied trying to rile Talbot.

'You know nothing about my dad,' Talbot spat back.

'I think I know quite a lot. Bob told me was a bit of a cunt and used to beat you and your mum, drank too much and killed his best mate while arguing about money. Everyone give a big round of applause for father of the year,' Ed said and clapped his hands slowly. He rarely used the C word, if at all, but today he wanted to push Talbot hard. It seemed to have the desired effect.

Talbot rose quickly, his chair toppling over. He was about to kick off but the landlord was next to Ed in a flash.

'I thought I told you last time you were in here you were barred for life?' the barman told Ed angrily.

'You did but I have some business with this piece of shit and unfortunately, he's in your shit hole of a pub,' Ed replied, never taking his eyes off Talbot.

'If you two wanna start trouble again, take it outside. I won't have brawling in my pub,' he said.

Talbot jabbed a finger towards Ed. 'Outside,' Talbot ordered.

Ed walked towards the door, aware of where Talbot was, fearing he might try and take Ed while his back was turned.

There was a small grassed area where a couple of wooden tables and benches were, looking as unloved as they did unused. Grass grew almost as tall as the legs of the benches, where whoever cut the grass couldn't be bothered to trim around them.

Ed turned and faced Talbot and his three mates.

'Let's see how you do against someone nearer your own age,' Ed said provoking more anger.

'I hope you put up more of a fight than Brown did. Doddery old bastard didn't land a single punch.'

'In his day he was as hard as ten men. He still is pretty good, but not as good as me. I reckon you either took him by surprise or those arseholes helped you, Ed said and grinned.

'Who you calling an arsehole? You hear that lad's? He called us arseholes.' One of the three men said.

Ed made a point of theatrically sniffing the air.

'You smell like arseholes. Either that or Talbot has filled his underpants at the thought of a fair fight,' Ed said and laughed mockingly.

The four men fanned out. Talbot and one other, a big burly farmer, stood in front of Ed, staring menacingly. The other two were wiry much like Ed, but looked like they lacked any real intelligence. Ed took a step forward and stamped his foot as he did so. As he expected the two smaller men, took a quick step backwards. That was all Ed needed to know; they didn't want to be here and wouldn't be very good in a brawl unless Talbot was winning and they'd join in; cowards. He put on his fight face and stared back at the four men with a face that showed no emotion, with his hands by his sides. He was ready.

A small crowd of curious drinkers had gathered and were cheering the four men on. Ed did his best to ignore their suggestions that Talbot should rip his head off and wipe his arse with it. Another man wanted Talbot kill to him and kick his dead body all the way to the harbour; much to the amusement of the crowd. Ed would silence their inane banter in time.

The four men facing him put their fists up. The burly man next to Talbot was the first to make a move. He took a step forward and jabbed with his left. As Ed expected he was slow, and he avoided the punch by moving his head to the left and repeated the action when he followed up with his right. His next punch was a wild haymaker borne of anger and frustration. Ed ducked under the blow, inched forward and slammed a fist squarely on the end of the burly man's nose, which exploded in a spray of blood. His hands instinctively clutched his broken nose. Ed followed up with two right hand blows to the man's stomach. The big man fell to his knees, struggling for breath. It was all over in a matter of seconds.

The crowd urged the other three men on, continuing with their childish banter, although a little more subdued than it had been.

Ed, ever aware of his surroundings saw one of the smaller men to his left, tentatively edging forward. With the odds still three to one, he needed to be decisive and kicked the man hard between the legs. He crumpled to the ground like he'd been shot. Talbot hadn't moved but the second of the smaller men, put his hands in the air and walked away; obviously the odds of two against one weren't quite to the coward's liking.

Ed smiled at John and took a step closer, now within striking range. Ed was usually happier on the counter attack but today, he had a point to make. He wanted to hurt Talbot for what he'd done to Bob. He flicked out a fist, which smacked into Talbot's cheekbone. It wasn't a hard punch, one merely trying to gauge his opponent's speed. Talbot grimaced, but seemed unconcerned and stood his ground. The crowd got behind their man once more 'Kick him to death John", "Kill the skinny little prick", Ed heard, but was unfazed.

Talbot moved quicker than Ed had expected and threw a barrage of left and rights to his head. Ed blocked them, but the bigger man was powerful and Ed rocked from side to side. His forearms would be a mass of angry bruises in the morning, of that he was sure. Talbot as well as being big and strong was fit and continued throwing punches, although Ed could feel the punches were becoming weaker and Talbot definitely slowing slightly.

Talbot changed tactics and threw a right to Ed's stomach. Ed worked hard in the gym and although he was slim he had stomach muscles like iron doors. He saw the punch coming, tensed and let it connect. The crowd roared at Talbot's success, expecting to see Ed doubled up and Talbot following up with a winning blow. Instead they were silenced as Ed looked Talbot in the eye and smiled.

'What the f…..' Talbot began to say, but Ed was done warming up and his words were cut off as Ed slammed his fist into Talbot's cheekbone, opening up a deep gash, sending the bigger man staggering backwards under the power.

Ed prided himself on his speed and ability to read a fight and was also blessed with a powerful punch, which seemed to take Talbot by surprise. Blood flowed freely down Talbot's cheek as he came back to face Ed. Anger showed in his face, but his eyes showed fear. Ed was quick to seize the advantage and smashed a fist into Talbot's eye. Talbot covered up his face powerless to stop the onslaught of punches Ed threw. Unlike Talbot, Ed wasn't one to waste energy and made sure every shot connected to his head and face. Talbot couldn't protect every part of his head and face at once and Ed was quick to find openings.

Ed was scoring easily, but changed to work on Talbot's body. He threw powerful left and rights that powered into Talbot's ribs. Talbot grunted, but to give him credit, he still stood his ground and even managed to throw a counter punch. It glanced off Ed's temple but he hardly felt it. He landed another left right combination to Talbot's ribs and switched back to headshots, seeing his opponent's arms drop slightly. Ed turned on the speed and landed blow after blow into Talbot's face, splitting his lips and opening up cuts around his eyes and face, but still Talbot stood his ground. Ed took a step back and looked at Talbot; he was a mess.

'Bring it on,' Talbot said breathlessly.

Ed shrugged, stepped forward and smashed a right hook into Talbot's cheekbone. Talbot's eyes rolled and he staggered forward. Ed landed a left hook into Talbot's other cheekbone and was rewarded with another satisfying gash. Talbot staggered again, doing his best to keep upright. Ed grinned and moved aside, and kicked him up the arse helping him along. Talbot staggered and dropped to his knees. Ed put a foot on Talbot's hip and pushed him over. Talbot toppled and lay on his back, breathing hard with no strength to rise. Ed was tempted to carry on kicking him until he was unconscious, but he wasn't a malicious person. He looked down at John Talbot and decided his face looked like he'd more than evened the score on Bob's behalf. He took out his smartphone and took a photo so Bob would know he got even, no not even, better. Nobody fucked with Ed's friends and family.

Ed looked at the crowd and the other two men who were now on their feet.

'Are we done?' Ed asked.

The crowd went back inside. The three men who'd stood with Talbot went over to take care of him but said nothing. Ed grunted, walked to his car and drove off to the hospital to see how his best friend was.

CHAPTER TWENTY-SEVEN

It was a short drive to the hospital, but now that the adrenaline had worn off so the pain started. Ed looked at his knuckles resting on the steering wheel. They were a little tender and one or two of them cut. He'd run them under cold water once he arrived at the hospital. Perhaps if he asked nicely a nurse might be inclined to find him an icepack to help with the swelling that was sure to follow. He parked up and asked the man at the reception desk where he could find Mr. Brown, who was brought in by ambulance earlier after being mugged. He was directed to the day ward. He wanted to get some flowers for Bob just to see if he'd lost his sense of humour, but was told by a nurse that flowers and fruit baskets were no longer allowed in hospitals due to allergies and the risk of infection, so he arrived at Bob's bedside empty handed.

Raechael was sitting on the only chair watching over Bob who seemed to be sleeping peacefully. Ed approached and smiled and asked how Bob was. Raechael explained that Bob had suffered concussion, and right now was just resting but the doctors were sure that no permanent damage had been done. Ed gave him a look over, and now that he'd been cleaned up, he didn't look so bad. He was going to have a nasty black eye and apart from a few other small cuts, grazes and bruises he looked to be OK.

'Your hands look a little sore,' Raechael said to Ed and gave him a knowing look.

Ed shrugged and looked at his cut and puffy knuckles, desperately trying to think of a good excuse.

'I had a blocked drain and had to get my hands in to unblock it. It was a tight fit and I scraped my knuckles.' Ed replied after a while.

'On both hands?'

'My right arm got tired so I had to swap,' Ed told her with a straight face.

I've no idea how many times I've told you, but you're a terrible liar, Ed.'

'Yeah, I know,' he replied and said nothing more.

Raechael gave him a withering look, the way only women can, that can make a man's resolve crumble in an instant. Ed was scared of no man, but women made him decidedly nervous and he felt compelled to confess.

'I bumped into John Talbot and a few of his friends on the way here,' he said nervously.

'That was convenient. You were driving to the hospital and just happened to bump into the man who assaulted my husband.'

'I know. I'm not a great believer in coincidences, but yeah, what are the chances, eh?' Ed replied, feeling more confident.

Raechael gave him another withering stare. Any confidence he had, disappeared like a puff of wind.

Ed told Raechael about his trip to The Dog and Whistle, but saved her the gory details.

'You fought four men?' she asked.

'Only one really. One ran away and the other two didn't put up much of a fight,' Ed replied trying to make light of it.

'Judging by the state of your knuckles and the lack of any marks on you, would suggest you won easily.'

'Reckon he wore himself out earlier when he gave Bob a slap. Anyway, he got what he deserved for beating up a fat, old man,' Ed replied, reckoning Bob was feigning sleep.

'I'm not old and I'm not fat. I'm just big-boned,' Bob replied groggily.

'I thought you were faking it. I saw you frown earlier. How are you feeling?' Ed asked, happy to be away from Raechael's interrogation.

'Pissed off and thirsty,' he replied.

'Understandable after getting your arse kicked,' Ed replied happy to try and wind Bob up.

'He took me from behind and caught me off guard, if you must know,' Bob said indignantly, pulling himself upright.

'Just him or his mates too?' Ed asked.

Bob spoke after a pause.

'It was just him. He got a lucky first punch in, and after that it was only gonna end one way. Had he faced me man to man it would've been an entirely different outcome, I can assure you,' Bob said, trying to regain some pride out of the situation.

Ed nodded, not wanting to make Bob feel any worse than he already did, and held back on the sarcastic comment he had lined up, despite it being a good one that was sure to wind his friend up.

'Well if it's any consolation, he won't be doing it again any time soon,' Ed replied and pulled his smartphone from his pocket and showed Bob the photo of Talbot.

'Jesus Christ, Ed. If you didn't kill him, I reckon he might slowly bleed to death.'

Raechael grabbed Ed's phone and looked at the photo of the prone John Talbot.

'Good,' Raechael said handing Ed his phone back.

Ed was surprised at her comment but decided not to pursue it, thinking it'd be better to wind Bob up.

'Nobody beats up my grandpa and gets away with it,' he said and grinned.

'If I wasn't feeling so groggy, I'd give you such a slap,' Bob replied.

'I think today we finally put to bed the argument of who is the better fighter, so there's no need to spar in my gym.'

'When my concussion's gone, we're still gonna have it out in your gym. I was taken by surprise, it wasn't a fair fight. You're not getting out of this one so easily,'

'OK, it's up to you. I'll try not to put you back in hospital.'

Bob swung his legs out of bed and grabbed his clothes. Despite Raechael's protestations he pulled the curtain and changed out of his hospital gown. Ed couldn't help but notice the bruises to Bob's legs and ribs. He chose not to comment but was happy to have evened the score. He hoped that would be the end of the matter.

Despite still being a few years the right side of forty, that evening Ed felt like an old man. He was dog tired and his knuckles were still aching and sore. When he arrived home he immersed them in ice cold water and savoured the numbness that enveloped them. He didn't recall having this problem when he was younger. Ed thought that over the years his knuckles would be immune to being abused. As he thought about it, he decided it was probably because as he got older he got into a lot fewer altercations than he did in his teens and early twenties, therefore his knuckles had likely softened rather than hardened with lack of use. Whatever the reason for his discomfort it was worth it to get revenge on behalf of Bob. He shuddered at the memory of Bob's bruised and swollen face; the rest of his body wasn't pretty either.

His mail today didn't include any warning notices from Owen Moore, he was happy to find out. Now sitting down with a large gin and tonic, Ed opened his laptop and went to his email to have a look at the information sent to him from Data. He opened the email and typed a quick thank you before downloading the three files and printing them off, along with the mail itself which conveniently had Owen's car make, model and registration number. It was probably of no use as it was probably one of the most populous cars and colours on the road. He walked wearily to the study and picked up the four sheets of A4 paper and looked at each as he made his way back to the living room. All of the transactions were in Bodmin apart from one which was from a store in Penzance. He gave the mobile phone location file a cursory look and that revealed the same that he spent most of his time in Bodmin with a few excursions to his old stomping ground, Padstow. It was a long list, but it told him all he needed to know. It was almost a certainty that Owen Moore would be found in Bodmin.

Ed searched the internet for a street map of Bodmin. He eventually found one that wasn't too fuzzy and with enough detail for what he needed, which he also printed off. For the next two hours Ed plotted all the locations of card transactions on the map of Bodmin, using information from Data, the detailed addresses from the internet and Google street view to get them mapped as accurately as he could. It was slow and laborious but it had to be done. A supermarket next to the police station seemed to be a popular place for buying lunch, judging by the times. He wasn't a policeman so perhaps he worked in the supermarket, Ed thought. Evenings and weekends the usage was more scattered as he expected, but still all within Bodmin. He was glad that Owen Moore like most people these days used the contactless facility on his debit card rather than cash. It'd made his task a lot easier.

Ed got his highlighter pens out and colour coded each of the locations where the cards had been used on the printouts from Data so he could see any patterns. Again all it told him was the supermarket was the most popular place and where he'd start his search by asking staff if Owen worked there.

At the end of two hours, Ed had come to the conclusion that Owen Moore worked somewhere in the vicinity of the supermarket but where he lived was unclear. Tomorrow he'd drive into Bodmin, buy an Ordnance Survey Map of the town, map the locations again on the bigger more detailed map and hang out at a few of the most frequented establishments. Before turning in for the night, he sent a quick message to Bob, to let him know Owen Moore was in Bodmin as he'd promised him earlier. He hoped he didn't get a message back from Bob insisting he came with him, as Ed knew he needed to rest for a few days. Ed showered and checked his phone, but the message to Bob hadn't been read which he was happy about. Ed was tired and sleep was quick to come.

CHAPTER TWENTY-EIGHT

It was a later start than Ed had intended, but the extra time in bed was much needed. He was going to set his alarm and start early but decided if he woke early he didn't need sleep, and if he slept in, it was because his mind and body needed it. After a quick workout in the gym in his basement and a coffee, he showered and headed for Bodmin. A little under thirty minutes later he parked his car in the supermarket car park and set off with his map and the credit card information from Data that he'd combined into a single sheet to see if there were any patterns. About the only trend was the fact the ATM at the supermarket was the main source of cash withdrawals and it seemed the go to place for lunch. There was the odd lunchtime contactless card transaction at other places nearby but the supermarket was most weekdays and the occasional weekend too. It was 11:30am and it seemed that Owen Moore usually frequented the supermarket between twelve and one o'clock so Ed decided to sit in the coffee shop to kill thirty minutes until he hopefully arrived.

Ed looked at his watch and decided it was time to start his vigil. He walked outside and found a nice place to keep an eye on the front of the supermarket and the ATM. While he waited he scanned the car park for Owen's car, either parked up or arriving, but didn't want to spend too long looking and miss his primary objective, Owen Moore, who was just as likely to arrive on foot as by car. After thirty minutes Ed decided to move to another location, not wanting to arouse too much suspicion; despite this being unlikely in a busy town. He'd ask Bob about surveillance tactics next time they caught up.

The supermarket was extremely busy and Ed's eyes were

constantly darting left and right at anyone who was Owen Moore's size and build. At 2pm Ed realised today wasn't one of the days Owen was going to turn up at the supermarket to buy his lunch. Ed wandered the aisles and showed Owen's photo to a young lady restocking shelves but she was confident the man didn't work at the supermarket. To be sure he asked a second member of staff who gave the same answer. Ed stepped outside, looked at the map and decided to head towards the nearest of the other locations used by Owen. Little knowing he himself was being observed; the hunter was now the hunted.

DI Phil Reynolds lay back in his chair and pushed the palms of his hands into his temples and made circular motions to try and alleviate the stress-headache that was building. The case was frustrating. He reviewed the facts in his mind. It was confirmed that none of the victims were linked either socially or via business. The only factors they'd got in common was that each man had recently been charged with domestic abuse, given restraining orders, fined and in the case of their last victim, Pete Quigley, received a suspended prison sentence at Bodmin Magistrates Court. All three men were killed by the same person, which could be male or a strong female and was either doing it for someone called John or was called John. Phil wasn't ruling out any possibilities, but was thinking it was most likely the killer was called John. None of the three murder locations had provided them with any forensic evidence to assist with finding the killer. Neighbours had heard nothing. Friends and family had noted nothing different in the victims' demeanor, and knew of nobody called John who would benefit from their deaths, or a John who would want the victims dead.

Phil's biggest concern was that whoever it was, would strike again and that would pile on the pressure from above. It could even result in him being replaced as the lead investigator. This was a fantastic opportunity to shine and perhaps earn a promotion or at least earn him recognition that would help with a promotion in the future; opportunities like this didn't happen every day, and he needed to make the most of it.

A polite cough made Phil open his eyes. DC Shaun Edwards was standing over him. Phil looked up and suggested they grab a coffee or what passed as coffee from the vending machine in the canteen; he needed a change of scenery which might galvanise his thoughts

'I had a thought,' Edwards said once they were sat nursing a plastic cup of brown, faintly chemical tasting coffee.

'Go on then, I'd like to hear it. I'm sick of going over the same thoughts I've had,' Phil replied.

'We know all three men were fairly recently convicted of domestic abuse at Bodmin Magistrates' Court. Maybe our man is looking at a fourth victim. If so, why don't we go to the court and see what cases for domestic abuse are scheduled or if there are any recent cases that might give us the name of a potential fourth victim,' Shaun said enthusiastically.

Phil sipped his coffee and thought about it. It was a valid point and worth pursuing.

'You're a good detective Shaun. That's a good point, but all the schedules are online, so we don't have to go.'

'I was thinking that we might be able to view CCTV, ask if they have any regular attendees at the courtrooms, or ask if they have anyone working there called John,' Edwards replied his enthusiasm not waning.

'Good point. I'm sure what we can find out online is going to be limited. Let's go pay them a visit and see what we can get out of them. It's only half an hour's drive.'

There were plenty of parking spaces at the court. Either it was a quiet day or all the cases for the day had been heard. Phil walked up to the reception desk and showed his ID to the young man.

'How can I help you?' he replied after looking at the ID.

'I was after information on recent domestic abuse cases and future scheduled cases,' Reynolds asked.

'You do know our scheduled cases and past cases can all be accessed online?' he replied.

'I am aware of that, but some of the information is withheld. Usually the important information that I'm interested in,' Reynolds replied unable to hide his annoyance.

'I see. I'll have to refer you to Mr. Williams,' the young man replied and picked up the telephone.

Before the man could dial, Reynolds put his hand over the keypad.

'Anyone can view a case here, can't they, either online or in the public gallery?' he asked.

'That's correct. We don't screen all cases online but most,' he replied.

'If someone wants to view a case, do they have to sign in?'

'No. They need to tell me what case they want to view. Some cases that have commercially sensitive data or involve juveniles aren't open to the public. We don't keep a record of anyone who does attend or view cases online.'

'Do you have any regular visitors to the courts who sit in the public galleries?' Phil asked.

'There are a few old women who come in a couple of times a month but I don't recall anyone who could be deemed a regular. Most people who sit in the public galleries are friends and family.'

'Is there CCTV of the hearings and the building itself?' Phil pressed.

'Yes we've got cameras in and around the building, but in the courtroom the CCTV is interested only in the proceedings for online viewing and security reasons, but there aren't any cameras covering the public gallery. All footage covering the courtrooms and the building, I believe, is only kept for thirty days but security should be able to confirm that.'

'Thank you. You can call Mr. Williams now.'

After a short wait a tall, gangly man around sixty years old appeared and led them through to an office. After introductions Phil explained what he needed.

'Let me see,' Williams said his hand flashing across the keyboard. 'Right,' he said and made a few more keystrokes. Pages began spewing out of the printer on the adjacent desk.

'That's interesting. All three cases were in the first week of last month. Must've been a bad week for wives,' he said dryly.

'Indeed,' Phil replied. 'So as they were over a month ago, all the CCTV will have been overwritten?'

'That's correct.'

'Have there been any other domestic abuse cases since then and do you have any scheduled?' Phil asked.

Williams again showed his prowess on the keyboard.

'No cases have been heard since then,' he said and began typing again. 'And only one scheduled to date. A Mr. Harry Sutherland, age thirty-two from St Merryn has a hearing a week tomorrow,' Williams replied.

'I don't suppose you have an address for Mr. Sutherland do you?' Phil asked.

Williams shifted uncomfortably. 'I'm not at liberty to give out personal information. I'm sorry inspector.'

'I understand. However, a man's life might be at stake here. I can easily obtain the information elsewhere, but it'll save me some time if you can give it to me right now. I just want to pay Sutherland a visit and ensure he's in no danger.' Phil said tersely.

'Very well, do you have a pen inspector?'

Phil wrote the address down and thanked Mr. Williams.

'I assume the number of staff working at this court is quite low?' Phil asked.

'Yes, quite small. I don't know the exact number but security will have that information.'

'Do you know if anyone by the name of John works here?'

Williams paused to think about the question.

'No. I'm pretty sure we don't. There are actually more women working here than men. I don't know everyone well, but I know most by name and don't recall a John.'

'Perhaps you could call security or HR to find out?'

A few minutes later William's confirmed they employed nobody by the name of John. Phil thanked him and headed out to the car and a journey to St. Merryn to see Harry Sutherland.

CHAPTER TWENTY-NINE

They sat in the car, both men in reflective silence, while they waited for the lights to change. Phil Reynolds drummed his fingers on the steering wheel, wondering if they were on the right track. It was the only real tangible lead they had. John Talbot had solid alibis for all three nights the murders took place and were backed up by his friends, the pub landlord and his wife. He doubted even the most loyal of friends would lie to cover up three murders for a mate. Perhaps one or two might, but not all of them. Despite Talbot ticking all the boxes, he was a dead end. With no further leads as yet, it seemed that they could be on the right track with the courts but with no further clues as to the killer's identity they'd have to wait a week for Sutherland's court case to come up and speak to everyone who came to the public gallery. It was certainly an option, but a week of no progress wouldn't sit well with the hierarchy who were applying pressure to get a result; even more so as Brandon Taylor was a prominent local entrepreneur and unfortunately one who had friends in high places.

'Do you think we're on the right track or barking up the wrong tree, boss?' Shaun asked.

'It's the only probable lead we have, but we need to pursue other angles. We can't go a week without any progress or we'll all be getting a kick up the arse from the higher echelons of power. You know how it is with high profile cases. The Chief Super shouts and the likes of you and I get our arses kicked.'

Phil pulled the car over, gave a short toot of the horn and opened the passenger window.

'What brings you to Bodmin, Ed?' he asked.

'Looking for a needle in a haystack,' he replied with a smile.

Phil and Shaun got out of the car.

'That makes two of us. Your elusive Owen Moore, eh? What makes you think he's in Bodmin?' Phil asked.

'My friend in MI5 did me a favour and pulled credit and debit card records for my man and most of them appeared to be in Bodmin. Most days he goes to the supermarket where he buys lunch and sometimes a coffee shop and other times a pub, or buys a takeaway. I reckon if I'm at these places about the same time he's been here, one day our paths will cross. Right now I'm just checking out where these places he goes to are as I've got a little time to spare and he wasn't in the supermarket today,' Ed replied.

'It must be nice to have friends in high places. Don't suppose he can find my triple murderer, could he?' Phil asked tongue in cheek.

'He's good, but I think even Data would struggle to find him with the lack of evidence you've got,' Ed replied and grinned.

'Thanks for the reminder, Ed. I hope you have better luck than we're having. We need to get back to the station now and look at our pitiful excuse of evidence,' Phil replied.

Phil and Shaun got in the car and drove to the junction and waited at the red light. Ed tapped the top of the car, waved and took a left towards his next location, which was a pub. Perhaps he'd treat himself to a nice cold pint.

As Phil pulled away, Shaun looked left to see where Ed went. He shook his head as he saw Ed enter a pub thinking how lucky he was. Just as his view was blocked by the building on the corner of the junction, Shaun could've sworn it looked like Ed was being followed. He shrugged. He didn't know Ed well, but knew of his reputation and knew he was more than capable of looking after himself so said nothing and turned his thoughts to his own problems.

In the pub he decide against a pint and ordered a gin and tonic not wanting to spend too long there; just long enough to show Owen Moore's photo to the bar staff. He knew he'd been there at least twice since his disappearance, if not more, depending on whether he used his debit card each time he bought a drink or sometimes used cash, so the bar staff confirming his presence wasn't critical to finding him. He showed the photo anyway. The barmaid said she didn't recognise him but she only worked until 5pm. The landlord scratched his chin and said he looked familiar but couldn't be certain, and could only say that if he did come in for a drink, he wasn't one of his regulars. Ed thanked them and sat down with his drink and looked at his map. He came to the conclusion that the supermarket was nearby to where he worked, and the other locations were on his way home, assuming he walked to work. A quick look at the credit card information he had showed very few transactions at petrol stations, and all were at different stations. Normally, people who did regular journeys to and from work used the same facility. Owen almost certainly walked to work. Using that train of thought he drew pencil lines on his map from the supermarket to each of the locations. Almost all the lines were in the same direction and didn't really tell him a great deal, only confirming that Owen most likely worked somewhere around the supermarket and possibly lived somewhere beyond the end of his lines. He would check that out later to see if he could narrow it down. There couldn't be too many companies in the area large enough to warrant an onsite maintenance engineer, he thought.

Ed scratched his head and turned back to the credit and debit card details provided by Data. There was only ever one transaction on any given day. He was hoping to find a few days where there was more than one transaction, which might indicate a possible route home from work but it wasn't to be. He recalled reading a book or seeing a movie where police looked at where murders took place on a map and drew connecting lines between the points to find the centre, which was the approximate area where the murderer might live. Ed looked at his map and knew from the locations that it wouldn't work for him as all the locations were in a wide corridor so there was no central point as such. Ed finished his drink and returned to walking the streets.

At a couple of the places he visited, members of staff had said Owen Moore looked familiar, but again, they couldn't be sure. It was frustrating, but if someone showed him a picture of someone that he'd seen fleetingly in a crowd, he was sure he wouldn't be able to say for sure if he'd seen them. Ed looked at his watch and decided to call it a day. Tomorrow, now he knew exactly where and what type of businesses the cards had been used at, he'd come back and make sure he was at the location at the time the card had been used. He still felt the supermarket was his best bet as that was the most frequently used location and mostly around lunchtime, although one or two were between 4pm and 6pm. One of the pubs he'd visited had been used a couple of times around 7pm, and a Costa coffee was also used several times between 4pm and 5pm.

Ed reached his car; it was now almost dark and he was tired. He was grateful that there was no parking ticket on his windscreen, so perhaps the supermarket didn't enforce the rule of no stays longer than three hours as the sign suggested or he would be faced with paying a hefty fine, which would be a kick in the teeth after what he viewed as an unproductive day, results wise anyway. There was always a possibility he'd get a surprise in the post in the coming weeks, but he could add that to Mrs. Moore's invoice. He knew he was being hard on himself as the ground work he'd completed today was a necessity. Tomorrow would be a better day he told himself. The impromptu pep talk did little to lift his spirits. He turned the air conditioning down low to keep him awake and drove out of the car park, unknowingly observed all the way by the man he'd come to find.

CHAPTER THIRTY

On the drive home, Ed decided he'd head into Padstow. He could get parked easily this time of day as the tourists would all be heading back to their hotels or caravan sites that were so abundant in the area. Ed himself owned a caravan and had done for over ten years, inheriting it from his parents when they died in a coach crash. The original held a lot of memories for Ed; not all of them good. He used to come and stay every summer then return home to Hertfordshire to carry on his business, refurbishing houses to sell on at a profit. Later he used it when he was refurbishing the farmhouse he purchased. He and his now deceased wife, TJ, lived in it for almost six months, until the farmhouse was habitable. Sometime later she and Bob's wife were held hostage there until Ed and Bob, with the help of former sniper and hitman, John Stone, embarked on a daring rescue. Later it was blown to pieces by a gang of hired thugs working for a politician and all-round sleazebag called Reece Greenfield. Bob had bought a replacement one for him after his wife was murdered and his house was burnt to the ground in an arson attack. Ed had stayed there until his house was rebuilt. He hadn't been there for some time as he'd been so busy. There was a time he would've been happy to live in it permanently as his house felt so empty and lonely. It was only after meeting and becoming romantically involved with Angel that persuaded him not to sell the house, despite its value now being around three million due to the property price boom. It was a family house and needed a good family living in it; he often thought about downsizing and cashing in. The only positive about the house was it was remote and gave him some privacy and he didn't have to worry about noisy neighbours. Also if he did sell it, Angel wouldn't be happy as she loved the place. God he missed Angel and looked forward to seeing her in a day or so.

Ed parked up in the harbour car park, which as he'd banked on had plenty of free spaces. He walked round to find a coffee shop that was still open. He looked at his watch and knew that the bistro at the far end of the harbour would be open. He just hoped they had a free table as it was a popular place. He was in luck and sat down at a spare table and waited to be served.

'You can come and sit with us, you unsociable sod,' someone said.

Ed turned and saw Phil Reynolds and his fiancée Emma. He smiled and shifted seats.

'Sorry, I was lost in my own thoughts and didn't see you,' Ed replied and gave Emma a hug when she stood to greet him and shook Phil's hand, who didn't bother to stand as they'd met and spoken earlier.

'Thinking about your missing man?' Phil said, noticing Ed had his sheets of paper with him.

'No, I was lost in the past for a few moments. I just brought these with me for something to read. I'm planning on going for a meal in the pub, but needed a coffee to wake me up a bit. I don't like drinking coffee in a pub; it's just wrong,' Ed replied.

'What's wrong with cooking a hearty meal in that beautiful kitchen of yours?' Emma asked after a pause, while Ed ordered his coffee.

'I didn't fancy going back to the house. As I've said to you before, I rattle around in it like a pea in a bucket. Some days I enjoy the solitude and peace and quiet, and others, I hate it.'

Emma smiled. 'Missing Angel, I think,' she replied.

'Of course I am; a lot in fact. It feels like home when she's there. When I'm alone... it's not,' Ed replied. 'Anyway, how's your new place coming along?' he asked, steering the conversation away from himself.

'It's not, because my wallpaper putter-upper is too busy with trying to solve murders. He manages a couple of strips some nights but that's it. I'd do it myself, but I can't. Maybe I'll get a man in. It's only the stairs, hall and landing to do really and a little bit in one bedroom. On the plus side, I've managed to do all the painting,' Emma replied.

'As I told you the last time we met, I think I'll have my missing person case done and dusted in a day or two. If Angel hasn't come or I haven't gone to London, I'll do it for you. I like a bit of DIY,' Ed replied and thanked the waitress for his coffee and took a sip of the strong, black brew, already beginning to feel better.

'Thanks Ed. I could be tied up on this triple murder for some time yet. As always it's frustrating. We just haven't got anything to go on apart from we might be looking for a man called John,' Phil replied.

'I know how you feel. As I said to you earlier, this time I had to resort to calling in a favour otherwise I think I'd be at a complete loss. That's why Bob doesn't get involved in missing persons. He said it's tedious and often heart-breaking when the person you're looking for is dead or a junkie or turned to prostitution to pay for their drug habit. Fortunately, I've never experienced that. I know this guy is alive, unless someone out there's using his mobile phone and credit card, which is unlikely, at least I hope it is. I just need to get lucky and be in the right place at the right time,' Ed replied.

'Lucky you; I wish I could say the same,' Phil said.

Ed could feel the genuine desperation in Phil's voice.

'At least you'll get your wallpapering done for free, if it drags on,' Ed replied.

'I might have plenty of time on my hands if drags on as I'll be looking for a new job,' Phil told him.

'I assumed you'd got a solid lead as you were mooching around Bodmin,' Ed said.

'To be honest with you, it's probably tentative at best. All three victims had recently been charged with domestic abuse and given restraining orders, so we thought maybe the person we're looking for might've been hanging around the public galleries on cases involving domestic abuse. If he was, there are no records as CCTV is only kept for thirty days and nobody can recall regular attendees to any hearings. We checked the dates of the hearings and all the victims were killed just after thirty days of being found guilty. So our hunch could be correct as it seems it's someone who knows how the system works. Mind you that said, there's so much available online these days, he could probably find out they only keep the CCTV for thirty days.

The next case is a week away so we want to find our man just in case our hunch is right and we end up with another victim in five weeks. We went to see the man on trial next week and told him if he sees anything suspicious to give us a call. That put the wind up him, I can tell you. We'll also put a man in the public gallery for his hearing' Phil explained.

'That sounds feasible. Let's hope your man only attends Bodmin Magistrates' Court.'

'That's a good point. I'll take a trip out to Truro as that's the only other magistrate's court in Cornwall. It's also the only crown court too.'

'There are only two magistrates' courts? That surprises me. I assumed there'd be a lot more,' Ed replied.

'It's a big county, but the crime rate is low. Did you know that Devon and Cornwall have the lowest crime rates in England? In fact, I think in the UK we have the fourth lowest crime rate behind the Orkney Islands, East Renfrewshire and some county out in the sticks in Northern Island,' Phil told him proudly.

'Maybe that's why my business is slow,' Ed replied.

'Good for you though, as that gives you plenty of spare time to go gallivanting around the world with MI5,' Emma said jokingly.

'Even if I was busy, I'd drop everything to help Jack Griggs. I owe him a lot and I'd get to see more of Angel. I did say to Jack after he asked me to go to prison we must be even by now. We agreed that sometimes he needs me and sometimes I need him. He still wants me to become an agent, but I don't think that's for me. I'll help him when he needs a scapegoat who can be hung out to dry to save the good reputation of MI5, and in return I get to tap Team Nemesis for a bit of help, like I did with those bloody diamonds, and tapping up Data to get me into what I can't through legal channels. It's a cosy little arrangement.'

Ed finished the last of his coffee, got the waitress's attention and signalled for the bill. When it came it included Phil and Emma's orders. Ed put enough money on the table to cover it all and a healthy tip. Phil protested but Ed waved it away, letting Phil know he was happy to pay as compensation for intruding on their date. He knew that when Phil was on a major case, he had precious little time to spend with his fiancée.

Feeling much better for having had some company, Ed decided a noisy pub wasn't what he wanted and opted to drive home and stick a frozen meal in the microwave and open a bottle of wine. While his meal was cooking in the microwave, Ed realised he'd left his notes in the car. He went outside and looked in the car; they weren't on the passenger seat where he thought he'd left them. It then dawned on him that he'd left them in the bistro. He went to the study and printed off more copies that he'd saved to his hard drive. After his sad meal for one, Ed polished off the bottle of wine and fell into a deep sleep on the couch.

CHAPTER THIRTY-ONE

Truro was a forty-five minute drive from Padstow. Phil Reynolds and Shaun Edwards set out early and arrived just after 9am when the courts opened. They walked up to the reception desk and Phil showed the receptionist his warrant card and explained why they were there. The lady nodded and told them they'd need to speak to John Downard who was in charge of the records and archives. After a phone call and a short wait a tall man that Phil guessed to be in his early forties approached them wearing a navy suit. He was average build with a mop of dark hair. Phil was expecting an older man like Mr. Williams at Bodmin Magistrate's Court. Phil introduced himself and Shaun Edwards and they were led through a door to the administrative offices.

Downard's office area was small and had three desks. His occupied a corner of the room by the only window and was larger than the other two, which were occupied by two women who were busy typing data into the computer. Downard found a spare chair and placed it next to the one already opposite his desk for Phil and Shaun.

'How can I help you, inspector?' Downard asked. His voice was much more public school than his hair suggested, and was a little unexpected.

'I'm interested in domestic abuse cases from say the last twelve months,' Phil told him.

'OK, that should be easy as all the recent files are stored digitally. A lot of the older ones would require a trip to the archives as we're likely to only have the physical copies. We are slowly digitising all the historic records but it takes time and money and as with most jobs, we're understaffed and underfunded,' Downard replied and smiled.

'You and me both,' Phil replied. 'So can you print me a list of all domestic abuse cases for the year? I'd like names and addresses and the result of the trial. That's cases where the defendant was found not guilty as well as guilty. I'd also like a list of scheduled cases for the next six months, if that's possible.'

'That's past and scheduled cases and is a very easy thing to compile, but I'll need authorisation,' Downard told him.

'I can easily get that but I'm running a murder investigation. It's a distinct possibility that the man we're looking for is targeting men found guilty of domestic abuse. Right now around Padstow, but there's possibility he's been active elsewhere in the county. It could be that someone on your database is the next victim or has already been a victim, and there might be vital clues to help us bring the perpetrator of these crimes to justice. If you delay giving me this information, you might cost someone their life. The nature of these murders is very gruesome. The victims endured extensive torture and died in agony. Now I can make a phone call or you can save me time and just print the list,' Phil said keeping his voice polite but authoritative.

Downard seemed to be thinking about this.

'Of course, that's not a problem. I can overlook the procedural aspect just this once,' he replied and began typing commands into his computer. 'Do you want a printed copy or a digital copy?' he asked.

'Both,' Phil replied and handed him a thumb drive he'd finally got round to purchasing.

Edwards looked to his boss and nodded, letting him know he was impressed he'd finally got round to buying one.

'Mr. Downard, do you have access to all the magistrate's courts files or just Truro?' Edwards asked.

'Every magistrate's court is linked on a common platform,' Downard replied proudly.

'So you could access the court in Bodmin and vice versa?' Edwards asked. Phil was intrigued as to where Shaun was going with his questioning.

'Yes, if there was a need to, but the police also have access to this information, which is why I'm surprised you've come all the way to Truro when you could get the information online.'

'You being an expert can probably save us a lot of time as you're more familiar with the system, John.' Edwards replied using Downard's first name.

Phil nodded in understanding.

The printer spat out a few pages. Downard handed them to DI Reynolds along with his thumb drive.

'Say thank you John,' Edwards said, keeping his eyes fixed on Downard.

'Why do I need to say, thank you?' Downard said after a pause, and looked warily between the two detectives.

'I was reminding my boss. Sometimes he's got a bad habit of forgetting,' Shaun said.

'Oh, I see. It's not important. I'm just happy to be of help,' Downard replied and gave a quick smile, thinking it strange that a constable would speak to a senior officer in such a way.

'Thank you for your time, Mr. Downard. Do you have a security manager here?' Phil asked.

'Yes, Don Pervis. His office is at the end of the corridor, I'll take you there.'

Don had the look of an ex-military man. He stood ramrod straight, shoulders back and had the sharpest creases in his trousers and shirt, Phil had ever seen.

'How can I help?' he asked.

'Can you confirm that CCTV is deleted after thirty days?' Phil asked.

'Yes, I believe it's standard across all the courts,' he replied.

'I also assume, like Bodmin, anyone can attend a court hearing?'

'Correct, if it's an open hearing, and before you ask, there's no register to sign. They just have to check with the clerk manning the front desk. If I had it my way, I'd change that, as to me it poses a security threat.'

'Quite right. It would certainly be helpful to me on this case. I assume everyone who works here has a pass. If so, can you give me a list of all current personnel and any former employees from say the last six months?' Phil asked.

'Easy enough to do,' Pervis replied and began tapping away at the keyboard.

Phil handed him his thumb drive and asked for both a printed copy and soft copy.

They thanked Pervis for his help and made their way back to the car park.

Phil took out his thumb drive and connected it directly to his smartphone, uploaded the files given to him by Downard and Pervis, and sent them across to Fiona Walsh as an attachment. Edwards looked on clearly impressed with Phil's new gadget.

'Nice bit of kit,' Edwards said to his boss.

'I was in the mobile phone shop looking at buying a bog-standard thumb drive and the salesman asked me what I wanted it for and suggested this one as it's more versatile and lets me send immediately without having to download onto a laptop first. It connects to a phone one end and the other is a USB for connecting to a laptop. It even has a little adaptor so it can connect to a phone that has a different charging port. It wasn't that much more expensive than a standard thumb drive,' Phil said proudly.

'Nice. I might look into getting one myself.'

'Good work back there with Downard. Do you think he could be our man?' Phil asked.

'I don't know, but as you always say, it's always a good idea to be thorough and to keep an open mind.'

'He seemed confused rather than concerned with the "the say thank you" comment, but I'll get someone to run a check on him.'

Phil looked at his phone, selected a number from his recent calls list and made a call.

'Fiona, I've just sent you some files. It's the names of all the people who have stood trial for domestic abuse from the Truro Magistrate's Courts and a few who will be standing trial in the near future. It's not too big. I'd like you to run some checks on these people and find out if they're alive or dead and if they're dead were they murdered or did they die of natural causes. Don't worry about those awaiting trial. I'll give them a call myself at some point,' Phil asked her.

'Sure, shouldn't take too long. I'll have all that by the time you arrive back at the office,' she replied.

'There's also a list of employees past and present who work or have worked at Truro Magistrates'. If there are any John's on the list run a check on them. I'm particularly interested in a John

Downard who is definitely on the list. He looks after the records and archives. Just a cursory check to see if he's got any previous.'

'Is he a suspect?' she asked.

'I just want to be sure. His name's John and he's got access to all the records for all magistrates' courts in the UK.'

'OK, no problem. Is there anything else?'

'No thanks,' Phil replied and ended the call.

'Right Shaun, let's head back, get some lunch and see what Fiona digs up. Oh, and put the paperwork from Downard in the glovebox will you,' Phil said.

Shaun took the A4 sheets from his boss and opened the glove box, as he did more paperwork fell on the floor out of the very full compartment. He picked it up and saw the top page was the email to Ed from Data.

'This is an email to your mate Ed,' Shaun said.

'Oh that stuff, he left that lot in the restaurant last night. He came into the same place Emma and I were eating. I stuck it in the car so I wouldn't forget to return it to him and of course that's exactly what I did,' Phil explained.

Shaun flicked through the pages paying them only a little interest.

'Where did he get this from?' Shaun asked.

'He's got a few mates in MI5 and one is a computer genius. It's useful having friends in high places as I think he'd be struggling without them on this case. He can't get that level of information by going to the banks or phone companies and as he told me, his man could've been anywhere in the world, but he now knows, as do you, from bumping into him the other day, he's most likely to be in Bodmin, based on his credit card usage,' Phil replied, somewhat envious that Ed could get all this information without going through the official channels and getting authorisation from a judge.

'It must be nice to be well connected. It's got his car registration and colour, credit and debit card usage for contactless transactions and tracking of his mobile phone,' Shaun replied impressed.

'Ed always has been a lucky bastard. Even by his own admission he says life has blessed him with a lot of luck, but has also dealt him a lot of bad luck so it's karma finding a natural balance I reckon. Anyway, put it with the paperwork from Downard and I'll try and remember to return it to him at some point.'

Shaun opened the glove box and managed to shove it back in, without anything else spilling on the floor, and stared ahead deep in thought.

CHAPTER THIRY-TWO

Ed was full of renewed energy after a long nap on the sofa and a few more hours sleep in his bed. He had time to go for a run and workout in the gym before heading back to Bodmin. The earliest time a transaction had been made on either of the bank cards was lunchtime. He decided he'd spend the first couple of hours seeing the locations he'd not had time to visit the previous day and then be in the vicinity of where the cards were used and at the time they were used later that day, assuming he failed to find Owen Moore at the supermarket at lunchtime. A look at the list showed the next location was a coffee shop and if that failed the Indian restaurant. Logic said he couldn't keep missing him; their paths had to cross at some point. However, Owen Moore knew Ed was looking for him, so perhaps if he was desperate to remain unfound he'd change his routines or even shop elsewhere. It was a possibility and it'd be something Ed himself would likely do if he knew he was being tracked. If that happened he'd have to ask Data to run another check on his cards to see where and when his new places were. He hated having to do it but needs must, and Jack Griggs was never shy at coming forward and pulling favours from him, so why should he be? All Ed was after was information, which seemed a small return for what he'd been asked to do by Jack. Prison was the worst experience of his life to date and one he'd never agree to again, ever. Ed shuddered involuntarily at the memory and parked his car at the far end of the supermarket car park, where he hoped it would be out of sight and unseen by Owen Moore; he was being cautious. Moore knew where Ed lived so it stood to reason that he was likely to know the car he drove.

Ed looked at the map and decided he'd got enough time to view a few of the places and stepped up his pace. The previous night, before he fell asleep on the sofa, he tried a number of ways to try and find out where Owen Moore might live by drawing lines connecting the locations north to south and east to west, to try to find the centre point but to no avail. Each attempt put him nowhere near any housing estates. One attempt put him in a small industrial area and the other in a school. He checked out both locations and decided that the school was a place that might be worth exploring as there were a number of properties and housing estates within walking distance and after all his calculations were just approximations, or perhaps just wild guesses. Also, his job as a glorified handyman might mean he took a job as a caretaker at the school. The other, the industrial area, he decided was one he didn't need to consider as there was very little housing at all. He doubted Owen would be living in a lock-up or factory.

His diversion to kill time had not filled him with any confidence at being able to find his missing person. Wandering around aimlessly was just pointless. If he failed to find him at the supermarket he'd stick to his intentions and be at the locations about the same time the transactions were made. Alas, what Ed also found was apart from the supermarket, which was a daily haunt, none of the other locations were used on the same day of the week and some only used every other week, which made his task even harder. As much as he liked Indian food, the thought of eating it every day for a fortnight wasn't a prospect he relished.

Ed walked back and decided on a different strategy and went inside the supermarket and stood where he could keep an eye on both the coffee shop, which also sold baguettes and cakes, and the supermarkets own selection of sandwiches and meal deals. To avoid too much suspicion Ed picked up a basket and put in a sandwich and a packet of crisps. He walked over to the newsagent section and looked at the selection of newspapers. Being lunchtime a lot of them had sold out. He was left with a choice of one of the broadsheets or the Star. He opted for the Star as the others were bulky and heavy and if he needed to use one as a prop, it might be cumbersome. He recalled his commutes to London back when he was working, and remembered the train passengers who read broadsheets had a very precise way of folding their newspapers to make them easier to hold within the limited space in the carriages. It had always impressed Ed, but he was sure he couldn't mimic this, thus it was the Daily Star. As an afterthought he dropped in a four pack of Doom Bar, despite not drinking that much beer at home, unless Bob or Bulldog paid him a visit.

He made his way back to where he could easily walk back and forth to see the two areas he was interested in, deciding that standing in one place too long would make him seem suspicious to any in-store detectives and he didn't want to blow his cover by being targeted as a potential shoplifter. Even if they didn't have in-store detectives, he was sure to be picked up on the security cameras and challenged.

Ed looked at his watch and felt despondent as it was nearing the latest time Owen had used his card in the supermarket. If this failed, he'd have to hang out near the coffee shop or the Indian restaurant on what he'd decided was Owen's route home, which wasn't good as he wanted closure on this case as Angel was likely to be arriving soon and he wanted to spend some quality time with her.

Ed took another look at his watch and decided to go to the checkout to pay for his few provisions. The queues were long, especially the one basket only queues, so he headed for the self-service checkouts, hoping he'd get though quickly. He only had to wait a couple of minutes and began scanning his few items. Completely forgetting that beer had to be checked by a member of staff, he ran it through and the light came on and he had to wait for an assistant to confirm he was old enough to purchase alcohol. The only assistant was busy helping out another customer. As he was looking for another assistant to help him, he saw a familiar face.

The man seemed oblivious to Ed or decided to ignore him if he had seen him. Ed pulled up the photo of Owen Moore on his phone and took a look at the man walking to the meal deal section. The man in Ed's photo had natural blond hair, almost white. He knew it was natural as the eyebrows were also the same shade of blond, whereas the man in the store had brown hair with matching eyebrows. Ed scrutinised the man, whilst trying to remain nonchalant. There was no mistaking the facial features. The pale-blue eyes were the same as his mother's, as was the small, narrow nose.

So distracted was he that he failed to hear the assistant asking him if he needed any help, until she put a hand on his arm.

'Sorry,' he replied. 'My beer needs to be authorised,' he replied. The assistant used her ID card to authorise it.

'Do you have your own bag, sir?' she asked.

Ed had forgotten about that and said that he didn't. The assistant picked up a shop provided bag and scanned it for him and finished off the transaction. Ed thanked her and tapped his card on the reader to pay for his items. He knew there was only one entrance and exit to the supermarket so he left and took up position outside and waited.

CHAPTER THIRTY-THREE

No sooner had DI Reynolds and DC Shaun Edwards entered the office they were approached by DS Fiona Walsh who seemed to be in a buoyant mood. That cheered Phil, hoping that her smile was due to getting a good lead on their suspect. He had three murders on his hands and although he was making some progress, it was pitifully slow and he expected to be up in front of the boss very soon if things stayed that way.

'What have you got for me, Fiona?' Phil asked.

'We checked out all the names of those found guilty of domestic violence and most of them are still alive...'

'OK, is there anything suspicious?' Phil interrupted DS Walsh, wanting to know if there was anything of interest and a possible breakthrough.

'Unfortunately not. One died of drink related issues. One died of a drug overdose and another was involved in a car accident and died in hospital after a few days in intensive care. Nothing suspicious, the man stepped out in front of a car as he was too engrossed in his mobile phone. All the others are alive and well, in various parts of the country, but sadly no murder victims,' Walsh told Reynolds.

'The smile on your face suggests that you might have something of interest,' Phil said.

'Possibly. I checked out all the John's on your list. There were only three. One retired and now lives in Spain and hasn't returned to the UK in the last six months. Another retired through ill health when his mobility became too severe to work and is now in a nursing home. However, your John Downard has form. It might be a case of jumping to conclusions, but your man has a couple of convictions that might be of interest.'

Phil nodded for Walsh to continue eager to hear what she'd got to say about John Downard that might give them cause to bring him in. The optimist in Phil was already thinking about wrapping the case up, but the realist in him knew it was just wishful thinking.

'When he was eighteen he was charged with actual bodily harm and given community service. He was out with friends in a pub when a girl and her boyfriend were having an argument. She slapped her boyfriend round the face and he retaliated by punching her in the stomach and face. John Downard intervened and the boyfriend ended up in casualty with a couple of broken ribs and needing eighteen stitches to his face. Fast forward fifteen years he was again found guilty of ABH and was given a suspended sentence and ordered to pay damages. The victim was his brother-in-law who'd cheated on his wife, Downard's step-sister. When the step-sister confronted her husband they rowed and had a fight. She went to stay with her step-brother, John Downard, and when he saw the black eye she was sporting, he went mad, drove to his step-sister's house and beat up her husband, who like his victim fifteen years previously, ended up in casualty with a dislocated jaw and needing nine stiches to a gash on his cheekbone. He also needed two dental implants, which was the reason for damages being awarded. So quite a history of violence,' Fiona told him.

'Good work, Fiona. No wonder you look pleased,' Phil replied.

'Shall we bring him in?' she asked,

'Not just yet. Run some checks on him. See what car he drives and see if we can match the car to anywhere near our three victims. We know the murderer used the victim's own car to dispose of the body for his first murder, but if it was Downard, he had to get to Padstow and Rock somehow and presumably park somewhere convenient, as he would likely be covered in blood. Do that and let me know the results, then we can make a call on whether to bring him in or not.'

'OK boss, I'm on it.'

Phil smiled and went to get a coffee. Edwards, still clutching the paper copies of the files given to them by Downard, dropped them on Phil's desk and went to his own desk to check his emails and in-tray. Unfortunately for Phil, he never made it to the coffee machine as he received a summons to the chief super's office. Hopefully, he'd be offered a nice cup of proper filter coffee when he got to Clatworthy's office. Miracles did happen, but not often.

It was only a few minutes until Ed spied Owen Moore leaving the supermarket. He looked around and took a seat on one of the benches and began unpacking his lunch. Before he could take a first bite of his sandwich, Ed was sat next to him on the bench.

'Hello Owen. You're a difficult man to find,' he said and smiled at the man next to him.

'I'm sorry, I think you've mistaken me for someone else,' he replied not bothering to look at Ed and took a bite of his sandwich.

'I don't think so. Same height and build as Owen Moore. Not quite as blond as the photo I have of you, but there's no mistaking those eyes, pale blue with the darker ring round the iris, just like your dear old mum's,' Ed said happily.

'OK, good for you, you found me, despite me sending you a warning not to. You're a stubborn man, Case.'

'It's been said before by more than one person so I guess there must be some truth in what you say.'

'Believe me there is. I made it quite clear in my note for you to stay away. I don't want to be found,' Owen said, making it obvious he was unhappy at being found.

'I know, but I have a job to do, what can I say? Your mother is paying me good money to find you. Don't worry, my rates are reasonable so there still might be a little inheritance for you one day,' Ed said, hoping to antagonise the man who he'd taken an instant dislike to, which seemed to be a frequent occurrence these days.

'OK, so now you've found me, your job is complete. Go tell my mother you found me and collect your wages. How did you find me out of interest?'

'Well, it wasn't easy. I checked every pub, cafe, restaurant, coffee shop and public places, like libraries and swimming baths, but nobody had seen you since you quit your job. Obviously someone had as they told you I was asking about you, which is how I think you found out and put your little note through the door. When I was at a complete loss, I called in a favour from a friend who's got access to just about anything he wants on the internet. He gave me all the details of your credit and debit card uses and even a traced your mobile phone usage, so when you went from Padstow to Bodmin for example, it showed the new cell it connected to. He also provided me with your car make, model and registration, so if I didn't find you at the supermarket or other locations where you regularly use your card, I'd search the car parks for a car matching your make and model. The details elude me but it's all here.' Ed said making a show of flapping his printouts for Owen to see.

'Well done. Now go away and leave me alone.'

'I will, but first of all I need a selfie to prove to your mum that I found you. I'll also tell her where, as she's bound to ask. She is my client after all, and paying for a service, so she's got the right to know. But tell me, why does a grown man who's lived with his mother for so many years, suddenly decide to pack his bags and go and leave his poor old mum worried sick and resorting to getting a PI to find you?' Ed asked.

'Do I owe you an explanation? You're just the lackey my mother hired,' Owen replied, unable to contain his growing frustration.

'You don't, but I'm just curious,' Ed replied matter-of-factly.

'Why doesn't that surprise me?' he replied.

'You sound like you know me well,' Ed replied and shrugged his shoulders, letting Owen know he didn't care what he thought.

'I know a lot more about you than you might think, James.'

Ed was surprised he knew his real first name, but didn't show it. He looked across at Owen Moore, challenging him to say more.

'Case isn't a particularly common surname. Only about zero point four percent of the population to be exact...'

'That's still around two-hundred and eighty thousand,' Ed interjected quickly.

'You maths is very good. I also know you've murdered people in self-defence and you've had two wives, both who died in mysterious circumstance...'

'How do you know this?' Ed asked shocked that this information was readily available to anyone who was interested enough to find out.

'Surprised are you? Well it's no big secret. I was in the church some years ago when you made a ridiculous bid in the auction just to get one over on that awful red-headed woman. That was quite a passionate speech. I'm also friends with Julie Mortimer, the local reporter, and gave her a call. I remember she told me about you some time ago when she was helping your wife to find John Trevithick's treasure. She embellished me with some information. The rest was looking at obituaries from newspapers and open records for births, deaths and marriages,' Moore told him, his voice lacking any emotion; cold.

'Congratulations on your detective work. It seems you've gone to a lot of trouble to find out about me. I wonder why? You know I could probably use someone like you in the office,' Ed replied.

'Same reasons as you; curiosity,' Owen replied.

Ed shrugged and pulled the Star newspaper from his bag.

'Give your mum a nice big smile,' he said and held the newspaper up and took a few quick snaps of Owen Moore.

'I always think a person's choice of newspaper says a lot about a person's character and intelligence.'

'Don't judge me from this rag. It was all they'd got left and was cheaper and lighter than the broadsheets,' Ed replied and gave Owen a brief smile.

'Cheaper? Why would that be a concern for the man that became extremely wealthy as a result of his parents death and no doubt even wealthier after the death of your first wife and possibly your second wife too,' Owen replied, returning the terse smile Ed had given him earlier.

'You've really have done your homework. However, the deaths of my family aren't something I want to discuss with a stranger or anyone else for that matter,' Ed replied.

'Hmmm something to hide perhaps, Mr. Case?' Moore pressed.

'Nothing at all. My past is filled with a lot of unpleasant memories I'd rather forget. Dragging up those details just to satisfy your curiosity isn't something I want to do. By and large I'm trying to put my unhappy past behind me and concentrate only on the here and now and my future.'

'If you say so, Case.' Owen Moore replied disinterestedly.

'I think my job is done here. I'll be seeing your mother when I return to Padstow. Perhaps you should have a think about how she's feeling and reconsider contacting her to put her mind at rest.

It's what any decent son would do. Goodbye Owen,' Ed replied, picked up his shopping and headed to his car, watched all the way by Owen Moore.

CHAPTER THIRTY-FOUR

DI Reynolds went back to his desk, slightly dejected, even the coffee did little to lift his spirits. His conversation with Clatworthy was not a pleasant experience. Both the local and national press were circling, knowing they were investigating three murders the perpetrator of the crime was now officially classed as a serial killer, and he had no prime suspect. The press always went into a frenzy when the words "serial killer" were mentioned. The top brass seemed to be siding with the press and were pushing for a result; one that Phil was unable to provide at the present time. They were quick to point the finger when things weren't going as well as they needed to, but equally quick at patting themselves on the back when people like himself got a result. They'd all be clambering over each other to get their mugs on TV, telling the world what a good job they did. He guessed the police force was no different from any other profession.

In a bid to have one piece of good news, Phil told Clatworthy about his conversation with John Downard, hoping that it'd be seen as a positive in what was otherwise a floundering investigation. Clatworthy's response was "So because his name is John and he's got previous for ABH he automatically becomes a suspect. That's clutching at straws at best and I think you know that DI Reynolds" it made Phil cringe even now as he knew that it was true and he was just trying to make it look better than it actually was. In truth the case had got nowhere.

Fiona Walsh came over and pulled a chair up.

'I hope you've got some good news,' Phil said wearily.

'Did the boss give you a hard time?' Fiona asked light-heartedly.

'Just a little. Basically he told me I was desperate thinking Downard was our man, just because his name was John and had a couple of old charges for ABH. To be fair he's got a point but it's never nice to have to admit that, is it? Especially to the big boss.'

'Well we might actually be onto something with Downard.'

Phil leaned forward, praying it was enough to bring him in, despite what Clatworthy thought.

'We ran some background checks on John Downard. He drives a white Ford Focus. While trawling through the traffic cameras and available CCTV, we spotted a white Ford Focus around Rock an hour before Brandon Taylor was murdered. Unfortunately the car registration wasn't captured on any of the cameras as they weren't traffic cameras. We're trying to trace its journey via other cameras, but it's a popular make and model, sir.' Fiona informed him.

'Nice work, Fiona. Have you dug up any information that might lead us to believe Downard would have a problem with wife beaters?' Phil asked, his interest in Downard piqued; despite what Clatworthy thought.

'We're still working on that one. So far all we know is both his ABH arrests were related to men hitting women,' she replied.

'Doesn't really help, even I have to admit it's a tad thin. If our friend, Ed Case, was called John, we'd be arresting him. He's got into more fights over women being treated badly than anyone I know,' he replied.

Just then DC Will Pascoe rushed over to Phil's desk, smiling broadly.

'Sir, John Downard was fostered at an early age. His real name is John Finch. His parents divorced and neither wanted custody of him, so social services got involved and he was sent to a foster home and eventually he was adopted and changed his name to Downard. His birth parents have both since died. Both his mother and father were known to the police; they were both substance abusers and alcoholics and he had a very unhappy childhood by all accounts. There was no record of any reports of domestic assault, but I think it could be a pretty good bet that two alcoholic drug addicts living together would be a tempestuous relationship,' Will informed Phil enthusiastically.

Phil thought about this. The name fitted. The same make and

model car he drove was seen in the vicinity of one of the murders and might even be at all three now they knew what they were looking for. Downard had a history of violence and both instances were for protecting vulnerable women. He clearly had an unhappy childhood and would likely have seen a lot of stuff a young boy shouldn't have to see and, which would have likely left him with some very unhappy memories.

'Bring him in,' Phil replied and smiled for the first time in a long while.

Ed was pleased that he'd found Owen Moore. Missing person cases were particularly frustrating but until this case, he'd been quite lucky. He recalled his very first missing person case, which was also his first case as a private investigator. He'd been tasked by an old friend of his to find her best friend and fellow exotic dancer, Jade Wickham. That time he persuaded Detective Sergeant Kevin Holt to help him as he was investigating a string of disappearances of call girls, exotic dancers and prostitutes across London and it seemed likely that their investigations were into the same person or gang. It turned out to be a good call and between them, ably supported by Bob they had managed to find Jade.

'The beginning of the end,' Ed muttered inside the empty car.

Becoming a private investigator was supposed to be a way of keeping him out of trouble, as trouble had an uncanny knack of following Ed around, like a bad smell. Alas, becoming a private investigator did nothing to shake off his personal nemesis "bad luck" which almost destroyed his life. It was only his cowardice at not pulling the trigger and blowing his brains through the top of his head that saved his life.

Ed shook his head to dispel those unhappy memories. The past was the past and was something that couldn't be changed. He made it a point these days to live each day to the full and look to the future. Something Angel had told him daily, as part of his rehabilitation after his near breakdown. God he missed her. He hoped she'd be back soon so he could drive up to London and spend some quality time together in a posh hotel room.

He parked the car outside Mrs. Moore's home and strode up to the door and rang the doorbell. After a short wait the door was opened by Mrs. Moore who seemed surprised to see him.

Ed smiled and Mrs. Moore invited him in and he sat in the same chair he'd sat in when he was last in the house. He heard the same clattering in the kitchen and knew that Mrs. Moore was rustling up a pot of tea and a plate of biscuits; no doubt rich tea, Ed thought and smiled when that was exactly what she put on the coffee table between them.

'Have you found Owen?' she asked.

'I did, which is what I came to tell you,' Ed replied.

'Well if you found him, where is he?'

She seemed put out that Ed had turned up on his own.

'I would imagine he's back at work right now…'

'Well that just won't do!' she replied forcefully, interrupting Ed.

'Mrs. Moore. I was hired to find your son, which I did. There really is no easy way to dress this up, but for reasons which Owen didn't tell me, he didn't want to get in touch with you, despite me telling him that you'd be very happy to hear from him. I'm really sorry about his attitude, but what Owen does is out of my hands.'

Mrs. Moore's brow furrowed.

'Well, why didn't you arrest him?' she asked.

Ed tried not to laugh and smiled back politely.

'I'm a private investigator and I don't have the authority to arrest anyone. Technically, I could make a citizen's arrest if he'd committed a crime, but he hasn't done anything wrong. Well morally I think he has, but legally he hasn't.'

'Is he still in Padstow?' she asked.

'No, he now lives in Bodmin and I assume he works there too. He wasn't very forthcoming with information, Mrs. Moore. He seemed very resentful that I'd actually found him.'

'I see. How do I know you've found him? You might be lying to me just to collect your fee?'

Ed was quite shocked at her attitude. On the outside seemed to be a sweet and mild natured lady but underneath that façade she was quite a different person. Maybe she suffered from some kind of bi-polar disorder and her son, Owen, had left home after having had enough of her mood swings. He wouldn't be the first man to leave a woman on those grounds.

Ed pulled his phone from his pocket and showed her the photo he'd taken of Owen a short time before.

'My Owen has blond hair, who's this man?' she asked indignantly.

'I can assure you this is your son. For reasons known only to him, he's dyed his hair brown. The eyes are pale blue just like yours. In fact the resemblance to you is uncanny. Just in case you're wondering, if you look at the newspaper you'll see that it's today's copy of the Star.'

Mrs. Moore looked blankly at a space above Ed's head, seemed to gather her thoughts and poured them both a cup of tea. Ed noted her hand trembling slightly as she poured. She used her other hand to steady the pot. Ed felt rather sorry for her. Mrs. Moore placed a cup of tea in front of Ed and smiled sadly.

'Help yourself to a biscuit. I can't drink a tea without a biscuit to dunk,' she said repeating the phrase she used on his previous visit.

'Thank you. I know your son told me he didn't want to get in touch with you, but that doesn't mean you can't try and get to see him. I don't have an address for him as he hasn't registered to pay council tax and isn't on the electoral role yet. Perhaps as it's only been a few weeks his paperwork is still pending. However, I do have a list of places where you might find him. Would you like me to give it to you?'

Mrs. Moore nodded, and pulled a handkerchief from her sleeve, dabbed at her eyes and blew her nose softly.

'I'll just get the information from the car,' Ed said and left Mrs. Moore alone to regain her composure.

Ed took his time, much more than he actually needed to allow his client a little time to compose herself and come to terms with the situation. Ed returned a few minutes later, closing the front door, he'd left on the latch, behind him.

He found the right A4 sheet and gave that to Mrs. Moore along with the map.

'He seems to go the supermarket most weekdays. I assume he works somewhere nearby. As you can see most of the other places I've noted are predominantly in one direction so I assume that these places are on his way home, but as I said to you earlier, I didn't manage to get the information. As I already told you, Owen wasn't exactly very chatty and forthcoming with much information. I hope that's of use?' Ed said feeling genuinely sorry for the woman.

Mrs. Moore nodded; resigned to the fact her son had left and didn't want to see her. Ed quickly finished his tea and placed the cup and saucer back on the tray with the untouched biscuits.

'I'll send you my invoice in the next few days, Mrs. Moore. It won't be a large bill as it basically involved a couple of trips to Bodmin and a few hours at the computer. Is that OK?'

Mrs. Moore nodded and blew her nose again. Ed said he'd let himself out, relieved to leave the oppressive atmosphere in the house.

In the car Ed put the phone back in the cradle and called Bob.

'I've found Owen Moore and now I fancy a beer. Are you busy?' he asked.

'When you say a beer, is that one beer or a lot of beers?' Bob asked.

'Does it make a difference?'

'If it's 'a' as in a single beer you can piss off and stop wasting my time. If it's a lot of beers I'll go get my coat and we can still be friends,' Bob told him.

'In that case, I'll see you in The Ship in a few minutes.'

'Good man. You know it makes sense.'

CHAPTER THIRTY-FIVE

Two uniformed police officers from Truro brought an angry John Downard to the station in Padstow. Phil thanked the officers asked them to wait in the canteen in case Downard wasn't charged and would need to be returned to Truro. The two officers seemed to like that idea as it meant a cushy shift. Phil left Downard to stew for ten minutes before he entered the interview room along with Fiona Walsh. Phil thought the presence of a woman, considering the nature of the murders and Downard's past convictions for ABH, might act as a calming effect. Judging by the look on Downard's face he'd need calming down.

'Am I under arrest?' Downard asked when he and Fiona took seats opposite.

'Were you cautioned when you were brought here?' Phil asked.

'No.'

'Then you're not under arrest, and before you ask, you're free to leave any time you want, although I think that would be unwise as it'd make us think you have something to hide, and the next time we talk it would be under caution. Do you understand?' Phil replied, keeping his voice flat and cold.

'Yes. I'm well aware of police procedures. However, I told you everything you wanted to know when I spoke to you earlier,' Downard replied his tone still angry.

'Well, we ran a few more checks when we got back. We like to be thorough before eliminating people from our inquiries; especially when it's a murder investigation. '

'So tell me what you found out so I can clear my name and go home, I've got better things to be doing than wasting my time here.'

'Perhaps we'll get to the bottom of what better things you're talking about as the interview progresses,' Phil said and deliberately smirked to make it seem he'd got something on the man.

'What do you mean by that?' Downard asked.

Phil ignored the question, deliberately trying to rile Downard.

'You've been to court twice and been found guilty of ABH so clearly you have a bit of a short temper,' Phil said and waited for Downard to reply.

'That was bloody years ago. I was just a kid,' he replied quickly.

'I agree you were only eighteen when you hit a man in the Red Lion public house and put him in hospital.'

'He beat his girlfriend up. What was I supposed to do, look the other way and pretend it never happened like a lot of the other arseholes in the pub did?' he replied his anger rising. 'I don't like bullies. Especially bullies who pick on women.'

Phil shared a look with DS Walsh.

'The sensible thing to do would've been to comfort the girl and tell her to call the police and advise them she'd been assaulted and wanted to press charges against the man,' Phil replied.

Downard scoffed.

'Clearly you don't live in the real world. Look, I'd had a few drinks and my judgement was clouded. What can I say?'

'Was that the case fifteen years later when you put your brother-in-law in hospital? You were a little more than a kid then.'

'That bastard was no good. My sister loved him, but I'd got him marked as a flash bugger and a playboy the first time I laid eyes on the arsehole. It turned out I was right. He was a turd on the doorstep of humanity; it was only a matter of time before he revealed his true colours.'

'So you drove thirty-five minutes and were still so angry that you beat him badly enough that he needed hospital treatment. Seems like you have real anger issues. To be expected considering what family life you must've had growing up,' Phil said trying to provoke a reaction.

'What do you know? I'm sure you grew up in a great family. Never went without, no coming home wondering what state your parents would be in. Having to put up with continual fighting and arguing, not knowing if one day you'd come home from school and find one or both of them dead from an overdose or having choked on their own vomit in a drunken stupor. Having the kids at school ridiculing you and taking the piss because they'd seen your parents' drunken, drug addled rants in the street. So yeah, I was angry. My step-sister was the closest thing I had to family. I warned that bastard if he did anything to upset my sister I'd make him regret it. I'm true to my word detective. I want a coffee,' he replied.

Phil nodded to the uniformed police officer standing by the door to go get a coffee for Downard.

'You drive a white Ford Focus, correct?' Phil asked.

'Yes, me and a million other people most likely.'

'But I'm guessing that those other million people weren't seen on traffic cameras at three murder scenes,' Phil lied, as so far they'd only linked the car to one of the three murders, but Downard didn't know that. He hoped that the bluff would work.

'I couldn't say, but I can assure you, it wasn't my car. I don't tend to drive much after dark or not long distances, because I don't have great night vision thanks to glaucoma that I inherited from my disgusting parents. The glare from the headlights of oncoming traffic makes me a risk to myself and other drivers. Everything I need is in Truro. I drive to and from work and make the occasional trip to Penzance, if I can't get what I want locally or online,' Downard replied.

The uniformed police officer put a cup of coffee on the table. It was black no sugar. He gave Downard an unfriendly look that said take it or leave it. Downard sipped at the tepid liquid and pulled a face. Phil could sympathise with the man; it took a lot of getting used to.

'If you're lying we'll find out, John. There are traffic and CCTV cameras everywhere. Do you know a Mick Woods?' Phil asked pressing ahead with questions to put Downard under pressure.

'No. I don't think I know anyone called Mick.'

'What about Brandon Taylor?'

'No never heard of him.'

'What about Pete Quigley?'

'No, I don't know any of these people.' Downard replied

Phil was surprised he'd managed to keep his temper in check. He almost seemed resigned to being assaulted with a barrage of questions.

'What were you doing on the night of the fourteenth?' Phil asked.

'At home I would've thought,' Downard replied quickly.

'What about the eighteenth?'

'The same; I don't go out much.'

'What about the twenty-second?'

'I was most likely at home again. As I've already told you, I don't go out much in the evenings. I'm a gamer,' Downard replied.

'You're a bit old to be a gamer, aren't you?' Phil replied, surprised a grown man would be hooked on online games.

'Guess it comes of a deprived childhood. Some men play darts or snooker; I like the game, Soldier of Fortune, amongst others.'

Phil considered the reply and thought it was a good answer. Darts and snooker probably seemed strange games for adults to enjoy to a gamer.

'We will need to check your laptop to confirm this. What times do you play?'

'I get home from work, eat dinner and settle down for the night. Some days I finish early around eleven o'clock or midnight. Other nights perhaps later, but most nights it's quite late. It just depends who is online and how good they are. I don't live far from the office and traffic is usually quite light so I don't have to be up at the crack of dawn like many people have to be to commute to work for a nine o'clock start, ' Downard replied.

Phil could detect the relief in Downard's voice at potentially having an alibi, albeit a tenuous one, Phil thought. He wondered if a game was continuous or if it could be paused for some reason, like nailing a man to the floor and mutilating him with a hammer, and then continuing as if he'd been playing all that time. He was sure the computer techs would know and be able to find out.

'OK John. I think we should take a quick break here. Myself and DS Walsh will go grab a coffee and see you back here in ten minutes.

Phil and Fiona Walsh left, leaving the burly uniformed officer to watch over Downard.

Outside the interview room Phil turned to Fiona.

'Gut feel?' he asked her.

'I'd say he's not our man,' she replied,

'What do you base that on?' Phil asked, wanting to know why she thought Downard was innocent.

'Body language for a start and the way he gave answers without thinking. There was nothing calculated about him. Perhaps he's a very clever guy. I know his previous makes him a suspect as does his car, possibly, but he seemed surprised to be pulled in. His anger quickly faded after you stopped baiting him, and the answers he provided were without too much thought. A guilty person normally thinks about an answer to detract any more questioning, or to provide a tangible lie. He didn't seem to care,' Fiona replied.

'He could be clever and anticipated the questions on the ride up from Truro and already had answers prepared, but unfortunately, I have to agree. He was casual with his answers, not cagey, as you'd expect of a guilty person. We'll hand him back to the two uniforms from Truro and tell them to take his laptop or whatever he uses, for analysis to make sure he's not lying about his whereabouts. What we really need is a definite sighting of the car at all three locations and at least one with the number plate. If we can get that, we can eliminate him and concentrate on finding our man. I just hope Clatworthy doesn't get wind of this, or he'll haul me over the coals as he told me not to bring him in.'

'To be fair, boss, new information came to light which warranted him being questioned,' Fiona replied.

'Thanks, let's hope Clatworthy sees it that way too. Let's get a coffee and get back to the interview room and let Downard go home or he might put in a complaint and that'd sure come to the attention of Clatworthy and get his back up.'

In the canteen they found the two uniformed officers from Truro and told them to be ready in reception to meet Downard and take him home. Phil and Fiona grabbed coffees and headed back to the interview room.

'You're free to go, Mr. Downard,' Phil informed him.

The relief was clear on Downard's face.

'Thank you, I didn't murder those three men,' Downard replied.

'You will need to hand over your laptop or gaming consul or whatever it is you use so our experts can verify your alibi of gaming at the time of the three murders. I know that's going to be an inconvenience, but I'm sure you'll understand,' Phil said.

'It's OK. I understand and I have an old laptop I can use until you give me my one back.'

'Right, come with me, I'll escort you to reception where the officers from Truro will take you home. Thank you for your time and co-operation, Mr. Downard, and my apologies for taking up your time this evening,' Phil said, hoping to end on a friendly note and stop any complaint being lodged.

'That's OK. I appreciate you're just doing your job officer,' Downard replied, but his tone suggested he didn't mean it.

Phil went to his desk and scooped up a pile of paperwork to look through at home. The clues had to be there. He was missing something. Emma wouldn't be happy with him working late but she understood that there'd be times when work had to take precedence and tonight was one of those nights.

CHAPTER THIRTY-SIX

Padstow some years previous

Being an only child was both a blessing and a curse for the young boy. A blessing that he didn't have to compete for the attention and love of his mother, but on the other hand it was a curse in that when his father was drunk, which was most of the time he wasn't working, he was the brunt of his anger. He sometimes wished for a brother who would take a beating on the days when his still painful bruises were kicked and punched even blacker and bluer than they already were. In the summer he was forced to wear long sleeved tops and long trousers to hide his embarrassment and his mother's shame, even on the days when it was blisteringly hot. He'd dearly have loved to wear shorts and T-shirts like his classmates did, but knew to do so would draw unwanted attention. He knew how to avoid unwanted attention. He'd spent his entire short life avoiding unwanted attention from his brutal father, cringing with every creak of the stairs in house. He knew the sound every one of those thirteen steps made by heart. He'd hold his breath, rigid with fright, and listen to his father make his way up them when he returned from the pub. On a good day his father would walk past his room and collapse in a drunken stupor on the bed in the room next door to his. On a bad day the door would burst open and his father would stagger in take off his belt and whip him until he cried out for his mother.

This evening the boy was on the floor in his bedroom, writing up his English homework as he did every Sunday night. At school on Monday, each pupil would stand up and read what they did at the weekend. The boy hated that as he didn't do much as he had few friends and there was no money for trips to the zoo in Newquay like some of the other kids did; the lucky ones. The boy often lied. He couldn't write the truth that he spent every weekend in fear, and when he wasn't in fear he was being beaten and abused by his father. This time he made up a story about going to the supermarket with his mother and being bought a bag of sweets to eat while watching TV that night. He wrote in detail of every type of sweet in the pick 'n' mix selection, describing the taste and which one he ate first and how he held back on his favourite sweets until the end of the half pound bag, thus ensuring the first taste was as good as the last. In reality he couldn't remember the last time his mother had any money left over to buy him any sweets, but he had to write something. He was sure the other kids saw through his lies, but his teacher always smiled and gave him good grades for his English, if only for their creative content.

The front door slammed shut with great force; the boy knew his father was very drunk. He could hear his father as he mumbled something about being hungry and demanding his dinner from his mother. The boy breathed a sigh of relief knowing that if he was going to get a beating it wouldn't be until his father had eaten. He prayed his father took his time eating his meal. While is father was eating he wasn't being beaten; merely living in fear of another beating. He continued to write up his homework; his keen ears were listening out for his father. He didn't have to wait too long before his drunken father began lumbering up the stairs. The boy knew every stair by its creak and knew his father was now just two stairs from the top. Involuntarily the boy's legs began to tremble as he was overcome by fear. His body ached all over from the beating the night before, and he knew another beating would leave him in great pain and with difficulty in walking or sitting if his father decided to take his belt to him. His father's footsteps stopped outside the boy's bedroom door, he let out an involuntary whimper and hoped his father hadn't heard. His father belched loudly and broke wind even louder. The boy stifled a giggle. The bedroom door burst open.

'What's so funny, boy?' he father demanded.

'N…n…nothing,' the boy stammered.

'I'll give you nothing, you useless piece of shit,' his father shouted.

The man bent down and lifted the young boy off the floor by the front of his jumper and threw him onto the bed. The boy's head connected with the wall but he knew better than to cry out, it'd only spur his father on to more violence. He learnt a long time ago if he remained silent the beatings were less severe; showing weakness or defiance only spurred his father on; submissive acceptance was his only defence.

The man cuffed the boy around the head, stars danced across the boy's vision, but his father didn't care, even if he was aware of the pain he was inflicting on his son. The blows were relentless and the boy gritted his teeth together to stop himself from making any sounds.

His father, a heavy smoker, was breathing hard from the exertion of beating the boy and paused. The boy didn't believe in god. If there was a god he surely wouldn't let this happen to him day after day. God was supposed to be good; a benevolent god he'd heard his mother say, which was a word he wasn't familiar with, but assumed it was a good thing. The boy screwed his eyes up and prayed to a benevolent god that he hoped existed, that his father was done for the night. Alas, he was only just starting.

The boy heard the oh-so familiar sound of his father's leather belt slipping through the belt loops on his trousers. His own trousers were forcefully pulled down to his knees and he was dragged backwards across the bed so he was half on half off the bed his buttocks already covered in nasty red welts were presented to his father. Thwack. The first blow landed. The boy grabbed his pillow, his knuckles white as he pushed his face deep into the feathers biting into it to mask his whimpering. Thwack. The second blow, even harder than the first, landed. His skin was on fire, the pain excruciating. Thwack, thwack, thwack. His father was into his stride now. The boy could take no more and screamed.

'Stop, stop, stop it! I hate you, I wish you were dead,' the boy screamed at his father between sobs.

'Is that so, you snivelling little shit. You'll be wishing you were dead by the time I'm done with you.'

The boy saw the belt thrown onto the bed and wondered what was coming next. The man put an arm under the boy's waist and lifted him into the air. With his free hand his father pulled his own trousers down followed by his underpants.

'I'll make you hate me now, just you see you ungrateful bastard,' his father said. His free hand grabbed his penis and he pushed it between his son's cheeks.

The boy screamed repeatedly for his mother as his father tried in vain to penetrate the boy. Years of heavy drinking had taken its toll and fortunately for the boy, the man was virtually impotent. He slapped his flaccid penis across the boy's scarred buttocks trying to coax it into an erection.

'I'll show you. I'll show you. Wish I was dead, do you?' his father ranted.

All the while the boy screamed for his mother who never came.

After what seemed an eternity his mother appeared at the doorway. There was blood on her torn dress and one eye was closing over. She held her great-grandfather's old service pistol in her hand and marched resolutely over to her husband a look of utter hatred in her eyes. In a few steps she was in striking distance and raised the gun ready to kill her husband. Alas, even drunk he had his wits about him and wrenched it from his wife's grasp and hurled it at the wall. He dropped the screaming boy back down on the bed, pulled up his own trousers and casually backhanded his wife across the face, sending her sprawling onto the bed with her son; they clung to each other sobbing.

'Useless fucking bitch!' he screamed and marched of the room.

The mother gasped involuntarily as the front door slammed shut.

That night the boy's wish came true and his father never returned home after falling into the path of a speeding juggernaut. There was a god after all and he was a benevolent god, he thought.

The man wiped away the tears as the final memory of his unhappy childhood intruded into his thoughts yet again. Why now after all this time, he wondered and shook his head to dispel the last lingering visions of his childhood. The man blew his nose and took a deep breath. It was time to go to work.

CHAPTER THIRTY-SEVEN

Padstow present day

Finding a parking space in Padstow was always a challenge but lady luck was shining down on Ed Case today and he found one of several in the harbour car park. He'd pay a premium for leaving his car there overnight but money wasn't a major concern for him. The cost of parking galled him and normally he'd park in the cheaper car park at the top of the town and walk in. However, despite the low crime rate in the town, he didn't want to leave his car in what would become an empty car park come a little later that evening and make it a temptation for vandals or thieves. He recalled a day when he went back to his car in that car park and his car exploded, knocking him over with the blast. He had a certain gangster called McGuire to thank for that. He'd rigged his car with semtex as once again Ed was poking his nose where it wasn't wanted. Fortunately for Ed, he'd activated the remote to unlock the doors from some distance away or he'd probably have been blown into more pieces than his car had been. Ed was unlucky with cars. His last one had also been blown to pieces by two rogue police officers working on behalf of the Illuminati and the one before that had been written off by Bob in a car chase. Ed had just advised his insurance company about a change of vehicle rather than try and explain the truth.

Ed had lived in Cornwall for a number of years and now considered it home. The people in the village where he lived were initially unwelcoming, due to a certain Felicity Trevithick spreading malicious gossip and turning the locals against him.

Once he'd overcome that hurdle, he and his wife had been accepted and welcomed by the villagers. He was in no doubt he'd always be considered an outsider, but he fit in and was enjoying life.

It'd been an eventful few years. He renovated his farmhouse and made it into something beautiful, only for it to be burnt to the ground and for it to be rebuilt again. It was a fabulous house but only ever felt like a home when Angel visited. It held too many bad memories of his now deceased wife and daughter and it required too much gardening. Ed did his best to keep on top of it but had hired a local gardener a few times this year when he'd been a bit lapse with the pruning.

He looked across at the building site that was once a warehouse owned by a former London gangster called Harry Daniels. He smiled at the memory of him and Bob, throwing hand grenades into the warehouse packed with munitions stolen from the IRA and destined for the Middle East. The blast had shattered the windows of the nearest properties and the blaze lasted for two days. Ed and Bob had jumped off the harbour into the freezing water and only just managed to escape the fireball that erupted through the open warehouse doors, revenge for blowing his car to bits. The IRA took care of Harry Daniels.

He walked around the harbour noting the two speedboats owned by his friend Colin, who was married to Lisa, the barmaid at the clubhouse on the caravan park where Ed had his caravan. It reminded him he should go and see Sue McLeod who ran the clubhouse as it'd been a while since he'd last been there. Ed wondered where all the time had gone. It seemed to be flying by at an alarming speed. 'Dead soon,' he mutter to himself and shook his head.

The Ship was half-full, a few tourists grabbing a beer or dinner before heading back to their caravans or hotels, and the other half being local workers, grabbing a beer or two before heading home. Then there were people like Bob and Ed who would no doubt be in there drinking until late. Angel would berate him if she knew how much he'd been drinking lately. Angel liked a drink, but also took her fitness very seriously. Working with fellow elite ex-soldiers, in a clandestine group within MI5 hunting down and eliminating members of the Illuminati, she had to keep on top of her game. Ed also took his fitness seriously but as a private investigator didn't need to be as concerned about it as Angel did. It was more about personal pride for him. He always seemed to find trouble and had on occasion worked with Angel and the team, and as such he needed to be fit enough to keep up with the team and be able to defend himself. It was a skill that he'd honed to perfection since his teens. Angel was as good if not better in combat than he was, but he was good enough for his needs. He didn't have to go toe-to-toe with mercenaries, well not on a regular basis. The one time he did, it was terrifying. Angel and the rest of Team Nemesis took it all in their stride but Ed never wanted to go through that experience again. The only good thing to come of his time with Nemesis was meeting and becoming romantically involved with Angel, being taught how to shoot straight with a handgun and machine gun and being able to tap up Data for help with difficult cases. The thought of Angel made him miss her as it always did. He knew that was all part of the relationship and they both knew they'd spend a lot of time apart. They trusted each other implicitly and knew cheating on each other would never happen. Ed had saved Angel's life more than once and vice versa and they had an unshakable bond.

Ed spied Bob in his usual seat and noted the almost empty glass in front of him. He ordered a couple of pints of Doom Bar and made his way over to Bob.

'Congratulations, Magnum,' Bob said when Ed took a seat and pushed a fresh pint towards him.

'A piece of cake. Didn't I say I'd have this one wrapped up in no time at all?' Ed replied smugly.

'Only by virtue of the fact you've got useful mates in MI5,' Bob replied grudgingly.

'It still counts. I'm glad I have Data to tap up for info otherwise you would've been right and I wouldn't have had a cat in hell's chance of solving this one. I might've got lucky, but as you said, if someone doesn't want to be found it can be very difficult to find them.'

'Maybe we should put on the website that we don't do missing persons?' Bob suggested.

'We don't get too many cases now. If we cut back on our remit, we'd just be in here every day getting pissed,' Ed replied.

'Personally, I don't have a problem with that,' Bob told him. There was humour in his voice, but Ed thought there was probably a lot of truth in it too.

'Angel will be back in a day or so and if she finds out how much booze I've been necking since she's been away, she'll give my arse a good kicking and make me run around Trevose Head until my feet drop off.'

'She won't hear it from me or you'll grass me up to Raechael.'

'What do you tell her when you go to the pub and come back stinking of booze?' Ed asked, thinking he might pick up a few tips on dodging the wrath of Angel.

'She knows, but she also knows not to say anything. She knows she'll be wasting her breath. She likes a drink too but prefers to have a glass or two of wine in the garden while reading a book,' Bob told him.

Ed looked at Bob, his face still badly bruised but not as swollen.

'How are you recovering? Your face looks like it's a little less painful. What about the rest of you that I can't see, and don't want to see?' Ed asked genuinely concerned for his friend.

'My ribs are still painful. The x-rays showed that they weren't broken but they're still severely bruised. The bruises on my legs are still tender, but I can walk without wincing now. If I'm honest Ed, my pride hurt more than anything. He took me by surprise, but still he was quicker, I didn't even manage to land any punches. I know we say "we're getting too old for this shit," quite a lot in fact, but I really think I am.'

Ed had never heard Bob sound so down. Normally he'd joke something off and just pick himself up and get on with it.

'Oh well, Talbot will be feeling a lot worse than you after what I gave him. Anyway, what's with all this bullshit, defeatist attitude? I got my arse kicked twice in one night at Aldbury House. It was only Anna who saved my arse. How do you think I felt, only being alive because of a fourteen year-old girl? I got back up, worked harder in the gym and got over it. Since then, I've managed to give a bloody good account of myself when I've needed to.'

'It's alright for you. You're still the right side of forty. I'm nearer sixty than I am fifty.' Bob replied.

'Come to the house and workout in the gym. We can spar

together and we can learn a thing or two off each other. That's what I do when Angel comes over for a few days.'

'Really? What a waste. If I had a girl like yours, I'd be sparring in the bedroom to keep fit.'

'We do that too, but you don't want to hear about how I drive Angel wild in the sack, do you?'

'You're absolutely right I don't. You know, I really do think I've reached that stage where I really am too old for this shit.'

'So what're you saying? Are you gonna quit on me?' Ed asked genuinely concerned.

Bob shrugged.

'C'mon Bob. You can't quit. I'd be like the Lone Ranger without Tonto, or Batman without Robin, or beer without alcohol.'

'Beer without alcohol; what an utterly joyless experience that would be.'

'My point exactly. Bob, it's OK to be a fat, old bastard, but being a selfish, fat, old bastard isn't a good thing. We've only been partners a short time, we've got years ahead of us. Tell you what. You come to the house, and I'll get you fighting fit and Angel will too when she's around. Then we'll go and see Talbot. If he kicks your butt… again, you can quit, if not we carry on,' Ed told him.

'Go and get a beer in and I'll think about it,' Bob replied.

'I think it's your round.'

'I can't think and order a beer, can I?' Bob replied and smiled.

'You sure you're not a Yorkshireman, you tight bastard?' Ed asked as he got to his feet.

'Wash your mouth out, you cretin. Cut me in half and you'll see London right through the middle of me.'

Ed shook his head and went to get beer. What did he care?

Working late was an occupational hazard. At least tonight Phil had the option of doing it from home. It wasn't a great night for Emma, but at least tonight they were in the same room. This week, most nights he'd had to stay late at the station worrying about his triple murder case, what Clatworthy would be thinking with the lack of progress and whether or not the murderer would strike again before they could make an arrest.

Emma came up behind him and began to massage his shoulders. Phil sighed softly, appreciating the comfort Emma was trying to give him.

'Penny for them?' she asked.

'Ah, just the usual. I really thought we'd nailed the case earlier, but it wasn't to be,' Phil replied.

Emma wasn't slow to pick up on the downbeat tone in her fiancé's voice.

Ordinarily they never discussed work but tonight Phil needed an outlet for his pent up frustration. His DCI was in hospital and normally they'd discuss cases and try to buoy each other by being positive. He didn't feel he had that option with Shaun Edwards or Fiona Walsh, so this time he'd break his rule about discussing work with Emma.

'We think we're looking for a guy who's got an issue with domestic abuse. We believe he was likely to have been in a family where the father used to beat his mother and quite likely him too. Again, it's an assumption that the murderer has access to the magistrates, courts or their records and targets men convicted of domestic abuse. We thought today we'd got our man, but now I'm not so sure.'

'Why's that?' Emma asked.

'He drives a car that's the make and model that was seen at the scene of one of the murders but unfortunately we didn't manage to get a number plate. His mother and father were alcoholics and drug users so he was fostered out. He works at the magistrates' courts in Truro, so has access to all the records for all magistrates' courts as that's his job, so he ticks all the boxes assuming our assumptions are correct. Also, his name is John and the killer leaves a note that reads "Say thank you John" which is another tick in the box'

Emma continued to massage Phil's neck and shoulders, trying to relieve the stress.

'So why don't you think he's your man if he ticks all the right boxes?' she asked.

'Gut feel. You learn to go with your instincts in this job. Also, he said he was a gamer and spent all his nights playing computer games. We'll take his computer and verify that, but I'm pretty sure we're barking up the wrong tree. Whoever we're looking for is smart and knows that CCTV footage at the courts is deleted after thirty days. All three victims were killed thirty or more days after their trial. That means if they were at the trial in the public gallery or even at the courts, there'd be no record of them. Perhaps a coincidence, but I don't think so.'

Phil flicked through the paperwork in front of him as Emma continued to massage him. He analysed every page then frowned and sifted through a few sheets and tossed them aside.

'What are those that you're not interested in?' Emma asked, as so far Phil had scrutinised every single sheet of paper.

'They're Ed's notes that he left behind at the restaurant the other night. I called him and he said he didn't need them as he'd already printed off new copies. They must've been in the stack of papers I picked up that somehow got embedded in the mass of paperwork that lands on my desk,'

'Mind if I take a look at it?' Emma asked.

'Sure it's nothing related to my case and maybe you can see something that might help your old mate. If you don't mind me asking, why didn't you two become an item? I know you think highly of him, as he does you.'

Emma leaned forward and kissed Phil tenderly on the neck.

'For starters he was too old for me…' she said.

'He's only a couple of years older than me,' Phil interrupted.

'That's true, but he fell in love with Laura, Raechael's daughter. He stopped me from committing suicide and brought me to Cornwall to start a new life as you know. He's one of the most generous unassuming guys I've ever met, but our friendship is more brother-sister and was never going to be anything but.'

'So you were never going to be lady of the manor. I thought every girl's dream was to marry a millionaire and live the life of a princess,' Phil said.

'You know Ed as well as I do. If we'd got together, I'd most likely be living a life wondering about if and when he was gonna get himself killed. You know his history as well as I do and that's the reason Laura gave him the elbow. I actually think him and Angel are a perfect match; both live dangerously. Anyway, that's all in the past. I met you, via Ed in fact, and found my very own prince charming, albeit not as rich, but I'm happy with what I've got.'

Phil reached out and gave Emma's forearm a squeeze to let her know he appreciated the fact. He was a little in awe of Ed. He seemed to live a charmed life and despite his wealth and the knocks he'd received in his life, he was a very likeable person.

'Oh my god!' Emma exclaimed as Phil turned over a sheet of paper to reveal a photo of Pete Quigley.

Phil quickly turned the photo over.

'Sorry I didn't realise that was in the paperwork.'

'What kind of sick bastard would do that to another human being?' Emma said.

'Welcome to my world,' Phil replied.

Emma turned her attention to the paperwork belonging to Ed to take her mind of the horrific injuries inflicted on Peter Quigley and sat down opposite.

'Data is Ed's friend at MI5, isn't he?' Emma asked having looked at the email print out

'He is and judging by the information he gave Ed, he's a good friend to have. It would've taken us days to get a judge to give us the go ahead to ensure the relevant banks and mobile phone companies gave us that kind of information. Ed gets it all with just one phone call,' Phil replied, a little jealous of Ed's connections.

'Owen Moore. Who is he?' Emma asked.

'Just a missing person, Ed's looking into.'

'This Data guy has been very thorough, even though he still apologies for not giving Ed any call details. He's given him his car make and model and number plate; although I reckon he's got his work cut out with finding that. There must be thousands of white Focus's on the road.'

'Needle in a haystack for sure,' Phil replied, barely listening, more intent on reading through the interview notes for John Talbot.

'Can every mobile phone really be tracked and recorded?' Emma asked.

'Of course, all mobile phone companies have this information. Every time your phone passes from one cell to another it's recorded. How else do you think someone can call you? Mobile phones are continually in communication with the network. If I call you, the network searches for the last know location for your number and routes the call,' Phil told her.

'Well this guy seems to have a very boring life, based on this information. I reckon he lives in Bodmin and never ventures further than Padstow…or Rock and once went to Penzance.'

'I know people who rarely leave Padstow,' Phil replied still distracted by John Talbot's interview notes.

Emma flipped over the page and looked at Ed's map and studied it.

'It seems like Ed's missing person spent a lot of time at the supermarket.'

'Probably works there,' Phil said a little annoyed at the distraction,

Emma continued to look at the map.

'Maybe he does but the supermarket is right next door to the Magistrates' court. Maybe he worked there?'

Phil looked up on hearing 'Magistrates' court'.

'Maybe he's worth looking into?'

'Pass me that stuff will you?' he asked.

Emma slid the sheets across the table. Phil looked at the map and frowned as he looked through the mobile phone locations and car details. Just a coincidence, he thought.

'Shame his name isn't John or he might be a person of interest,' Phil replied, placing the papers on the desk.

'His middle name's John,' Emma replied.

'Why is that important?'

'Plenty of famous people use their middle names as they prefer it to their first name. Maybe he doesn't like being called Owen so goes by John?' Emma replied.

'Like who? I've never known anyone use their middle name.'

'Meghan Markle for one. Her first name is Rachel. Jason Momoa's is Joseph. Tom Hardy's first name is Edward. Brad Pitt was William...'

'OK, OK, I get it, Phil replied, looking at Ed's notes with renewed interest.

Phil studied the map and came to the same conclusion that Ed did; that he worked in or near the supermarket and the other places he visited were on his way home from work. Phil looked up at Emma who was smiling seeing Phil taking an interest in Ed's information.

The mobile phone information was interesting. Most of the locations were Padstow for the first week or so but became predominately Bodmin for the last five weeks, with the exception of a couple of visits to Padstow, Rock and Penzance. Phil looked at the dates and times.

'Shit,' Phil muttered and checked his own notes for dates and times. 'Oh shit,' he said again.

'What's up?' Emma asked.

'The dates and times of Owen Moore's mobile movements tie in with the dates and times of the three murders more or less. I think Ed is searching for the same person I am,' Phil said.

'Oh my god. Call him, Phil. Let him know he could be in serious danger!' Emma said beginning to panic.

Phil looked through the notes again.

'He drives the same car we're looking for too, a white Ford Focus. Surely it's just a coincidence?' Phil said.

'You told me you don't believe in coincidences. Just call him to make sure he's safe or at least warn him until you've caught up with the guy and eliminated him or arrested him,' Emma said, genuinely concerned for Ed's safety.

Phil picked up his mobile and dialled Ed's number. It rang then diverted to voicemail. Phil ran a hand over his chin and dialled again with the same result. He looked at his watch, it wasn't late not even ten-thirty.

'He's not answering his phone. Maybe he's gone to bed already. He's probably been out with Bob who drank him under the table again. I'll try him again in the morning,' Phil replied.

'Phil, what if Ed found him and he's in trouble?' Emma replied, fearing for her friend's safety.

'Unlikely, I'd think. Even if he did find him, Ed just wants to get him to talk to his mother or will just take a photo as proof he found him. Ed isn't connected to these murders as he doesn't fit the profile of the victims. That's assuming Owen Moore is the man we're looking for. In any case, he's unlikely to get one over on Ed. I've never seen anyone fight like him; he's a machine and a match for anyone.'

'You told me the killer sneaks up and bashes them over the head with a hammer. If Ed's had a few he might not be in a position to defend himself.'

'I guess so. Let me call him again.'

'Call, Bob. If Ed's out and has his phone on mute, he's likely to be out with Bob. I need to know he's safe or I won't be able to sleep,' Emma said flustered and thinking the worst.

Phil dialled Bob's number and waited.

'Hi Phil, need some help with your triple murder?' Bob said his voice a little slurred.

'In a roundabout way. I don't suppose you've seen Ed today, have you? I can't get him on his mobile and Emma's worried about him.'

'He left the pub about forty-five minutes ago. We had a few pints to celebrate him winding up his missing person case. Lucky bastard has MI5 to help him out. It would've taken him a month of Sundays to find him otherwise; if he was lucky.'

'Oh that's not good...' Phil started to say.

'Not good, why's that?' Bob asked.

'Well, we think that Owen Moore could, and I stress could, be the man I'm looking for,' Phil replied uncertainly.

'OK what makes you think that?' Bob asked sobering up quickly.

Phil relayed all the similarities with the profile of the man he was looking for and what Ed had found out.

'I can't drive, I've had too many. Come and pick me up. I have a key to his place so we'll go and make sure he's OK.'

'Hopefully, he'll just have his phone on mute or switched off,' Phil said optimistically.

'Ed never switches it off in case Angel calls. Hurry up, I'm waiting for you,' Bob said and ended the call.

CHAPTER THIRTY-EIGHT

Ed left the pub and managed to get a taxi, having finally persuaded Bob to have a serious think about quitting the private investigation business. He argued that if anything tasty came up, Bob would be chomping at the bit to get involved because he'd be bored. He didn't have any hobbies, unless you could call binge drinking a hobby and would just get in Raechael's way and drink himself into an early grave, dying of liver failure, a fat, bored ex-copper.

He knew Bob was still licking his wounds from being on the wrong end of a nasty seeing to by John Talbot, and Ed said he'd help him get back to his fitness levels of twenty years previous. Bob had given Ed a look of incredulity and told him twenty years ago he was probably in worse physical shape than he was now. Twenty years or so ago when he was still in the Met and working under Jack Griggs, now the director general of MI5, he knew everyone and therefore was out drinking more and there was always a kebab shop or late night greasy spoon open to provide a full-English to anyone with the munchies after a few beers.

Ed compromised and said he'd help him get his speed and agility levels up and weight down. Ed smiled at Bob's reply when Ed said with the right training, he might even get a six pack in a few months. Bob replied the only six pack he was interested in was the ones in his fridge. In the end, he thought he'd put a strong case forward to make sure Bob stayed on as a partner in the business.

Ed stepped out of the taxi, which had dropped him at the top of his drive and made his way to the house. He recalled putting the key in the door and nothing else. How he ended up naked as the day he was born, with nylon cable ties around his wrists and ankles, which in turn were nailed to the floor was a mystery, but Ed knew just how serious his predicament was from speaking to Phil. What he didn't know was why him? If Phil was right, he didn't fit the profile of the other victims.

His head was pounding and he could feel the congealed blood at the back of his head, resting on the cold tiled floor of his living room. That he knew, as he could see the sofa swimming in and out of focus along with a pair of legs, clad in black. Whoever the legs belonged to got up and made their way out of the room. Ed could hear them in the kitchen, making themselves a cup of coffee. He hoped the person was making him one too, he had a raging thirst and unfortunately the need for the lavatory from all the beer he'd consumed with Bob.

The person was a man, Ed could tell from the shoe size and his build. He'd finished in the kitchen and sat down on the sofa, and took a noisy slurp of his coffee.

Ed's vision was beginning to settle but the pain in his head was still just as fierce. He tensed his arms and tried the bonds; they were strong and Ed was too weak. Exerting even the slightest tension made his head throb even more painfully.

'Who are you?' Ed asked his voice was hoarse and sounded like it belonged to a stranger not him.

'You already know who I am,' the man replied.

Ed craned his neck and looked at the man who was doing nothing to conceal his face. Whatever happened tonight the man on the sofa had no intention of letting Ed live; he'd seen his face.

'Owen Moore,' he croaked.

'You can call me, John,' Owen replied.

If Ed had any linger doubts about his situation they dispersed quickly at hearing the name John.

'Fuck,' he muttered.

'You are indeed fucked, Case. So now you know who I am and what I am and why I moved out of my mother's,' Owen replied and smiled.

'Why, John, when your name's Owen?' Ed asked, both curious and stalling for time. The more he talked the longer he stayed alive.

'Let's just say I had a difficult birth and that left me with a few minor mobility and learning difficulties, which over time I overcame, quite quickly actually, despite the odds. One of those problems was mild dyslexia. Whenever I tried to write my name, rather than writing Owen I wrote Omen or Nemo and I used to get teased by the other kids in my class. You know how cruel children can be. However, I didn't have any problems writing John, so I started calling myself John. Only my mother refused to call me John. She told me I was christened Owen and that was the only name she'd call me by. She always was a stubborn woman,' Owen told him.

'She misses you. It broke her heart when I told her I'd found you but you refused to contact her. She didn't like the new hair colour by the way,' Ed said, desperately trying to think of a line of conversation to keep him alive. The longer he was alive the better his chances of escape. It'd worked before, but this time, his situation was dire. Nobody knew of his predicament and nobody would come to his rescue. This was one Houdini act he'd have to fathom out by himself. He just needed time; assuming Owen Moore wasn't in a hurry to kill him.

'Why me, John? Why am I nailed to the floor? I thought you were doing this as revenge on wife beaters?'

'That's a good question. Nobody has asked me that. Most people just care about their own well-being and try to beg me to let them go.'

'I'm guessing that as the police are looking for a triple murderer there's no chance of me getting out of here alive, is there?' Ed asked.

'Absolutely none whatsoever. To answer your question, you know too much. You said you'd got my bank card transactions and mobile phone locations and car details. If you gave that to your police friends, I would become their prime suspect, and correctly so, and that would make things awkward and I can't allow that to happen. I still have work to do; a lot of work to do. That aside, even if you don't fill the criteria I look for in my other victims, I want to find out what makes you tick.'

'I think you'll be disappointed. I'm not a wife beater, John,' Ed said his tone flat and even. He didn't want to give Owen any reason to start smashing him up with the hammer that he knew must be somewhere nearby, so called him by his preferred name. Phil had told him some of the gruesome details of the injuries he'd inflicted on his victims. The thought of having his privates ripped from between his legs and stuffed in his mouth was a terrifying thought. Ed only hoped when his time came it was mercifully quick.

'You say you're not a wife beater, yet both your wives died in mysterious circumstances as we discussed earlier. I did a lot of digging around when I knew you were looking for me. If you'd heeded the warning, you wouldn't be here now. Curiosity killed the cat as they say.'

'My first wife died in a car accident,' Ed told him.

He kept the facts brief hoping to drag the conversation out by Owen asking lots of questions. Ed just hoped he was curious, if not he'd change tactics and give him verbose answers.

'I know. The van was parked up and rolled all by itself into a gulley and blew up, killing your wife and her lover. Very convenient for you, I think,' Owen said, leaning over Ed and sipping his coffee. He let some of the liquid spill onto Ed's stomach. The liquid was piping hot. Ed hissed in pain.

'I must commend you on your choice of coffee. So far all my victims had been drinking instant coffee, cheap instant coffee at that. Blue Mountain, very nice. Thank you for making my short stay a pleasant stay.'

'Perhaps if the coffee is that nice you'll try and keep it in the cup and not spill it over my stomach,' Ed replied,

'Carry on, Case. You were telling me about your first wife.'

'That bitch married me for my money. My parents died in a bus crash while on holiday. They left me money and being young and stupid and hurting at losing my only family, I invested it in a bunch of shares that were doing badly as I wanted nothing do with that money; it was no substitute for my parents. My wife didn't know this and when she found out she started a string of affairs. The guy in the van was the fitter who laid the wooden floors in the house and was the last in a long line of casual affairs. Not a happy marriage, but I never killed her. Her own infidelity killer her,' Ed told him.

'It seems like there are a lot of car accidents in your life. You made a lot of money out of them too. Coincidence? I think perhaps not. I think you're cold and calculating,' Owen said, staring at Ed intently.

'I had nothing to do with my parents' tour bus crashing; how could I? In any case, I'd rather my parents were alive and be a relatively poor man. My wife, she hated me because she thought I was rich and I wasn't. I was hurting, I hated her even, but I never killed her. The police said the handbrake was off or faulty and while they were screwing in the back of the van it rolled down the slope into a gulley. The van was full of chemicals used in laying floors and they think one of the tins came open on impact and was ignited by a cigarette. I confess I didn't shed a tear when I was told by the police, but it was just a freak accident,' Ed couldn't help but feel angry having had to dig up a past he hadn't thought of in some years.

'Plausible story, although still difficult to believe. You got incredibly rich very quickly. Perhaps like me you were very clever and covered you tracks,' Owen said, his pale blue eyes with the darker rings bore into Ed's own green eyes.

'I did become rich very quickly. The shares instead of bombing like I hoped they would were actually worth a fortune. I also had life insurance on my wife and she had a death in service plan with her company pension, so yes I was sitting on over three million quid. I can't deny that, but there was no murder involved. It was just bad luck or good luck, whatever you choose to call it.'

'Your old friend, Julie Mortimer, told me this story. Either you're a consistently good liar or you're being honest,' Owen replied and gave him a look of contempt.

'I forgot I told her quite a lot of my life story. But why do I need to lie? You're gonna torture me and kill me like the others regardless. I have nothing to gain by lying. So what makes you tick, John? Why are you killing men found guilty of domestic abuse?' Ed asked, all the time testing his restraints. There was no slack, no give. His situation was helpless.

'Because men like that don't change. Men like that despite being found guilty and fined are still menaces. They'll hook up with another woman or family and the cycle of abuse will start again. A leopard never changes it's spots. You put a paedophile in prison; he's still a paedophile when he comes out. It's how the brain's wired.'

'You sound like that's something you know from personal experience.' Ed said, hoping to buy himself some more time.

'I think I'll get myself another coffee first. Might as well, I made a pot of it.'

'Bring me back one will you John, I'm parched.'

'If I bring you one back, you'll be wearing it,' Owen replied.

'In that case I'll just have a glass of cold water, if that's OK with you.'

Owen Moore stared down at Ed and shook his head.

As soon as he left the room Ed was tugging at his bonds; he wouldn't go down without a fight; it wasn't in his nature.

CHAPTER THIRTY-NINE

Phil grabbed his car keys and set off to pick up Bob. He was only a few minutes away and there was no traffic at that time of night. When he pulled up outside, Bob was leaning on a lamppost, by the edge of the kerb waiting. Even from inside the car Phil could see his body was tense, his face, despite the cuts and bruises, was anxious. He got in without saying a word; he just nodded at Phil to drive and drive fast.

Ed's house was only a few minutes' drive away. The atmosphere in the car was tense as Phil sped around the narrow country lanes as fast as he dared and prayed nothing was coming in the opposite direction. Neither man spoke a word. Visions of Mick Woods, Brandon Taylor and Pete Quigley filled Phil's head.

'Are you positive that Owen Moore is the same man you're looking for? Only it'd be a bit embarrassing to go crashing into his house only to find him shagging Angel,' Bob said half-jokingly, trying to alleviate the tension a little.

Phil shook his head.

'That's something I don't want to see. To answer your question, I'm as sure as I can be. If he's not, then there are a lot of coincidences, and you and I both know there are no such things as coincidences.'

'Go on then tell me,' Bob replied, wanting to know the facts.

'Both men drive a white Ford Focus which was seen at one crime scene. I know there must be hundreds, if not thousands in Cornwall alone, but that's the first coincidence. When you look at where his bank cards were used, they're centred around a supermarket in Bodmin, which just so happens to be right next door to the Magistrate's court where our three victims made their court appearances and were found guilty of domestic abuse. The final one, and by far the most compelling to make me jump to the conclusion they're one and the same, is the mobile phone information. Ed has records of when Owen Moore's phone moved between cells. On or around the times of the three murders our man was in the vicinity of those locations. Oh and I forgot, his middle name is John,' Phil told Bob.

'OK, I agree with your point about coincidences, but it's a bit tenuous with the middle name, isn't it?' Bob replied.

'I thought so too, but Emma said a lot of famous people don't use their first name and go by their middle names. She rattled off a few celebrities who do just that, so I guess it's feasible for non-celebrities to do likewise.'

'I guess so. Anyway, I think your logic is good and there's a good chance they're one and the same. Let's hope Ed is just indisposed and not in any danger, either way he needs to be warned. Heaven forbid we're too late.' Bob replied solemnly. He thought he'd lost Ed once before, it was a horrible feeling.

'Any ideas on how we do this? You've had a lot more experience at this kind of thing than I have,' Phil asked the older, more experienced man.

'I think we park up outside the perimeter wall and walk down to the house so we don't make too much noise and panic the man. Then we split up and have a good look around the downstairs. Meet up by the back door and if we find nothing we go in and do a full recce of the house. If he's not there, I've no idea. Maybe best not to dwell on that, but if he's in trouble with our murder suspect, he normally targets his victims in their own home. So, if he's not home, let's pray he's safe. If he's in trouble with the cops or been taken to hospital for some reason, we'd know as all the coppers round here know we're mates and one of us would've been called by the duty sergeant,' Bob replied, hoping he was right.

'What if Ed's in trouble?' Phil asked nervously.

'I have a key. We go in and save his arse and hope we're not too late.'

Phil pulled the car up outside the perimeter wall, a bag of nerves, and looked at the house in the distance down the long drive. A light went out in the kitchen. They glimpsed the silhouette of a man behind the blind before the kitchen was left in darkness. The two men looked at each other and shrugged.

'Don't read anything good in that. Our man likes his coffee. He's poured scalding coffee on all three of his victims,' Phil told Bob.

'Thanks for that great pep talk. Let's go check before we jump to any conclusions,' Bob replied.

The two men split up and went in opposite directions around the perimeter of the house, moving cautiously and as silently as possible. It was nerve wracking for both men as a lot was at stake. One mistake and Ed could be dead.

Phil carefully checked the back door to the kitchen but it was locked. The same was true for the rear door to the garden. On Bob's side of the house the only doors were the patio doors to the dining room and living room. The patio doors to the dining room were locked so he moved along to the living room. A crack in the curtains revealed a lamp was on somewhere providing soft lighting. Bob took a peek through the narrow crack where the curtains didn't quite meet. His heart leapt and his blood turned cold as he could see Ed's head and torso. He was lying naked on the floor. A man sat on the sofa appraising him, nursing a cup of steaming coffee.

'Fuck,' he said silently.

Bob looked up to see Phil creeping towards him. He held his hand up to stop him and motioned to meet up round the front of the house.

'It's the worst case scenario,' Bob whispered to Phil as they hunkered down under the window to the side of the front door.

'Ed's alive isn't he?' Phil asked.

'Yes, but for how much longer, I don't know. He's naked and on the floor, no doubt secured by cable ties. Owen Moore, I assume Owen Moore, as I could only see his lower body, is sitting there with a coffee looking down at Ed.'

'So what's next?' Phil asked.

'I only have a front door key so we have to go in via that door and soon, before things start getting messy. If we can get in unseen we can go to the basement where Ed keeps his safe, which I have the combination for, and I know he's got a few illegal guns in there. I was thinking we might need to get tooled up, just as a deterrent to get Moore to drop the hammer if he makes a grab for it. Are you ready?' Bob asked.

'Guns? I'll pretend I never heard that. This isn't good, but I'm as ready as I'll ever be,' he replied.

Bob pulled the key from his pocket.

As he did a gun was thrust into his back. 'Both of you, stand up and put your hands in the air where I can see them, and turn around slowly.' They were told in a voice little more than a whisper.

CHAPTER FORTY

As soon as Owen left the room for his second cup of coffee, Ed craned his neck to see the ties that held him firmly to the floor. The nails were not perpendicular, but had gone in at an angle. If he was going to free himself he needed to pull his wrists towards him not pull upwards, which would be futile. Ed began to pull his right hand. Nothing happened so he tried his left hand pulling with all his strength. The nylon tie bit painfully into his skin. He ignored the pain and pulled harder. Pain was better than the only other option of a slow death by repeated blows with a hammer. Was it his imagination or was there a slight movement? Encouraged, Ed began tugging, believing that movement would be more effective than a continuous pulling. It hurt like hell as each tug caused the tie to chafe his skin raw. Ed continued to ignore the pain and fire in his muscles. The nail was definitely moving.

Ed heard the pot being replaced on the hot plate of the coffee machine. He didn't have much time. He tugged even more furiously. The nail suddenly came loose. He almost smashed himself in the face as his arm became free. Ed looked and saw concrete dust and did his best to sweep it under his naked body. He just managed to put his hand back down in position before Owen stepped into the room and sat back down on the couch.

'I see from the sweat on your body you've been trying to get free. It won't do you any good. You'll only end up with bloody wrists and ankles just like the last three did.'

Ed made a show of tugging his right arm to show Owen he was unsuccessful.

'How did you know your victims were wife beaters?' Ed asked.

Again it wasn't through wanting to know, of course he was curious, but it was more stalling tactics.

'I found out about a job at Bodmin Magistrates' Courts. The buildings are relatively new, but as with many buildings they get old quickly and need constant maintenance due to cheap construction materials or lack of maintenance. The local council worked out a permanent employee would be cheaper than calling in specialists when needed. They needed a man of my experience as I'm CORGI registered and electrically qualified. Every day I would see the court schedule and was curious. My father was a nasty, mean-minded bully who made my childhood a living hell. He was a bully and a drunk who liked to beat me and my mother most days. I spent most of my childhood in abject terror.

Recently, I started experiencing these vivid memories and decided I needed a new life away from my mother, who for the most part did nothing to stop the abuse my father dished out to me, or her for that matter. I never had the chance to ask him why. I wanted to find out and I thought listening to men defending themselves in court would be a good way to understand my father. Alas, the courts just wanted to find them guilty or innocent and not delve into the reasons. I wanted more. I wanted to know; I needed to find out what made them tick. The rest I'm sure you can work out, from what you've read in the newspapers and from your friends in the police.'

'I see,' Ed replied not knowing if he did or didn't see his reasoning. 'Did you find out?' he asked.

'Oh yes. I always find out what makes them tick.' Owen replied and smiled.

It was a smile that never reached his cold, blue eyes. Ed was running out of stalling questions and had to think hard as he stared into the dead eyes of his killer.

'You were going to tell me about your personal experience of domestic abuse before you got a coffee,' Ed said.

'Was I?' Owen looked at his watch. 'Why not? We've got plenty of time before I have to say goodbye, and I've still got half a pot of coffee.'

Ed was feeling a lot happier now that he'd managed to get one arm free. His situation was far from perfect but with one arm free at least he had hope.

'My father was a bastard. I don't remember if he was always a bastard, but my earliest memories were of him coming home drunk and beating my mother. Then when I got a little older he began beating me. Sometimes with his belt, sometimes he'd just kick and punch me black and blue and seemed to enjoy it, and I never understood why.

You come from a well-balanced family. Your parents loved you and you loved them, I'm sure. I bet you have no idea what it feels like to be hated by your father and be ridiculed by your classmates. I'm sure you were a popular kid. All the kids at school were wary of me as I was withdrawn, as you'd expect from being severely beaten most nights, going to bed crying and scared, waking up scared, dreading the front door banging in the evening knowing the next day the cycle would start again, just like every other fucking day; day in day out. The last time he beat me, I told him I hated him and wished him dead. Because of that he tried to rape me but fortunately he was so drunk he couldn't get it up. I'm sure if he'd been able to he'd have buggered me and left me in a bloodied heap on the bedroom floor. That was the only time my mother came to my help. My father backhanded her and stormed out. That was the last we saw of the nasty, malicious bastard. That night he fell into the road drunk, into the path of a speeding juggernaut. He survived but fortunately died in hospital. That was the happiest day of my childhood. No child deserves that,' Owen told him.

'I feel for you John, I really do, but killing people isn't going to solve anything. There are cases of domestic abuse happening as we speak up and down the country, not just in England but in every country, one man can't stop it. You'll be caught. Soon you'll slip up or the police will find a connection and you'll spend a life behind bars. You kill me and the police will look into my recent cases and you'll be the first person they look into. They'll run background checks and you'll be caught; of that you can be certain. I spent a week in prison recently and trust me it was the most frightening experience of my life. I wouldn't wish it on anyone, not even you. Stop, go back to your mum and make your peace with her. No more killing,' Ed replied hoping to appeal to his better nature, which he was sure was there underneath the surface.

'It's too late. Even if I stop, as you've already told me, the police will make a connection. As for my mother, huh, she did nothing to help. She could've made him stop. Gone to the police, reported him to social services or whatever they were called back then. She did nothing. When I started to recall details about my past, I remembered. I remembered how she was never there for me, never, not once. I want nothing to do with her. If she wasn't my mother I'd kill her too.'

Owen paused and stared silently at Ed. Ed wondered if this was going to be the point where he'd have to try and fight for his life.

'Why were you in prison? So far you've led me to believe you're a good guy, maybe not such a good guy after all, tell me, I'm intrigued,' Owen said leaning forward.

Ed was happy answering another question. It was another few seconds of being alive and being able to work on freeing his other hand.

'I didn't do anything illegal, well not as such. Maybe if we have time I'll explain,' Ed replied continuing with the stalling tactics that would buy him enough time as he worked on his other wrist. With two hands free he stood a chance. A small chance, but one he'd pounce on.

'We have plenty of time, Case. Tell me, I'd really like to know.'

'I know some people in high places and owed them a favour. The favour asked, was for me to go to prison to get information out of a vicious criminal to help find the whereabouts of a person my friend wanted to find, who also happened to be a mutual friend; a friend who once saved my life. He couldn't use his own people because it would've caused a scandal if it was made public knowledge. So, I was a scapegoat, completely deniable if my presence was found out and completely expendable should things have gone wrong. On my first day I was put in solitary confinement when a man started a fight with me. A homosexual rapist tried to screw me in the showers and I was involved in a riot. So believe me when I say you don't want to go to prison.'

'Friends in high places such as the police?'

'Much higher than the police; I'm sure you can work out who that is.'

'What happened to your second wife and daughter? I read they were killed. I assumed that was by you to make yourself even wealthier. I read your house was burnt down and you rebuilt it and probably got more pay outs on insurance. Arson when you were away on business seems to be very convenient,' Owen said and sneered down at Ed.

Ed watched as his hand snaked across towards the hammer at the side of the sofa. His fingers caressed the handle of it, almost like a lover would. He took a deep breath, readying himself for the onslaught which wasn't far away. The look in Owen's blue eyes had changed.

'Since being a private investigator I've managed to piss off a very influential organisation on at least two occasions. I cost these people a great deal of money and ruined their plans to have the most powerful man in the country in their pocket. I was warned by an old man to keep myself out of this organisation's business or I'd find my life taken away from me.

I thought nothing of it. I thought it was an idle threat. I returned home from a business trip and found my house burnt to the ground, my wife and daughter kidnapped and my life erased. My money was cleaned out, my car was torched, my mobile phone number erased. Nobody had any record that I even existed. I was a non-entity. According to the world I didn't exist and never had. All I had was the hope that I could find my wife and daughter.'

Ed's own anger was rising. He'd put all these bad memories behind him, probably just like Owen, until those memories resurfaced.

'I was thrown a lifeline and was lucky enough to join up with a team of highly skilled, highly trained people who were searching for the same man I was. I spent a week fighting for my life to find my family. I was shot at by mercenaries who belonged to this corrupt group. I went through hell, but finally found the man in a remote estate in Scotland. I'd made a promise that I wouldn't kill the man regardless of whether my family were alive or dead as he was vital to the man who helped me. The old man assured me they were alive and well and being kept in a cabin by the lake. He was true to his word, but when I got there that miserable, fucking bastard had ordered them to be slaughtered. I found them sat a table as if everything was normal, but their throats were cut open to the spine. I kept my word not to kill him.

Every fucking day I thought of him. Every time I thought of my wife and daughter, the only memory I could drag up out of all the happy times we'd spent together was of them sitting in that cabin covered in blood. Every morning I woke up drunk and picked up the handgun I kept and put it to my forehead, willing myself to pull the fucking trigger and end my miserable life, but I couldn't and I'd cry like a baby and then pick up the bottle and start all over again. I was stuck in this endless cycle. Oh, a computer expert restored my life and my possessions, but it meant nothing. Money and cars were just trinkets. The only thing important in my life was my family and it was gone.'

Ed sniffed and blinked tears from his eyes.

'Then one day I got a call. The people who'd taken charge of this guy had finished with him and it was their turn to keep to their side of the bargain. I went to visit that vindictive old bastard and he taunted me right up to the end. He pushed the right buttons goading me on, but I couldn't kill him. He told me that he'd ordered his brother to kill them and laughed at me. I kicked him in the throat, crushing his trachea and watched him gasp for air, dying a slow and painful death. Then I tracked his brother down with the help of those same friends in high places and did the same to him. Does that make me a bad person? If it does I don't really care. I guess that makes me no different than you, but my reason was personal. I guess we've both played god.'

Ed sniffed again and wiped his tears with his free hand. It was an instinctive move, having completely forgotten the situation he was in. He slowly put his hand to his side and stared at Owen who seemed confused, but only briefly as anger quickly replaced the confusion in his eyes.

CHAPTER FORTY-ONE

Bob and Phil turned around slowly as requested, their hands still raised high.

'Angel?' they both said in unison quietly.

'Yeah, what the fuck are you two up to. I saw the car parked up outside and then saw you two creeping around the building. I thought you were burglars or worse, knowing what Ed's like,' Angel said keeping her voice low.

'Where did you come from I didn't see you?' Bob asked.

'It's my job not to be seen and I'm good at it. Now just tell me what the fuck's going on.'

'To cut a long story short, Ed is nailed to the living room floor by a serial killer. We were just doing a quick recce before going in and hopefully rescuing him and stop him being beaten to death with a claw hammer. I have a front door key,' Bob said holding up the spare Ed gave him.

'Jesus Christ. I can't leave him alone for five minutes, can I? The time for questions is later.'

Angel showed no surprise at hearing of Ed's predicament. She held up a bunch of keys.

'I've got a full set. Give me forty-five seconds to get round the back and then you two come in via the front door. I'm going straight into the living room and will blow that fucker's head off if he lays so much as a finger on my boyfriend.'

Angel sprinted silently away.

'She's got some balls that one,' Phil said as Bob inserted the key into the lock as quietly as he could, counting down from forty-five.

Bob was at eighteen, when they could hear a commotion coming from inside the house. Without hesitation he turned the key and rushed inside.

The coffee cup dropped from Owen's hand. The scalding liquid poured over Ed's stomach and the cup itself bounced off and rolled away. Ed didn't have time to concern himself with the blistering hot coffee on his skin as the hammer came up fast. Ed watched and reacted just as quickly, deflecting it away with his free left hand. The hammer smashed into the tiles. Owen had overstretched and was slow to regain his balance. Ed punched him in the face but the punch lacked any real power as he couldn't draw his arm back and land a telling blow, and it just enraged Owen more. The hammer came down a second time. This time Ed caught hold of his wrist stopping the blow a fraction before it pulverized his eye socket. Owen was screaming with rage, the hammer quivering millimetres from Ed's eye. Ed conserved his energy. Owen lashed out with his own left hand catching Ed on the jaw. He managed to jerk his head away but the punch was still powerful and made him see stars.

Ed held onto the wrist holding the hammer and tried to push it back into Owen's face. With his free left hand Owen rained punches down into Ed's face. The blows were heavy as Owen had room to draw his fist back and make the punches count. Ed tugged away at the nylon tie on his right hand, his attempts to free himself becoming more frantic. Still he held onto Owen's wrist trying desperately to ensure the hammer couldn't be used. A fist hurt, but a hammer would break bones and kill for sure.

Owen was screaming with rage as he continued to punch Ed with his left hand. Ed did his best to keep his head moving, but the blows hurt. He could feel blood trickle from his nose and a cut over his right eye. It was a desperate situation and Ed had no time to think as the blows kept coming. Owen had stamina and each blow landed with the same power and accuracy as the last; he was strong and the punches were relentless.

In a moment of clarity Ed acted. So far he'd been pushing the hammer away from him. He changed tactics and pulled it towards him, catching Owen by surprise. It was the chance he'd hoped for and powered his forehead into Owen's face. His nose exploded and blood flew in all directions. Ed held him there and pulled his head back landing another butt to Owen's right eye. Owen screamed in pain, or was it rage, Ed thought? It didn't matter, he was hurting Owen and that was the only important thing to concentrate on. Ed kept Owen's hammer wrist pinned to the floor and pulled his head back once again, battering Owen with a relentless onslaught of headbutts.

Ed's face and head was slick with blood, both his and Owen's. His bruised and blooded forehead was on fire with pain, but still Ed didn't stop. If he stopped he'd be killed.

Owen was punching the side of Ed's face. Ed could feel the blows, but due to the angle of Owen's body he was unable to land a telling blow. Ed was in a world of pain his entire face felt like it was on fire, but he had no choice but to continue to use his head. A few cuts and bruises were better than a slow death with a thousand blows from a hammer.

Ed's right hand flew up; his fight against the nail holding it to the floor was won. Owen was pinning Ed down by the shoulder with his body but that wasn't a problem. Ed drew his right arm back and slammed a fist into Owen's kidney, again and again and again. They weren't debilitating blows, but the relentless pounding was taking its toll. Owen's breathing became laboured and his face contorted in pain. He tried to pull away, but Ed held him firm, landing blow after blow into his side and slamming his head into Owen's face opening up cuts around his eyes and mouth. Owen was now desperate to get away. Ed let him raise his body a few inches and then launched his head forward with as much power as he had left. Ed's forehead crunched into Owen's temple with devastating effect. Owen's body slumped across Ed's torso. Ed was seeing stars and his head felt like it was going to explode. Still, he kept his wits about him and removed the hammer from Owen's limp grip keeping it nearby in case he needed to use it to defend himself later.

Ed pushed Owen off his chest so he could sit up. Ed slowly raised himself up to a sitting position. Owen slid down his body, slick with blood; his face fell between Ed's legs, just as the living room door and patio doors flew open.

Ed looked across at Bob and Phil, both stood there open-mouthed taking in the carnage. Neither man spoke. Ed turned towards the patio doors and gave as good a smile as his puffy cut and bruised face would allow.

Angel walked forward, her face full of concern.

'Are you OK, Ed?' she asked.

'It's not what it looks like,' Ed said, trying to make light of the situation despite the pain.

Angel didn't acknowledge the joke, in fact she looked angry.

'Jesus Christ, Ed,' she said looking at the amount of blood, and the cuts and swelling on Ed's face. 'Are you hurt?'

'Reckon I might have a bit of a headache in the morning,' he replied.

Angel bent down to lift Owen's face out of Ed's genitals.

'Wait,' Ed replied.

Angel gave him a strange look.

'Use that hammer to pull those nails out so I can swing my legs round. I don't want to show off my meat and two veg to those two.

Angel prised the nails out of the floor and Ed turned away from Phil and Bob and slipped on his jeans and T shirt, not caring about being covered in blood. Nothing he ever bought was expensive so it didn't matter.

Phil made sure Owen was still breathing and sat him up and cuffed him. Angel took Ed to the kitchen, opened the draw where she knew Ed kept a rudimentary first aid kit and helped him clean his wounds. None were severe enough to warrant stitches and the bleeding had stopped, but Ed's entire head ached.

'You'll do,' she said and gave him a hug.

Bob entered the kitchen and looked him over.

'I know how you feel,' he replied grinning. His own face was still sporting the results of being on the wrong end of a beating from John Talbot.

'Not a great feeling is it?' Ed replied.

Flashing lights filled the kitchen window as an ambulance and two police cars rolled down the drive. Ed saw Phil outside speaking to the officers, informing them that he was in charge. He entered the kitchen and wrinkled his nose up after looking at Ed's battered face.

'The paramedics want to give you a quick look over and I'll be needing a statement from you, but that can wait until tomorrow, he told Ed.

Ed nodded.

'How did you know to come?' Ed asked.

'You've got Emma to thank for that. She looked at your notes from your mate Data and connected the dates and times of his mobile phone moving from cell to cell with the murders. Also his middle name is John and he drives a white Focus. When I called you and there was no answer, I spoke to Bob and we came to the rescue. Although I think you coped pretty well without us,' Phil told him.

'It's the thought that counts,' Ed said, his sense of humour returning.

'I think you need to brush up on your combat skills. You're getting slow,' Angel told him.

'Very funny. He crept up behind me and bashed me on the head with that infamous hammer of his. There's nothing wrong with my combat skills. In fact, I think I can finally say I beat a man with one arm tied behind my back,' Ed replied indignantly.

Angel shook her head in despair.

The paramedic came into the kitchen and gave Ed the same look Phil had. Ed sat down and the paramedic checked out his wounds, agreeing with Angel's point of view that he didn't need to get any hospital treatment, but advised him to see a doctor if the headache persisted as he was concerned about his skull fracture from a couple of years before. Ed asked him how he knew and he told him he was the paramedic who was on duty when Ed had his accident in the garden. It was indeed a small world.

CHAPTER FORTY-TWO

The paramedic had left Ed with some super-strength painkillers that as well as alleviating the pain also helped him to sleep. He awoke, not exactly refreshed, but feeling better than he had the night before. The burns to his stomach hadn't been too bad. The coffee had left a few nasty red scalds but the skin thankfully hadn't blistered. After coffee, he even managed a run along the clifftops with Angel, albeit at as sedate pace. He skipped working out on the punch bag as his knuckles were now in an even worse state than after his run in with John Talbot. He also skipped shaving as his face was still too tender. His face was a mass of puffy cuts, grazes, and bruises that covered almost every inch of it and it ached. His forehead was almost black from the bruising courtesy of Owen Moore's head. Ed hoped Owen was in as much, if not more, discomfort than he was.

Ed called Phil Reynolds and said he'd come in and give his statement. It took a couple of hours, and as Phil was taking him back to reception they bumped into Chief Superintendent Clatworthy. Ed knew the man didn't like him, mainly through his association with Bob. Clatworthy considered Bob and Ed like two peas in the same pod; uncouth and having a lack of respect of authority.

Clatworthy looked at Ed and pulled a face.

'Good god, you look dreadful,' he told him.

'I feel as bad as I look, sir,' Ed replied, deciding on being courteous, knowing Clatworthy would expect the opposite.

It seemed to take Clatworthy by surprise. He looked at Ed for a few seconds before speaking. Ed inwardly smiled, as a physical smile hurt like hell.

'I suppose I should thank you for your part in the capture of our serial killer. You're a very lucky man, Case.'

'I don't feel very lucky,' Ed replied.

'Compared to Moore's other three victims you are,' Clatworthy replied and smiled.

'Reckon I must be fitter, stronger and smarter than they were, with more to live for. A year ago I would've been a dead man as I was a mess. It's a good job DI Reynolds here is good at his job and was smart enough to tie Moore in to the murders and galvanise the troops to come and save me,' Ed thought a little white lie might help his friend out with promotion.

Ed made his way to the harbour where he'd agreed to meet Angel, where she'd be waiting with a pasty for him from the bakers.

Ed ignored the looks of the people he passed and the comments from their kids who knew no better. 'Mummy that man looks ugly,' one young girl said. 'Harsh but fair,' Ed mumbled as he walked on.

Angel was easy to spot with her short blonde hair. She was sitting next to Bob on a bench, both munching on pasties. Ed walked up to her and kissed her softly on the cheek and sat on a mooring bollard opposite. Bob balled up his paper bag and tossed it in the bin. Ed looked at Angel expectantly.

'Oh sorry, I gave your one to Bob. He saw me and came over for a chat. You'll have to get your own,' Angel said to him.

Ed looked at Bob who smiled back smugly. Ed decided the pasty could wait. He wasn't that hungry and eating hurt his face.

'Bob suggested going for a couple of beers, which sounds like a great idea as I've been dry since we got back from Crete.'

'Why not,' Ed replied through his swollen lips.

They entered The Ship, looking like two prize fighters past their prime, both men battered and bruised.

Lewis came up to serve them and looked between the two men.

'Ed, I reckon that forehead of yours is blacker than me!' Lewis remarked and laughed.

'Yeah, yeah, and any of that chalky racist shit and I'll give you what I gave Gavin Lyn that time,' Ed replied and did his best to smile, referring to a customer who thought it'd be OK to call

Lewis, chalky. He'd even tried to kid Ed that it was a term of endearment. Ed had broken his nose and suggested he find another place to drink.

'What happened to you?' Lewis asked.

'I made a citizen's arrest and he resisted,' Ed replied.

Ed ordered the drinks and a basket of chips as he'd missed out on a pasty.

'What happened to you Bob? You face looks like it was worse than Ed's before it started healing,' Angel asked.

'We had a run in with a local toe-rag and his mates during the course of Ed's missing person case. He fitted the profile of the man Phil was after so I put him in the frame. He wasn't happy about being put in the frame for three murders and jumped me. Caught me off guard,' Bob replied.

'I kicked ten shades of shit out of him after I saw Bob being loaded into an ambulance. I can assure you he looks worse than me and Bob together,' Ed replied.

'Wouldn't have expected anything less,' Angel replied and smiled, letting Ed know she was proud of him.

'Any other cases ongoing?' she asked.

'Nothing right now. So we've got a little spare time to lick our wounds and recover before the next exciting instalment of being a private investigator. Although… I might be doing it solo as Bob reckons he's too old and is going bail out on me. As I said to Bob, it'd be like beer without alcohol; a joyless experience. And Bob will just get bored, fatter and drink himself into an early grave,' Ed replied, going for the guilt trip.

'I said I was thinking about it. I'll give you my answer in a few days once my wounds have healed,' Bob replied, a trace of indignation in his voice.

'I reckon Ed's right on the mark with drinking yourself into an early grave. You might find things to do, but it's my guess most of them will involve beer, and in large quantities,' Angel replied, trying to pile on the pressure, knowing how much Ed would miss his partner.

Ed grinned, liking her tactics. Bob raised his eyes to the ceiling.

Lewis came over with a basket of chips and a small dish of ketchup, which Bob helped himself too almost before the basket had touched the table.

Ed was going to make a comment, but was distracted by Mrs. Moore, walking purposely towards them.

'Here comes trouble,' Ed said to nobody in particular,

'She's the mother of the guy that tried to kill Ed,' Bob told Angel.

Angel said nothing, but regarded the woman's pinched features with suspicion.

'What kind of animal are you, Case? I paid you to find my son, I didn't pay you to try and murder him. I've just come back from visiting him in hospital. He looks like he's been run over by a bus,' she said enraged.

'Take a look at my face, Mrs. Moore. It seems we were hit by the same bus,' Ed replied angrily.

'You're a bloody animal,' she screamed at him.

Before Ed could speak he was staring down the barrel of an ancient revolver. In fact, it looked identical to the one he'd stared down years ago. That one was being held by a nasty vindictive thug call Mack. When he pulled the trigger of the world war one relic, the bullet intended for him, hit one of his best friends, Jackie, straight through the heart, killing her instantly. Ed looked at Angel sat next to him.

'Not again, please, not again,' he said quietly.

Bob heard and shook his head; he'd been thinking the same thing.

There were gasps and screams from other customers. Some left their drinks and meals and ran out into the street. Ed was dimly aware of people shouting, 'that crazy lady's got a gun,' and 'someone call the police'. Others believing they were far enough away to be in any danger watched in morbid fascination, smartphones recording, completely unaware of the danger they may be in.

'Mrs. Moore, your son knocked me unconscious and nailed me to my own living room floor and fully intended to kill me by mutilating me with his hammer, as he'd done to his previous three victims. I did what I had to do to save my life, nothing more. You see this face?' Ed said pointing and circling his finger at the many cuts and bruises he had. 'These were inflicted by your son. I was lucky to escape with my life, which is more than can be said for the last three victims. Now, the fact I escaped means he's looking at only going on trial for three murders and an attempted murder, rather than four murders. I've done him a favour.'

'Nobody beats my boy and gets away with it,' she shouted.

'Your husband did and that's why your darling son killed those three men,' Ed replied trying to remain calm.

'I should've killed him with the same gun. I was weak and made a mistake hesitating. I won't make the same mistake twice, Case.'

'You're as crazy as your son,' Ed replied.

Ed smiled as he was overcome with a feeling of wellbeing. He knew he wasn't going to die today. In fact, he knew that nobody would die today.'

Mrs. Moore regarded him suspiciously.

'I don't see what you've got to smile about,' she said sharply.

Ed shrugged.

'Nobody's gonna die today Mrs. Moore,' he told her emotionlessly.

Mrs. Moore extended her arm fully. The barrel of the old revolver was still a few inches out of arms reach

'That looks like a .455 Webley officers revolver from world war one,' Angel said.

'You seem to know a lot about guns for a woman. I've no idea what it is. It was my great-grandfather's and it's loaded and at this range it won't miss,' she replied, turning her attention back to Ed.

'Did you know, the .455 Webley is one of the few revolvers made that has a safety catch,' Angel said and stood up. Uncertainty flashed across Mrs. Moore's face. In one fluid movement Angel disarmed the frightened woman with a speed that surprised Ed as much as it did Mrs. Moore, who was desperately trying to pull the trigger.

Angel pointed out the safety catch that was on and took it off.

'Now it's ready to use,' she said and pointed the gun at Mrs. Moore's chest. 'So I strongly suggest you take a seat as I'm sure the police will be here shortly and will take good care of you.'

Mrs. Moore wept. Bob was nearest and patted her on the shoulder and made a few comforting comments, probably feeling as awkward as he looked. Mrs. Moore seemed oblivious to everything as she was too wrapped up in her own guilt and failure.

'I take it you saw the safety catch was on?' Angel said to Ed.

'No. I've never fired a revolver so I've no idea if they even have one,' Ed told her.

'I assumed when you said nobody is going to die today, you'd seen it.'

'Nah, I just had a feeling. I knew I wasn't going to die and then I knew nobody would die. A bit like that time that merc was running at me firing his machine gun at me. I knew he wasn't gonna kill me. He ran out of bullets and I shot him when I thought I couldn't miss. It was the same thing today. It was the opposite in Corfu, I'd had a bad feeling the entire mission and I would've been killed if it wasn't for that Kevlar vest. You know how it is with me. It's some kind of sixth sense or something,' Ed replied and shrugged his shoulders.

'Your boyfriend's weird, Angel,' Bob said.

'You only just worked that one out?' Angel said,

'I've known it a long time, but he does seem to live a charmed life, so maybe there's something in it,' Bob replied shrugging his shoulders.

'Lewis, same again,' Ed shouted across the near empty pub. 'Oh and whatever Mrs. Moore wants.'

Ed leaned across the table and put a hand on top of Mrs. Moore's.

'Would you like a drink?' he asked.

'I just tried to kill you and you want to buy me a drink?' she said, finding Ed's behaviour very strange.

'Yeah well, nobody died, nobody got hurt and I don't harbour grudges. We all do stuff in our lives that we regret. I could bore you with countless tales of things I've done that I've regretted. Things that make waving a gun in my face seem like telling a little white lie. So have a drink as the cops will be here soon,' Ed said.

'Vodka and orange juice please,' she told him, and blew her nose.

Ed went to the bar and ordered the extra vodka and orange.

'I was thinking about closing for the day,' Lewis said.

'Why? I reckon once the cops go, this place is gonna be heaving with punters and the local journalists who'll all want a drink in the pub where the crazy lady pulled a gun on the infamous Ed Case. You'll be the star witness and will be able to regale them with heroic tales and bullshit,' Ed said with a wide grin.

'You and your girlfriend are bloody crazy.'

'Nah, I'm crazy, she's the smart one,' Ed replied, and tapped his card to pay for the drinks.

He heard the sirens and saw the blue lights as he put the tray of drinks on the table.

Phil was the first of the police to enter the pub. Bob had called him to let him know he didn't need to call in the Armed Response Unit as he didn't want the pub swarming with armed officers unnecessarily. Phil approached with two uniformed officers behind him.

'Mrs. Moore, I'm arresting you for…'

'Phil, let the lady finish her drink first,' Ed said

Phil was about to protest

'Please,' Ed said quietly.

Phil nodded. 'OK, but be quick.'

'Thank you, Mr. Case,' she replied and knocked the drink back in one. 'You might want to get that invoice to me quickly as I might not be around too much longer,' she said.

Ed nodded feeling sorry for the woman, who seemed to have aged in the last few hours.

Phil read Mrs. Moore her rights as they walked toward the doors of the pub. Angel slipped the safety catch on and pushed the weapon across to one of the uniformed officers who put it in an evidence bag.

'What will happen to her, Bob?' Angel asked, beating Ed to the same question.

'She's facing attempted murder and possession of an illegal firearm. Ordinarily she could face between twenty and thirty years. The judge will take into consideration that the weapon had the safety catch on and the circumstances. I think she'd be very unlucky if she got a custodial sentence. I think it's more likely she'll get a suspended sentence or community service and a fine, if she gets a compassionate judge and good solicitor.'

'I'll make sure she gets a good one,' Ed replied

'Crazy bastard. Why the hell would you do that?' Bob asked.

'I've done shit that I'm ashamed of, but I did it because I was hurting and angry, so I can relate to it. Like The Messenger and his brother I killed for murdering my wife and daughter, only because I wanted revenge and I was hurting. She's no different from me really and she deserves a second chance. She knows her son is gonna do life in prison or in an institution. She's harmless and doesn't deserve the same punishment as her son,' Ed told them.

'Agreed,' Angel said and raised her glass.

They clinked their glasses together.

'One day I'll work out what makes you tick, Ed.'

'I don't even know myself, Bob.' Ed replied and smiled, recalling that's exactly what Owen Moore wanted to know. 'But what I do know is that it's your round.'

'I think it was Mrs. Moore's round, but if she's being an illusionist, I suppose I'll have to step up,' Bob replied.

'You're a good man, Ed Case.' Angel said and kissed him softly on his cheek.

Ed smiled. Life was good once again. Everyone needed an Angel in their life.

ABOUT THE AUTHOR

John Morritt was born in England a long time ago, but in 2013 he made Thailand his new home.
John is the author of a book series featuring the likable Ed Case, who somehow seems to invite trouble. "Black Cockles" is the series debut novel, followed by "Nine Lives" with "Inglorious" being the third installment of what initially was due to be a trilogy. However, due to the popularity of Ed Case, "Nobody's Heroes" part 1 & 2 were soon to follow.
His stand-alone novels, "Vengeance", "Full Circle", and "The Last Hit" explore the darker side of human nature.

For more information visit www.johnmorritt.com

BLACK COCKLES
(Ed Case: Book 1)
by
John Morritt

Taking Emma to Cornwall to put some distance between her and her abusive, drug addict fiancé seemed like a good idea at the time. Unfortunately, Ed takes her to a place where she's in more danger as a serial killer is at large, targeting young, attractive women.

DCI Bob Brown is heading up the investigation and under increasing pressure to solve the case, as each attack becomes more frenzied and the killer, just as elusive. Could the answer be as simple as Ed suggests? Brown doesn't think so.

Ed, however, has other things to worry about. His holiday rapidly turns into a living nightmare after being singled out by Mack, a local thug, whose vindictiveness stops at nothing, not even murder.

NINE LIVES
(Ed Case: Book 2)
By
John Morritt

When Soho club owner Johnny Gold, tells Ed "I could use someone like you." Ed jumps at the opportunity of a job as a bouncer. Little does he know that he's entering a world of sleaze and corruption that will put his life in danger, because Johnny has a hidden agenda. It's only exotic dancer TJ, who stops him walking away. But even TJ has a secret.

After Johnny frames Ed for murder, he flees the club in an maelstrom of violence and is pursued the length of the country by two of Soho's most ruthless gangs, because Ed has something that belongs to Johnny and they all want it back – at any cost.

Surviving a terrifying orgy of death and violence, Ed heads back to London believing his ordeal is finally over, unaware that his real nightmares are just beginning.

VENGEANCE

(Ed Case: Book 2)

By

John Morritt

At the tender age of five, Peter Edwards witnesses the horrific death of his father by a drunk driver. Twenty years later, the nightmares that tortured him for a few years after the accident inexplicably return to haunt him, leading to the breakdown in his relationship with his girlfriend, Janet, and destroying his teaching career.

After a particularly graphic nightmare one night, Peter vividly recalls the face of the killer. He's filled with anger so strong, that he becomes consumed with avenging his father's death.

Though many dream of revenge, they lack the courage to act. Not Peter Edwards. An eye for an eye, a tooth for a tooth he tells himself as he embarks on a terrifying trail of vengeance.

INGLORIOUS
(Ed Case: Book 3)
By
John Morritt

When Ed unearths a 150-year-old mystery while renovating their house, as he and his fiancée TJ set about investigating it, they uncover damning details that take a terrifying turn, exacerbating the residents' hostility towards them.

Their situation becomes worse when Ed's friend, DCI Bob Brown, asks him for a favour. Ed knows it won't just be a case of 'give Roly a knuckle sandwich and job done'; life is never that simple for Ed.

With recent events and his fragile mental health, Ed is caught in a situation where he has to choose between breaking his promise to TJ to stay out of trouble, or help Bob. There is only one outcome and soon Ed finds himself drawn into the criminal underworld of ex-London gangster Harry Daniels.

FULL CIRCLE
by
John Morritt

Frank Smith looks forward to realising his dream of a comfortable life in sunny climes, after serving twenty years in prison for attempted murder.

His dream, however, shatters within days of becoming a free man, when he learns that duplicitous gangland boss Maurice Blair, now respectable businessman and head of a property development company, refuses to give him what is rightfully his.

As Frank unravels the web of deception spun by Blair, he returns to a life of crime, while he faces an uncertain future in a world that has moved on leaving him behind.

THE LAST HIT
by
John Morritt

John Stone, former army sniper and mercenary turned hitman, is sick of killing. When contracted by a shadowy government figure to take down an ex-member of parliament, testifying in an arms scandal that would embarrass the government, Stone decides it will be his last assignment. However, notorious North London gangster, Alex Brant, makes him an offer too good to refuse. What he believes will be one last run-of-the-mill job, turns out to be anything but.

Stone's life becomes more complicated, after a chance meeting with investigative journalist, Andrew Ferguson, results in several attempts being made on his life. With the help of MI5 agent, Nikki Miles, and Alex Brant's second in command, Kristina Kovac, Stone tries to work out who wants him dead and why. As he digs deeper, he realises his last two assignments are closely linked and why he's seen as a loose end. Stone struggles to understand who can be trusted and has to use all his skills to stay alive.

NOBODY'S HEROES
(Ed Case: Book 4)
by
John Morritt

Cornwall based, Private Investigator, Ed Case, gets his first assignment from an unlikely source. Pandora an old friend and exotic dancer, he once worked with in Soho, wants him to find her friend and colleague, Jade Wickham. Jade went missing and Pandora believes the police aren't taking matters seriously and fears for her friend's life.

Ed teams up with Detective Sergeant Holt, the officer looking into the disappearance of Jade and six other women working in the sex industry in London. Holt believes the women he is investigating are likely to be the tip of a very large iceberg. Holt's resources are stretched and, despite reservations, is quick to realise Ed's belligerence and scant regard for the law, could be an asset to moving the investigation forward.

As Ed and Holt close the net on the gang responsible for the disappearances, their lives are put in danger, as they pit their wits against, Agron Kastrati, one of London's most ruthless gangsters, with terrifying consequences.

NOBODY'S HEROES PART II – RETRIBUTION

(Ed Case: Book 5)

by
John Morritt

Kristina Kovac, the most powerful woman in London wants Ed Case and DCI Bob Brown eliminated. The two men thwart an attempt on their lives, but fear for the safety of their families. They believe only way they can keep their families safe is head to London and fight Kovac in her own back yard.

In London they meet up with two unlikely allies who want Kovac dead for their own reasons and form an uneasy alliance. With no plan other than to find and kill Kovac, they soon find themselves on the run but managing to stay one step ahead thanks to Ryan Jones.

None of the men trust Jones, who works for Kovac, but seems to be playing both sides. They know when things start to heat up, people like Jones will always choose the winning side. At Oakwood Farm events come to a terrifying conclusion and they discover exactly what side Jones is on.

LAST MAN ALIVE
(Ed Case: Book 6)

by
John Morritt

Private investigator, Ed Case, believes that if you're looking for someone, the first place to look, is where you least expect to find them. This reverse logic works to his advantage when hired by his friend, Chris Stevens, to find her missing fiancé, Lionel. Finding Lionel is the easy part. Keeping him alive is anything but, as Lionel's colourful past has caught up with him.

Reece Greenfield, a powerful and ambitious man, is trying to erase his past, systematically killing anyone who can derail his political ambitions. Lionel is the last man on that list, and it's now up to Ed and former DCI, Bob Brown, to ensure he remains the last man alive.

RELENTLESS
(Ed Case: Book 7)
by
John Morritt

Nothing is ever straight forward in private investigator, Ed Case's life. Returning from London after a successful missing person case, a series of perplexing events take place. His life falls apart then he learns his wife and daughter have been abducted. A chilling warning given to him by an old man he knows only as "The Messenger" seems to have been carried out, despite Ed doing as he was told and keeping out of trouble.

Fortunately for Ed, his mistrust of the old man, led him to take precautions, ensuring he still had the resources to find his family, and painstakingly sets about trying to locate the elusive Messenger. Unexpectedly, he receives an email from an unknown source, informing him that the man he seeks will be at Leadenhall Market, London at midnight the next day.

THE BOX
(Ed Case: Book 8)
by
John Morritt

Private investigator, Ed Case, is given a plain metal box to take care of after a chance encounter with a stranger on a train. The box is unremarkable apart from being highly polished and surprisingly heavy for its size. Intrigued, Ed has the box analysed and is astounded by what the analysis reveals.

However, the highly valuable contents are largely irrelevant as only the owner of the box can open it; any forced entry will destroy the contents. Ed has no choice but to take the box home and wait for the owner to collect it.

What ensues is a battle of wits. Ed must find the man who gave him the box in order to save his own life from two ruthless, rival criminals, who both want the box and the owner, to claim the priceless contents. Ed can only please one of the two and is faced with a difficult decision; who would make the most dangerous enemy?

INSIDE OUTSIDE
(Ed Case: Book 8)
by
John Morritt

Jack Griggs, Director General of MI5, has a problem, one that he is unable to resolve using his own resources without compromising the agency or risking the life of an agent. Jack is under pressure from both the Home Secretary, and the Lord Privy Seal who wants his nephew found.

Jack can think of only one man who has the tenacity and attitude to successfully complete the mission. He has no option but to ask his old friend Ed Case to help. Ed not being an agent is able to make his own rules, and gives Griggs deniability should anything go wrong.

Ed has a choice and can turn down Jack's cry for help but Ed owes Jack for past favours and the man he wants him to find once saved his life so Ed is compelled to help despite putting himself in the most hostile and dangerous environment he has ever experienced.

Printed in Great Britain
by Amazon